ESB

The Man Who
Never Stopped
Sleeping

❧

The Man Who Never Stopped Sleeping

Aharon Appelfeld

TRANSLATED FROM THE HEBREW BY

Jeffrey M. Green

Schocken Books, New York

Translation copyright © 2017 by Schocken Books, a division of Penguin Random House LLC

All rights reserved. Published in the United States by Schocken Books, a division of Penguin Random House LLC, New York, and distributed in Canada by Random House of Canada, a division of Penguin Random House Limited, Toronto. Originally published in Israel as *Ha'ish Shelo Pasak Leeshon* by Kinneret, Zmora-Bitan, Dvir Publishing House Ltd., Or Yehuda, in 2010. Copyright © 2010 by Aharon Appelfeld and Kinneret, Zmora-Bitan, Dvir Publishing House Ltd.

Schocken Books and colophon are registered trademarks of Penguin Random House LLC.

Library of Congress Cataloging-in-Publication Data
Names: Appelfeld, Aharon, author. Green, Yaacov Jeffrey, translator.
Title: The man who never stopped sleeping : a novel / Aharon Appelfeld; Translated from the Hebrew by Jeffrey M. Green.
Other titles: Ish she-lo pa-sak li-shon. English.
Description: First American edition. New York : Schocken Books, 2017.
Identifiers: LCCN 2016028875 (print). LCCN 2016036028 (ebook).
ISBN 9780805243192 (hardcover). ISBN 9780805243208 (ebook).
Subjects: LCSH: Jewish men—Fiction. Jewish youth—Fiction. Jewish refugees—Fiction. Young men—Fiction. World War, 1939–1945—Europe—Fiction. BISAC: FICTION / Literary. FICTION / Jewish. FICTION / Biographical. GSAFD: War stories.
Classification: LCC PJ5054.A755 I8413 2017 (print).
LCC PJ5054.A755 (ebook). DDC 892.43/6—dc23.
LC record available at lccn.loc.gov/2016028875.

www.schocken.com

Jacket photograph by Ludwig West/Flickr/Getty Images
Jacket design by Linda Huang

Printed in the United States of America
First American Edition
9 8 7 6 5 4 3 2 1

The Man Who
Never Stopped
Sleeping

I

At the end of the war, I became immersed in constant slumber. Though I moved from train to train, from truck to truck, and sometimes from wagon to wagon, it was all in a dense, dreamless sleep. When I opened my eyes for a moment, the people looked heavy and expressionless.

No wonder I don't remember a thing about that long journey. I ate what they gave out or, rather, from what was left over. If I hadn't been thirsty, I probably wouldn't even have gotten up to look for a slice of bread. Thirst tortured me all along the way. If some memory of that sleep-drunk journey still remains with me, it's the streams where I knelt to gulp the water. The chilly water put out the fire inside me for a while but not for long.

The refugees carried me and supported me. Sometimes I was forgotten, and then someone remembered me and went back to pick me up. My body remembers the jolting more than I do. Sometimes it seems that I'm still in that darkness, drifting and being borne along. What happened to me during those days of sleep will probably be unknown to me forever. Sometimes a voice that spoke to me comes back, or the taste of a piece of bread that was shoved into my mouth. But aside from that, there is just darkness.

That's how I arrived. The truck drivers rolled up the canvas. People and bundles tumbled out. "We're in Naples," the drivers announced. The sky was high above us, the sun blazed as it dipped into the sea, and the light was intense and dazzling.

I had no desire to push my way in to look for a bed in the sheds or to stand in line to get the used clothes that people from the Joint Distribution Committee were giving away. Everything around me buzzed with desire and a thirst for life, but the people looked ridiculous in their rushing about.

I could barely stand on my feet. At last I dragged myself over to a tree, sank down at its foot, and plunged into sleep.

It was a more diluted sleep. I could hear voices and the noise of the generators. I was borne along but without force. I felt the hard earth beneath me, and I said to myself, *In a little while they'll come and shake me.* At first that worry kept me from sinking into a deeper sleep, but, nevertheless, I eventually did so. In the evening a man approached, nudged me, and called out loud, "What are you doing here?" I didn't open my eyes and didn't bother to answer him. But he kept shaking me and bothering me, so I had no choice but to say to him, "I'm sleeping."

"Did you eat?" asked the man.

"I'm not hungry," I replied.

My body knew that kind of annoyance. All along the way people tried to wake me up, to shove bread into my mouth, to speak to me, to convince me that the war was over and that I had to open my eyes. There were no words in me to explain that I couldn't open my eyes, that I was trapped in thick sleep. From time to time, I did try to wake up, but sleep overpowered me.

Waves of darkness carried me along, and I moved forward. *Where are you heading?* I asked myself. *Home,* I replied, surprised at my own answer. Only a few of the refugees wanted to go back to their homes. Everyone else streamed to the sea in trains and trucks. People knew what they wanted. I had just one wish—to return to my parents.

As I was being carried forward, a hand touched me, and when I didn't react, the hand shook me again. I didn't want to answer, but the pulling disturbed me, and so I said, without opening my eyes, "Leave me alone. I want to sleep."

"You mustn't sleep for such a long time."

"My weariness isn't done. Leave me alone."

The man went away, but then he came back and prodded me again. My sleep was no longer deep, and I felt the man's determination to draw me out of it, no matter what.

I opened my eyes and was surprised to see that the man, on his knees and wearing glasses, looked like my uncle Arthur. I knew he wasn't Arthur, but still I was glad to see him.

"What are you doing here?" he asked softly.

"I came with the refugees."

"From where?" He stretched his neck toward me.

I couldn't answer that. The places where we had stopped slipped past me without leaving a trace.

The man stared at me and asked if I wanted something to eat. I was about to say, *A cup of cocoa*, but I realized that would be a foolish request. Only at home, at breakfast, and toward evening at supper would Mother make me a cup of cocoa.

"I'll bring you a sandwich and a glass of milk," the man said. Without waiting for my response, he went off to get it for me. I wondered about the man who resembled my uncle Arthur, not only in his build and face but also in his movements, and I decided to ask him whether he was a communist, too, like my uncle.

He came back with a tray of food.

"Thank you," I said. Since I had left the house, years earlier, no one had served me food on a tray.

"Hearty appetite," said the man, another term I hadn't heard since the war broke out.

I ate. The more I ate, the more my appetite grew, and I finished it all. The man watched without disturbing me. Finally, he asked my name.

I told him.

"What do you want to do?" he asked.

"Sleep," I said.

"I'll leave you alone," he replied, and went away.

I was by myself again, and I felt relieved. After the war, it was hard for me to be with people. Sleep was right for me. In sleep I lived fully. I needed that fullness like I needed air to breathe. Sometimes a dream floated up and threatened me.

The next day the man who looked like Uncle Arthur came back and knelt beside me. Again the resemblance stunned me.

He asked whether I had slept well, and I said yes.

I didn't hold my tongue and asked whether he knew a man named Arthur Blum.

"No," he answered curtly.

"You look like him. He's my uncle."

The man asked my age, and I told him.

"I'm sixteen years and nine months old."

"What do you want to do now?" he asked, as if he were a relative and not a stranger.

"I don't know yet."

That night I woke up and found a tray of fruit and a note. The note said, "Hello, my young friend. Tonight I'm leaving the camp and setting out. I wish you a fine awakening and a life of alertness, activity, and the ability to love." The note was signed, "Your friend who looks like your uncle Arthur."

I read it again and again, and tears flowed from my eyes.

2

I overcame the bonds of sleep and rose to my feet. The sea was already glowing. The grown-up refugees bathed in it, and a few swam. The sight was stunning in its strangeness.

My desire to return to slumber didn't fade, but the strong light, the bare shore, left me with no doubt that here one doesn't sleep during the daytime. I didn't see a shade tree nearby, or an awning, so I went back to my tree, closed my eyes, and waited for the night to enfold me and return me to the recesses of sleep.

Toward evening, hunger woke me up. Near the water there was a table where they were distributing rolls and glasses of milk. I stood in line and got my portion. The people looked ridiculous in their satisfaction.

Night fell, and I curled up next to my tree and fell asleep.

Apparently, the sun woke me up. Maybe the generator. But I was glad that people hadn't awakened me. I went over to the table and got breakfast. The light blinded me, and I went looking for cover. The whole seashore was lit as though with search-lights. I was puzzled by everyone's joyful shouts in the heart of that pounding light.

I didn't want to go into the sheds and live with the refugees. I found a long piece of sheet metal and bent it to protect myself from the sun.

For most of the day, I dozed or slept. Surprisingly, dreams filtered into my sleep and showed me images of days gone by but not images of the war. In one of my dreams I saw Father and Mother standing on the banks of the River Prut. In their faces there was amazement that I had found them. I told them that I had been looking for them for years. People hadn't helped me, and some of them misled me, but I was firm in my resolve to return home.

"Weren't you afraid?" Mother asked.

"No. I was sure that if I persevered I would get to you sooner or later. I refused to accept the verdict of those who insisted that no one who had left by train would return."

"Thank you," said Mother in a voice I didn't recognize.

"There's no need to thank me," I quickly replied. "I did it with a clear mind and the desire to be with you."

Upon hearing my words, Father smiled his full smile but didn't utter a word.

I was surprised that they weren't eager to approach me and hug me.

"Mother," I said, "when will we go home?"

"In a little while. We just got here. I didn't imagine we'd meet you." She spoke in a voice not her own.

"What's good to eat at home?" My voice from the past returned.

"All the things you love. Even meatballs stuffed with prunes."

"Mother, I've been longing for that delicacy for years," I said, and I was astonished by the words that came out of me.

The darkness had grown very thin. I could feel the ground beneath me. I was sorry that the darkness was fading and I would soon be exposed. I curled up in the hope that it would return, thicken, and swaddle me. The thought occurred to me that the man who looked like Uncle Arthur, who had brought me fruit and left me a note, was none other than a messenger from my uncle, and soon, if I could properly expect his arrival, he would appear. This thought roused me, and I opened my eyes.

3

That day I saw a boy my age. It seemed to me that I'd seen him on the trip here, and maybe even before that. I approached him and introduced myself.

The boy wasn't surprised that I'd spoken to him and said, "My name is Mark." I noticed right away that he was standing differently from the other refugees. His clothes were neat and his gaze was focused. I told him that I had been sleeping since the end of the war, and today, in fact, was the first day I'd emerged from sleep.

Hardly had the words left my mouth before I regretted that I'd revealed my secret, but Mark wasn't surprised. He looked at me gently. From his look, I understood that exceptional things were not strange to him.

"Where are you from?" I asked, trying to get closer to him.

"What difference does it make?" he responded.

I understood. He was guarding his privacy.

We walked along the shore. The light was strong and blinded me, but I was glad to be with Mark. He left me without saying a word. I didn't know then that the time would come when I'd get to know him well.

Most of the day I was curled up under the metal sheet. The refugees recognized me and called out, "Here's the sleeping boy."

They didn't pick on me, but it was hard for me to be close to them. It seemed that they hadn't forgotten the trouble I'd caused them. For that reason, and maybe for others, I kept my distance. I sat at the makeshift kiosk and drank lemonade.

A woman approached me. "Why do you stare at us like that?" she asked.

"I'm not staring. I'm thinking," I told her the truth.

"What are you thinking about?" She didn't let up.

"About what happened to me over the past few months."

"What happened to you, if I may ask?"

"Since the end of the war, I've been immersed in slumber. And even now, if I could lay my head on something elevated, I'd fall asleep. Light isn't good for me."

The woman studied me.

"Are you the one we carried from train to train and from truck to truck?" she asked.

"I guess so."

"We forgot you sometimes, but in the end we found you," she said, as though in wonderment.

I didn't know how to reply, so I just said, "Thanks."

"What's the matter with you?"

"I don't know."

"Impatient people tried to wake you, but the wiser ones realized it was wrong to shake you. You slept quietly, and you were handsome in your sleep. It seemed then that you, not us, were living properly. We were confused. And now are you awake?"

"Almost."

"Thank God. Some people thought that sleep would be your undoing, but the wiser ones said, 'Let the boy sleep. He's bound up in sleep, and we mustn't detach him. When the time comes, he'll wake and he'll be like the rest of us.'"

I looked closely at her and was stunned: she looked like my aunt Elsa. Only her clothes were different. Aunt Elsa always dressed with exaggerated elegance.

"You have to emerge from sleep." She spoke in motherly tones.

"I hope to do that soon," I said, but I knew it didn't depend on me.

"You're young, and your whole life lies before you," she said. That was a sentence I'd heard more than once from my aunt. It was one of her clichés. Everybody knew she had no words of her own, that clichés were her crutches, and they secretly made fun of her.

"You have to get away from us," the woman continued. "Our life has no purpose or meaning. The sooner you leave us, the better for you."

"Where should I go?"

"Anywhere, just not here."

"But—how can I say it—I belong to you. I was with you in the ghetto and in the forest, and you brought me here. Your language is mine, and in every corner I see a relative. You, for example, look very much like my aunt Elsa. I almost called you Elsa."

"Why didn't you?"

"I wasn't sure."

"Dwelling with us won't do you any good." She repeated her argument. "A boy like you must finish high school and not get involved in smuggling, in money changing, and in all sorts of dubious businesses." It was as though her voice came from elsewhere.

"You're right," I said.

Suddenly, I felt myself being swaddled by sleep. I stood up and said, "Sorry. I have to go. I have to go back to my place."

"Where is your place?" she asked matter-of-factly.

"Not far from here," I said, and I ran to my bent metal sheet. Sleep grabbed me, and I slumbered.

4

Every day I became more alert. The food was plentiful, the milk was fresh and tasty, and I gobbled down whatever came to hand.

"He's awake. He's come out of his sleep," a refugee said, pointing at me. I didn't know whether he was happy for me or happy to make fun of me. My exposed wakefulness wasn't easy for me. In sleep I was connected, with no barrier, to my parents and to the house where I grew up, and I continued to live my life and theirs. Now I felt that I had been expelled from a protected place into blinding, wounding light.

At night I no longer slept as before. Sounds penetrated me and tore up my sleep, and I was sorry to be cut off from what was a part of me.

As I was being struck by the light, I saw a man, not tall, dressed in a short peasant blouse, talking to the older boys. He looked like our pharmacist, who used to give a lollipop to every child who entered the pharmacy. But this man's temperament was different. He spoke in torrents of Yiddish mixed with German about another life, a life with much activity and pleasure. I was reminded of my uncle Arthur, who also spoke about another life. Father would listen and make occasional comments. Mother accepted his words without challenge. Arthur was her beloved big brother, and she admired everything he said.

I looked at the boys gathered around the man. They drank in his words thirstily. Some of them were tall and others were short, some alert and others bleary-eyed. For a moment it seemed that they, too, had been roused from deep sleep a short time ago.

"And how will we do it?" asked one of the boys.

"I'll explain," said the man calmly. "We'll start off the morning with a run, we'll eat breakfast, then we'll study Hebrew by speaking it, and later in the day we'll exercise and swim. We have two boats at our disposal, and we'll learn to row."

"And what will happen to us?" asked another boy.

"You'll change. In three months you'll be different. People won't recognize you. You'll be tall, strong, and tanned. The language will join with the body and become one."

I didn't understand everything he said, but I understood that if we did everything we were supposed to, we'd change and become different. In the process a part of me would be taken away, and I'd grow differently.

There was a frightening charm in his voice.

"My name is Ephraim. Call me Ephraim. We'll meet tomorrow after breakfast."

I went back to my metal sheet and tried to fall asleep. Ephraim's words, which enchanted me at first, now seemed like a recruitment speech for a unit where you trained night and day. The leaves were few and short, your only concern was obeying orders, and anyone who didn't obey them properly was punished.

I decided not to enlist and felt relieved.

I fell asleep and dreamed that I had gone home. Father was sitting in his room, writing. Mother was in the kitchen. The afternoon silence that I loved so much filled the rooms, but I was surprised my parents didn't notice that I'd returned. I decided not to approach them but to wait for the right time.

Later I heard Mother say, "Michael, lunch is on the table."

"I'm coming." Father's voice came promptly.

Father kept on writing, but after a minute or two he rose to his feet, closed his notebook, and went into the dining room.

"Vegetable soup!" Father called out from the doorway. "Just what I wanted."

"It tastes good, I think," said Mother softly.

"I'm sure."

That simple conversation, familiar to me in the marrow of my bones, brought tears to my eyes: they had gotten used to living without me.

5

After breakfast I saw the older boys gathered around Ephraim. I joined them, and we went to the seashore. The sea was already blazing.

"We'll make our own camp." Ephraim spoke without raising his voice. "We'll be separate from the refugees." I understood right away that he wasn't pleased with the refugees and that he wanted to keep us from them. I also noticed that he said "we."

Then we sat on the beach, and Ephraim spoke. He told us that we would train ourselves to be pioneers, going ahead of the camp and devoting ourselves to the general good, not like the refugees, who were concerned only with themselves.

I saw Mark, and I was glad he was there. Mark was wearing clothes that fit him, and his eyes glowed with maturity. I wanted to know whether Ephraim's words sounded right to him.

"We'll live and we'll learn," he declared. I had no opinion of my own, and so I agreed with him.

Then a wagon full of tents, field cots, and blankets arrived, and Ephraim showed us how to put up a tent. They were square tents, for two, and Mark asked me to put one up with him.

That's how our new life began. Wakefulness grew stronger in me with every hour. The sleepiness that had enveloped me for all those weeks diminished, and the dark cover that had protected me was torn away. Soon I would be bare.

Mark's experience in the war appeared to have been different from mine. He did everything coldly and methodically. I observed him and said to myself, *Those are the motions I'll have after Ephraim trains me.* Ephraim didn't rush us. He showed us how to stretch the tent cloths and pound the pegs into the sand.

By afternoon seven tents were standing. Ephraim checked the ropes and pegs and declared our tent stable. The look of the tent, the two field cots in it, and the blankets gave me the feeling that I had a protected space and that at night no one would push me anymore.

Later that afternoon we went out for our first run. We were to circle the camp twice. Not everyone managed to do it. Ephraim didn't give in to the laggards. In the end, they also did what they were supposed to.

At night we lit a bonfire, and Ephraim taught us the first verse of a Zionist song. We were fourteen boys, dressed in khaki shorts that the Jewish Agency had distributed. We sang and we roasted potatoes.

I felt that the road to robustness would be long. I would have to train in the spirit of Ephraim's words, to grow flexible and sun-tanned, to uproot the fears within me, and to peel off the remaining slumber that still clung to me.

That night, as though in spite, the overpowering slumber returned, and it seemed it was going to bear me away on its waves. I said to myself, *Ephraim wouldn't be pleased with my relapse,* and I tried to shake off the darkness that had gripped me. But it was stronger than I was, and it wasn't rooted out of me until the morning wake-up bell.

In my sleep the next night, Uncle Arthur was leaning over

me, asking how I was, and telling me that Ephraim's path was not the path to faith in mankind. I must understand that the body wouldn't save us, only the spirit. "Muscle Judaism" was a twisted idea.

I was surprised at my mild uncle Arthur's scolding.

"Anyone who wants the Jews to be muscular is living in a world of injustice," he shouted at me, without minding his manners. "The Jews also belong to the family of man, and the man comes before the Jew."

Suddenly, a tall, hairy man appeared and forcefully pulled my uncle away while hissing, "Communist!" Uncle Arthur was stunned by the man's violence and didn't say a word. Evidently, the tall, hairy man had no other words, just "communist," which he repeated endlessly. Uncle Arthur, who had been sensitive to noise for as long as I knew him, covered his ears with the palms of his hands. The huge man, seeing what my uncle was doing, burst into loud laughter, a triumphant laugh that shocked me. I awakened and sat up, while everyone else still slept.

6

⌒℮⌒

Our activities were extensive and well planned. Sometimes the training program seemed to be intended to change us completely, so that in time people would say, "They were trained by Ephraim." Ephraim's height and manner of speaking were unimpressive. Sometimes he seemed like an ordinary army man to me, training his recruits with a wise hand. He didn't shout, and he didn't harass. Though he spoke little, his gaze was determined. At night, on the other hand, at the campfire, he was relaxed, singing and rousing us to sing.

After morning lineup, we would go out for a run. "*Alef* is *ohel*, *ohel* is 'tent,'" we shouted. "*Beit* is *bayit*, *bayit* is 'house'; *gimel* is *gag*, *gag* is 'roof'; *dalet* is *delet*, *delet* is 'door'; *heh* is *har*, *har* is 'mountain.'" Every morning we added new words. The words I learned on that seashore were linked to the sea in my mind. Every time I said *ohel*, I saw the sides of the tent I pitched with my friend Mark and the pegs that refused to be gripped by the sand. The sea was so intense that every new word was filled with its blue water and tempered in the burning light of the sun.

One evening Ephraim spoke again about the need to attach the language to our bodies. Every Hebrew word added strength. I didn't understand how words became connected to the body, but

Ephraim's words seemed like correct instructions. If we listened to them, we would grow properly, and our thinking would be orderly and clear.

Slowly, imperceptibly, we distanced ourselves from everything that had been in us: the ghetto, the hiding places, the forests. From the southern coast of Naples, they seemed distant and blurry, as if they had lost their dreadful immediacy.

At night, after the ritual singing, we would flop onto our camp beds and fall asleep. It was a different kind of sleep, the kind I had known only from my childhood at home.

My mother was talking to me in a language whose notes, accents, and silences I knew. Her voice flowed to me clearly, but for some reason it was hard for me to answer her. As always, my mother understood me and was certain that it was only from "excitement," a word I hadn't heard for a while and which pleased me.

After a long silence, she asked, "What's the matter, dear?"

I tried to stitch together everything that had happened to me in the years since I last saw her, but I was able to come up with only one word.

"Mother."

That single word made her so happy that she ignored my difficulty in speaking, and her face filled with joy.

Later I managed to tell her, "I have a new language."

She looked at me in surprise and then grew gloomy.

"A new language," she repeated.

It was the language of the sea, I added. You learned at the seashore, and you absorbed it with all the colors and smells of the sea.

"Why do you need a sea language?" she wondered, wide-eyed.

"I'm a member of the Chosen," I said. I was surprised to hear that sentence leave my mouth.

"Won't you cultivate your mother tongue anymore?"

"Mother," I said, "don't worry. What you read to me every night from the storybook *Legends of the North*, before I went to sleep, that will last forever. I drank in that language from you, and it is in the marrow of my bones."

Mother was not convinced by my declaration.

"Why is it hard for you to speak to me?" she asked.

The language of the sea is a strong language, but the mother tongue is stronger, it occurred to me to tell her, but in my heart I wasn't convinced.

"What I had to give you, my dear, I gave with all my heart," Mother said in a choked voice. "Maybe I was mistaken. I was a young, inexperienced woman then. But don't doubt my good intentions. Please, son, don't transfer the secret of our conversation into a language I don't understand," she added and then disappeared. I woke up immediately.

7

The days passed without our noticing. Physical training and language instruction kneaded us. Ephraim was vigilant. At night he warned us against the refugees, their talk and their business dealings. We had to grow up without their influence, and only when we were immunized would we be allowed to help them. For the present, we had to invest all our might into shaping our new lives.

Ephraim was a man of many faces: When he ran with us, exercised, and taught us self-defense, he was cheerful and jocular and seemed like a man of thirty. But at night his face would change. He looked like a person with a heavy responsibility weighing on his shoulders. He stopped saying "I" and spoke as "we."

Some distance from our tent area the refugees lived in gloom. On our morning run or upon returning from field training, we passed by their sheds and heard our mother tongue being mumbled in their mouths. They were still living in the ghettos and the camps, trading goods for other goods, coins for coins. The smell of their food wafted over from their sheds, reminding us, as though in spite, of home.

Whenever I had a little time, I would sneak over to the refugees and sit by the kiosk. I had the feeling that before too long they would pick me up and carry me off. Sometimes a refugee noticed me and called out, "Here's the sleepy guy," as though I was about to run away. Anyway, they hadn't forgotten me.

It's amazing what the exercise and daily runs did for us. We grew taller. Our skin became tanned, and some of us were already looking at the refugees with arrogance, calling them rootless, as if they were inferior beings, stubborn people who refused to change, who burrowed into their prolonged misery and spoke in a language all of whose words were sorrow, depression, pain that could not be healed, or the unpleasant laughter of someone who was glad to have survived.

Ephraim told us that in the Land of Israel we would be far from them, in the heart of fields, orange groves, and orchards. We would have other names, and our bodies would move in a quiet and measured way, like tillers of the soil, without haste or panic.

The refugees sprawling in their sheds were not indifferent to us. They observed our changes, and not without pride. From time to time we would notice, in the distance, a bald head looking at us in amazement, a woman's look of desire, a skeptical old man who had seen efforts at change in his lifetime and no longer believed in them.

One evening a refugee approached me, a man of average height, wearing a secondhand suede jacket and a cap. He was a merchant or a money changer, and he asked me for my name and my family's name.

I told him.

He didn't ask anything else. He just looked gloomier and gloomier. I knew that for a moment he had taken me for one of his relatives, but disappointment hadn't been slow in coming.

"Where are you from, sir?" I addressed him, trying to bring him closer.

"It doesn't matter."

"Why not?"

"I don't like talking about myself," he said, and turned away.

He shuffled away, and his whole body said, *I was wrong this time, too. There's no hope.* I was sorry to have been the cause of his disappointment.

I returned to our area feeling somber. I ran into Mark, who shared my tent, and I told him what had happened to me. He looked at me and then astonished me by saying, "I guess we bear other people inside us, too."

My friend Mark was handsome, quiet, and introverted, doing all his duties seriously and precisely. He neither questioned nor complained, and he didn't like it when people asked him anything. We had been living in the same tent for more than two months, and I didn't know a thing about him. His mother tongue was the same as mine, but we obeyed instructions and spoke only Hebrew. Our conversations were brief and about current matters. Sometimes it seemed to me that Mark did things only because he had to. He had a world of his own, his fortress. No one knew where its entrances where, and there he lived his real life. Once, one of the boys challenged him.

"You aren't here," the boy said. "Where are you?"

Mark didn't reply. He just hit him. The boy fell to the ground and shouted, "He's crazy! What did I do to him?" Mark kept hitting the boy until he was pulled away. That night Ephraim asked Mark why he had hit his comrade. Mark made a strange gesture with his right shoulder and said, "He annoyed me." He responded to the rest of Ephraim's questions with only movements of his body.

Ephraim concluded by saying, "Promise all of us that from now on you won't hit your comrades. If you have a complaint, bring it before this assembly." Mark responded with silence to this comment as well, but Ephraim insisted that he say "I promise." After a short delay, Mark did utter those two words.

That night I was once again enveloped in a deep slumber. Every time I was in distress, it came to my assistance and swaddled me. Its contours changed over time, but its power was undiminished. Sometimes it isolated me, and I felt completely alone.

I saw Father again. This time he wasn't writing but engraving. His back was bent, and his hand held a chisel firmly.

"Father," I said, "you're exerting yourself more than I do in my fitness training."

"It's a chisel stylus. I have to get used to it."

"It would be better for you to exercise than to subdue the paper with a chisel."

"That's my fate, my dear. My fate led me to attempt the impossible and told me to persevere. You're right. It would be better to exercise. A person who exercises knows how to breathe properly. His body is sturdy and flexible. Eventually, he will reach old age in good health."

"The exercise is changing me, and it hurts."

"Let it change you." Father's voice was full of despair.

8

Toward evening, I went to the refugee camp to look for the man who had seen his relative in me. The men were short and broad. The years in the camps made them all look the same. Now they beheld the world with indifference and a touch of irony, as if to say, *Nothing can surprise us anymore. Man is a lowly creature.*

But then one of them raised his head and spoke directly to me.

"A little exercise and running don't change a person," he called out. "Don't get so arrogant. Your parents were with us in the camps, and they were no different from us. A little courtesy, a little modesty." He didn't expect me to answer him and went on his way.

I walked in the alleys of the camp. A stubborn feeling had been with me for days. If I returned here, I would easily mingle with these men. But, I kept repeating to myself, in a few months I'll change, the war years will be erased, and I'll be a new creature. The more I repeated those words, the more I saw their foolishness, and anguish mixed with sorrow consumed me.

I stopped and waited for the man who tried to find his relative in me. It seemed he was on his way to me. Meanwhile, another man approached and asked me what I was doing there. I didn't conceal that I was in the training group.

He looked at me sternly. "You ran away from us."

"I didn't run away. I'm close by. Just a few meters."

"And yet you ran away. Everyone who trains himself to travel to a faraway land—what is it called?—abandons us. Youth won't save you forever."

"I don't intend to abandon you."

"You have already abandoned us." He came closer, and I thought he was going to slap my face. But he just went away.

At this hour the comrades were already gathering at the campfire. I overcame my embarrassment at having abandoned the refugees and ran back to our area.

This time Ephraim spoke about manual labor, about the need to make our hands used to working. To demonstrate this, he brought us a hoe and showed us every side of it.

"A tool with many uses," he said, "one that every farmer is glad to have. In the next few days we'll bring you other tools and teach you how to use them," he promised. "By means of the tools, we are linked to the earth. The earth is the mother of all living things. It isn't love at first sight. You have to learn to love the earth; over time you become devoted to it and seek to be nearer to it."

It occurred to me that this was the way monks trained novices before they joined monasteries. But that thought also seemed preposterous to me because most of our training was physical. We weren't taught how to meditate or pray, only how to speak and argue.

With words they had acquired over the past few months and a few they had brought from home, some of the fellows among us already began to express their own opinions. It was hard for me to combine words into sentences. Every time I was asked, I became deeply embarrassed.

When I went for a shower, I looked at myself in the mirror: I saw that my body had filled out, and my muscles were thicker. But would my thinking change as well? Would I no longer think like my parents? Get excited by what excited them? Sit in an armchair in the afternoon and drink in the evening light? Would I become instead a man of the soil who was forbidden to contemplate? Who just worked and brought forth bread from the earth?

Ephraim was sure that bodily changes would also bring changes to the soul. A man who worked in an orchard—who harrowed, pulled out weeds, watered, plowed, pruned, propped up a fallen trunk, ate his meal in the shadow of a tree—he was the new Jew.

At first Ephraim sounded like an army man, but the more you listened to him, the more you grasped that he wanted to plant us into the soil of the Land even now. He was a member of the Haganah and served as a scout for them; the roads and footpaths of the country were familiar to him. But more than anything, he loved the orchards.

I asked Mark for his impressions of Ephraim's words. Mark made a dismissive gesture, as if to say, *What is there to say? In any event, I have nothing to say.* I felt that he was well enclosed in his fortress and that no one dared to approach the gate. I was sad for this handsome, talented fellow who could have been a faithful friend, but who shut himself off and didn't allow anyone to get close to him.

One of the boys asked Ephraim where he had been born.

"In the Land," he answered immediately.

Amazing, I said to myself. He didn't say in a ghetto or in the camps or in the forests. Every one of us had been in one of those places, but not Ephraim.

9

The language drills got harder by the day. Everything was oral, without notebooks or books. According to Ephraim's system, you had to learn the language with your senses, naturally, and the sound was especially important. As we ran, we recited the poems of Rachel, of Leah Goldberg, and of Natan Alterman. And here and there, a verse from the Bible.

"Don't worry. Writing and reading will come later," Ephraim assured us.

A few were already fluent in Hebrew. I tried but found it difficult. Still, I felt that the words were seeping into me and doing their secret work within my body.

Several times I promised my mother that I would guard her language with vigilance and that the bond between us would abide. Mother feared that the language of the sea would drown my mother tongue. Mother's speech was soft and fearful. I tried to console her, but I didn't know how.

She told me once that the division between this world and the one where she dwelled is much thinner than we imagine. "We will always be together," she said, using an expression I hadn't known.

I was pleased by that revelation and promised that at every opportunity I would tell her what I was experiencing. As an aside,

I told her that Mark, the boy with whom I shared my tent, was a fine fellow, but it was impossible to converse with him. His soul was imprisoned in a fortress, and he seldom uttered a word.

"You must watch over him," she said, sounding frightened.

"How can I watch over him?"

"Be by his side, just be by his side as much as possible."

My connection to Mother wasn't continuous. Sometimes the night exercises were so exhausting that I could barely drag my feet to the tent, and I immediately fell into a closed, dreamless sleep, with no sights or visions.

Ephraim started talking about the traits we had to acquire before going to the Land. First was to make do with little. Making do with little was the absolute opposite of living in luxury. Pioneers who lead their camp don't need luxuries. Eat bread and salt. Lust for wanton women is unacceptable and has to be avoided. You should know that whores wander along the seashore. You mustn't approach them and you mustn't resort to them, even when they offer their services for free.

That evening Ephraim spoke about purity of the body—not without a hint of preaching—and about interested and disinterested love. Someone who goes to a whore contaminates not only his body but also his soul. We were chosen, and we had to insist on cleanliness of mind. It was the first time this came up, and it had an ascetic sound.

"What are you doing, and what is it for?" Mother kept asking. She didn't understand the word "pioneer." Nor could I, to tell the truth, get to the bottom of its exact meaning. But since we had spoken the day before about the obligations incumbent upon the chosen ones, it occurred to me to explain to her that pioneers were the chosen of the nation.

"Is it a religious order?" she wondered.

"We don't pray, Mother, and we don't say blessings. We run all day and try to attach the new words to our bodies. Anyway, it's not a religious order."

"Is it an experiment? I hope it's harmless," she said, then added in a jocular tone of voice, "and is there food?"

"Plenty of it: vegetables and dairy products and Italian bread of the crispiest kind."

"Take care of yourself, my dear," she said and went away.

After six months of training—physical exercise and language drills, swimming, rowing, and, in the greatest secrecy, familiarity with two pistols—Ephraim told us that we would soon get on a truck that would take us to the port. Though our training program hadn't been completed, the first stage was behind us, and we could do the next, advanced stages in the Land.

From now on we were in service to the nation. Speaking in Hebrew was obligatory, day and night. In the Land, we would bind speaking Hebrew to the soil. A nation without land was a wretched nation.

10

We spent the final weeks on that concealed seacoast in intense training, leaping over hurdles and climbing walls. I was sorry that we would soon be leaving that place, which had sown previously unknown words and thoughts in me. But I mainly regretted that in the Land I would be separated from the refugees who had borne me on their shoulders and brought me to Naples.

Ephraim never ceased reminding us that we had to keep apart from the refugees and not even look at them, but I felt that this expression of reserve was ingratitude and a grave sin. I wanted to say that we mustn't be separated. We were a single body.

One of the refugees came to our training camp to remind us of that. He stood defiantly and called to Ephraim, "These boys are ours. You can't take them away from us. They are part of our experience. Your running and your drilling words and poems won't change them. They are flesh of our flesh."

Ephraim didn't respond. The man stood quietly and finally went away.

I stopped deluding myself. I knew that the day when we would be parted from the refugees was not far off.

I took advantage of every free moment—or "letup," as they called it—and stole over to the refugees. I was increasingly drawn to that forbidden place. There were already little kiosks there and spots with awnings where people gathered.

A few days earlier I had seen a woman making a gesture with her right hand that reminded me of my aunt Bettie. I approached her. She was indeed very similar.

Aunt Bettie suffered a lot in her life, but she never uttered a discouraging or reproachful word. She always found something positive in every situation and every person. To express her heartfelt beliefs, she always spoke with encouraging hand gestures—not exaggerated, but emphatic—and this was part of her charm. Even when she went to her death, together with dozens of other women, she parted from those remaining behind with an emphatic gesture, as if to say, *Don't worry; our separation won't be long, and soon we will meet again.*

I was glad that there was a woman in the world whose features resembled Aunt Bettie's, who used her gestures, and who shed light and warmth even in that remote place.

I wanted to say, *You are very similar to my aunt Bettie. In your eyes there is the same light of the love for your fellow man.*

But I didn't. It was nearly seven, and I ran back to our area, because at that hour we went out for night training. Night training was very exhausting, but it didn't expose us to the beating of the sun, as did our daytime training. The darkness, the coolness, and the sea breeze made crawling easier. We would get scratched and wounded, but the wounds toughened us. It was too bad the whores on the beach were forbidden to us. Some of them were tall and pretty, beguiling us at night in our dreams.

I struck up a conversation with a boy named Robert. Unlike Mark, my tent mate, he spoke without inhibition, mixing in German and Ukrainian words, and not insisting on pure Hebrew.

I noticed that Robert had about him an air of astonishment,

like that of a person who discovers something new even in monotonous daily life. He did everything, as we all did. It was impossible not to like him. He had a pleasantness that the war years hadn't snuffed out.

I asked him whether he was excited about the voyage.

"The future always bears within it some failure or defeat."

"In the Land, we'll be on a kibbutz," I said.

He didn't reply.

Ephraim's chief joy was the future. The past was worthless in his eyes. When he was informed that we would be departing soon, his eyes gleamed. He was apprehensive about the other refugees, who lay in wait and sought a way to reclaim us. "It's impossible to fight against that swarm," he said, and then explained the meaning of the word "swarm."

II

~ల~

The truck came at midnight. Ephraim issued his final instructions to us with great excitement.

"The truck will take us to the wharf. The ship will probably be full of refugees. You must set an example and help the weak, the sick, and the wounded. On the ship, too, you must take care to speak in Hebrew. You must obey the captain's orders and those of his officers, and make yourselves useful to them."

We listened with pride. We were no longer boys lingering about after the war whom everyone tried to exploit and maltreat, but an auxiliary force in the nation's service.

To our disappointment, reality was entirely different. Hundreds of refugees crowded on the wharf, surrounded by packages and cardboard boxes. No one obeyed instructions regarding the arrangements for boarding the ship and the size of the baggage. The quarrels were bitter and were accompanied by threats and shouts. Visions of the ghetto constantly appeared before our eyes. We, too, were forced to shove, but sturdy refugees pushed us aside.

Because of the disorder and quarrels, we were delayed, and the ship sailed only after two days of rioting.

The very next day a storm struck, and everyone began vomiting. No first-aid workers were at hand. Shouts of "Help! Help!"

went unanswered. Everyone took care of himself. The feeling was that here, too, as in the ghetto, the strong and violent would survive.

Ephraim was very upset. All our preparations and training for the voyage were of no use. The idea that we would be a good example and help the weak and the sick was quickly disproved. We lay prostrate on the deck, vomiting. Only Ephraim stood strong during the storm. Every time one of us fainted, he hurried to take care of him.

The ship was tossed about for three days. The sea did what it wished with us. The violent refugees had no consideration for either children or old people. The officers begged in vain, "Help the weak." Their cry fell upon deaf ears.

Abashed, we gathered around Ephraim. We hadn't done what we were supposed to do. Ephraim didn't demand the impossible. He asked only that we keep apart from the awkward refugees and make a corner for ourselves. We were so weak that we couldn't even obey this small request properly.

Surprisingly, in that mass of humanity, I discovered a family friend, a man as close to us as an uncle, Dr. Max Weingarten, the Latin teacher in the secondary school. He used to come to our house from time to time to play chess with Father. I couldn't believe my eyes and stood there, dumbstruck. I finally grasped his hand and said, "Dr. Weingarten."

I didn't tell him what had happened to me during the war. I told him a little bit about our physical exercises and language training, and about Ephraim's method for teaching Hebrew. Dr. Weingarten was surprised.

"Without notebooks or textbooks, everything orally?" he asked. For a moment, his surprise set him apart from the mass of humanity and made his face glow. "In medieval monasteries," he told me, "they employed similar teaching methods."

I asked him whether he had studied Hebrew in his youth. He said yes and immediately declaimed a few sentences. I was so moved that I cried out loud, "Dr. Weingarten!" I wanted to gather up all my joy at finding that precious man, but I was so weak that I couldn't find the words to express my happiness.

But then Dr. Weingarten recovered and said, "Wait, wait. I want to tell you some things you have to know." I didn't know what he meant. I was so weak that I couldn't stand up. I collapsed alongside him and said, "Once this storm is over, we can sit and talk. I want to spend time with you." But Dr. Weingarten was afraid of the storm that was raging, or perhaps he was afraid he wouldn't see me again. In any event, it was important for him then and there to reveal to me things that I might not have known.

"Did you know that when he was young, your father wanted to go to Berlin and study in the rabbinical seminary?" He spoke loudly, to drown out everyone's noise and the din of the sea.

"Was he religious then?" I was surprised.

"He was seeking his way to faith." Dr. Weingarten spoke to me with great intensity.

"Why didn't he go?"

"Because he started to write."

"Did he think writing would bring him to faith?"

"I guess so."

"I didn't know this," I said with my last bit of strength.

I was so weak that I couldn't absorb any more. I asked Dr. Weingarten's pardon and dragged myself to the corner where my comrades had gathered and collapsed.

Just then the storm died down, and I fell into a deep sleep that lasted two straight days.

12

When I awakened, I wondered why Dr. Weingarten had felt the need to tell me that Father once planned to study in the rabbinical seminary in Berlin. I looked around and couldn't see him. There was a huge commotion on the ship, and the air seethed with violence.

What am I doing here? I said to myself and tried to go back to sleep, but sleep was beyond my reach. My inner world was once again in shreds.

Meanwhile, our ship was intercepted by the British Navy. We knew that somewhere warships were pursuing us, but we didn't imagine that one would actually swoop down on us. We were surrounded by sailors who lined us up, took us off the ship, and brought us to a fenced-in camp in Palestine.

We arrived in Atlit toward morning. The Atlit Detention Camp wasn't like a ghetto or a concentration camp. We strolled about freely, without any of the soldiers shouting at us. Ephraim made sure we had our own shed so we would be separate from the other refugees.

I looked for Dr. Weingarten and found him curled up in one of the sheds. He came out and hugged me. I felt that my inner world hadn't been extinguished after all.

"Dr. Weingarten," I said and hugged his arm. I didn't hide the fact that it was now hard for me to talk about my past. But I very much wanted to hear from him, if he had things he wanted to tell me.

Dr. Weingarten recovered his bearings and told me that he had been with my father in a labor camp for a year and a half.

"Thanks to your father, a lot of people managed to hold on without being discouraged."

"How?"

"Every night your father would tell us a story by Kleist or by Kafka, or one of his own. He had a quiet voice, not soft, and people followed him wherever he led. Sometimes he would tell the same story night after night. People said his voice wasn't from this world. They said he was sent to bind our wounds after a day of discouraging work. They said that his stories were also parables to be deciphered in the future. He was himself one of the prisoners, humiliated and oppressed and no different from the rest of us. But at night, in the darkness, when he opened his mouth, his voice would unite us. Sometimes for an hour, sometimes for two."

I listened, and in my eyes Father's stature increased. He no longer seemed the way I had known him. Dr. Weingarten didn't fade away but continued speaking.

"In the tranquil years it seemed to your father that his writing had no purpose. But, amazingly, in a place where the world became hell, his voice was like one that came from on high."

I couldn't sleep that night. I saw Father telling a story slowly, as though counting the words, while his companions in suffering listened and drank in every syllable. Still, I was surprised that my father, a man of average height who never raised his voice, spoke every night to dozens of people tormented and in pain, and they all listened to him.

Precisely now, amid the commotion in Atlit, I heard my father speaking clearly, quietly, and full of nuances. Father didn't like ideological talk, neither Marxist nor Zionist, not to mention Orthodox. They pained his ears with their unequivocal statements. Sometimes he imitated their slogans to ridicule them.

Father had adopted several principles: A person shouldn't display his ego, either in speech or in writing. Expressing a position or a feeling before presenting the facts is forbidden. Attention to detail enhances speech. The subtleties are important. But never speak with total seriousness. You always have to maintain a bit of irony. Irony distinguishes a thinking person from someone who just spouts words.

During the war, I had lost those principles that had accompanied my childhood morning, noon, and evening. In fact, they were already lost in the ghetto. At that time people needed another language: muttering, grumbling, shouting, and cursing—the language of oppression.

During the war, I hardly spoke. I followed and listened in and was as cautious as I could be. No wonder it was hard for me to get a word out of my mouth after the war.

"Father was a shy man, not to mention a very private person. How could he stand in front of so many people, night after night?" I asked Dr. Weingarten. "Where did he get that spiritual courage?" Weingarten's answer surprised me with its directness.

"When he told stories at night, he was a different man. He had a different voice. That was everyone's opinion."

"Did he speak before he told stories?"

"No, he just told stories."

My desire to sink into myself grew stronger. In my spare time I would sit and observe, not observation in order to estimate distance or danger, but inner observation. That ability was apparently embedded in me, but I discovered it only in Atlit. In time I came to know that inner contemplation can draw up images of the soul that had sunk into me years earlier. Amazingly, when they rose up to the surface, they were as intact as when I first heard and saw them.

13

In the camp at Atlit I remained close to my brother refugees. I could still absorb the shadings of their speech, follow their expressions, listen, if only at a distance, to their clamorous skepticism.

"What was is what will be."

"True, the detention camps are a change for the better this time, but who knows what tomorrow will bring?"

"There's no certainty. Everything is a deception."

"Deception" articulated their experiences—in fact, my experiences as well. But I slipped away from them and from their experiences and took shelter in Ephraim's training.

In the depths of my heart I knew that the refugees were part of my family. I was bound to them by thousands of blood ties. I was fluent in their gestures. If I had been honest with myself, I would have stayed in their sheds, eaten with them, and drunk the bitter coffee from their pots. I would most likely have heard details about the way Father told them his stories. But in those days I felt obligated to follow Ephraim's training, and I observed the rules that kept the refugees at a distance. Because I kept my distance, I lost some of their bodily expressions, not to mention the life lessons that were expressed in their incisive sayings. Later, I would seek them out with longing and despair.

Dr. Weingarten was now like a member of my family. We would meet after night training. I learned things from him about my uncle Arthur, who had appeared to me on that hidden beach near Naples. Uncle Arthur never lost faith in communism, not even in the darkest days of the Party. He fled to Russia, then was imprisoned there, accused of treason, and exiled to Siberia. Dr. Weingarten received two letters from Siberia, brimming with optimism about a future that would be unblemished.

"From his youth, he was an optimist. He refused to see evil. He saw it as an error, a misunderstanding, a passing situation," said Dr. Weingarten, half praising, half mourning.

We kept practicing poems by Natan Alterman, Avraham Shlonsky, and Leah Goldberg, exercising, and ignoring the refugees. Fear that we would become like them—sitting in the doorways of the sheds, gaping and muttering, grumbling, getting angry or blowing up for no apparent reason—that fear settled within me, kept me apart from them. But the refugees recognized me from afar and called out in astonishment, "There's the sleepy boy. There he is." One of the refugees said to me, "You slept well. We watched you in your sleep, and we said to ourselves, what is the boy doing in his sleep? Where is he? What does he see? We forgot you several times, but in the end we went back and found you. Come back to us. Who knows what's in store for us? We'll watch over you."

Dr. Weingarten, the wisest of men, observed my rejection of those who had taken care of me. He knew that contradiction from within himself: as a boy he had been in the communist youth movement, had heard endless lectures about Marxism, and had been captivated by its doctrines.

In time he was sent out on several dangerous missions. Once, he was dispatched to set fire to a synagogue, and he obeyed the order: he poured kerosene on the entrance and the windows and set fire to the building. But the faithful Jews who had been alerted to save the Torah scrolls ignored the flames and burst in.

After the fire died down, the men tore the lapels of their shirts and mourned for the Torah scrolls—some of them very old—that had been burned. Toward dawn, after a night of lamentations and weeping, the rescuers rose from their mourning and began to dance with the Torah scrolls they had saved. The joy of the dancers and their spiritual devotion was so intense that Dr. Weingarten's action seemed to him not only stupid but also criminal. The next day he told his handlers he was leaving the Party.

That distant memory affected Dr. Weingarten. But I didn't understand that he was offering me a scrap of his living soul—in fact, of the souls of his entire generation. And that he was, in a way, warning me about what was to come. Years passed before I understood what Dr. Weingarten meant to me and what he gave me at that moment of life's passage.

My thinking at that time was so flaccid that everything that entered my ears in the Hebrew language sounded correct and just to me. The language and the poetry enchanted me. Because at that time the language was full of elevated words, slogans, and expressions of faith in the future, I, too, was charmed not only by the sounds of the new language, but also by the abundance of words.

In the evenings we read chapters from the book of Joshua. The counselor, a kibbutznik who was about thirty years old, spread a map out on the wall and showed us the places mentioned in the book. It was more a geography lesson than the study of holy scriptures. I didn't understand. Were we, too, required to be like Joshua and his army, who conquered Canaan by storm? Or was this only preparation for a trip, to familiarize us with the Judean Hills and the Jordan Valley, which we would plow with our feet when we were released from this prison?

Particularly in Atlit, far from any context, I remembered the long summer vacations in my grandparents' house in the Carpathian Mountains. I didn't see the mountains in my sleep, but when I woke up, I was face-to-face with them, in all their blue, green, and pink colors. Grandmother loved roses, and she had a large bed of them. Mother and Father used to stand and breathe in the fragrance, enthralled, and they would say, "Only here, only in these mountains, are there such heavenly smells."

Once, I saw Grandfather on a visit to the city. That tall, sturdy man seemed strange and lost on the sidewalks, as though constantly asking, *What am I doing here?* Then it occurred to me that Grandfather realized that the people around him no longer prayed, and that he would be better off returning to the mountains, where his comrades in prayer awaited him.

I asked Ephraim for a day of sleep, and he authorized it. I tried to overcome the bonds of sleep and not to ask for any concessions, but some days I felt suffocated: I couldn't go on without sleeping.

Once, in the midst of a conversation with friends, I collapsed into sleep. Ephraim leaned over and tried to wake me. Eventually, he understood that I was shackled to my sleep, and he left me alone. After that, whenever I asked Ephraim for a day or two of sleep, he allowed it, without even raising his head to look at me, as if it were a hidden weakness I couldn't control. My comrades ignored my weakness and didn't ask about it.

The High Holidays approached. There was a stirring throughout the camp but not among us. We kept on with our calisthenics, our drills in Hebrew words, the study of new poems and chapters of Joshua, and games of dodgeball and soccer.

On Yom Kippur a tense silence prevailed. Most of the refugees didn't attend services. They lay in their sheds and played chess, checkers, and cards. Here and there the rumble of a kerosene stove was heard, and the smell of coffee filled the air.

While we were busy among ourselves, a short man appeared. He didn't seem to be from there, with his crown of gray hair and prayer shawl. He approached us and called out, "The holy day is drawing to a close. The gates are being locked. Come to the prayer shed to be with the God of Israel at this time. Your grandfathers would be very pleased that you were privileged to go up to the Land of Israel. Come and pray together with your grandfathers."

The man stood there, expecting an answer, but we were as though frozen in place. No one dared to raise his head, ask a question, or object. The sun was low, and its fiery rays shimmered above us, but we didn't move. Seeing that there was to be no response to his request, the man quickly departed.

14

~~~

At that crossroad, between what was and what would be, I had very little time to myself. In those hours I didn't think of the future, as was expected of me, but looked inward and dredged up images that had been sunk inside me: Father and Mother and their bright youth.

The refugees continued to observe us. The calisthenics and language drills amazed them. They stood behind the pile of crates that separated us from them, watched, and were impressed.

"Look how tan they are," we heard someone exclaim.

But some of the refugees didn't hold their tongues.

"They're already arrogant," one said. "It doesn't suit them to come to us. They'll be sorry. A few muscles don't make a person excel."

Meanwhile, one of the refugees recognized me and came over.

"Is it you, the sleepy boy?" he wondered.

I didn't know what to say, so I replied, "I guess so."

"You should know," he said, "we carried you all the way. You weren't heavy, but, still, you were a bother for us. Your whole being annoyed us. You didn't seem to be beaten or in pain, but you clung to sleep with a mighty strength. Some believed we shouldn't let you sleep. It was a bad sleep that was liable to kill you. So they tried to wake you. But sleep was cast inside you like lead, and shaking didn't wake you. From the depths of our hearts, we pinned great hopes on you, if I may speak for us all. We said, *In a little while the lad will wake up and tell us things we don't know about.* So now you're awake. What or who roused you?"

"I have no idea," I said with all the simplicity I could muster.

"Still, what was shown to you in your sleep?"

"I don't know yet," I replied, and I meant what I said.

"When will you know?" The refugee wouldn't let me alone.

"When the time comes," I said, since I had no other words.

I didn't tell him of course that I still carried sleep with me to that very day, that every once in a while I would draw upon its darkness, and that recently I had slept for a whole day without anyone approaching me to wake me up.

Dr. Weingarten didn't come to our meeting place. I searched for him for several days and finally learned that he had fallen ill and was being treated in the camp infirmary. When I stood beside his bed, he opened his eyes and recognized me.

"It's nothing," he said. "A slight heart attack. It will pass. Nothing to worry about. It's not so easy to die." Even now, in this situation, irony twisted the corners of his mouth.

When I went to visit him the next morning, he was in a good mood. He was pleased by my erect posture and suntan, and he was interested in my doings. It was hard for me to talk. The words I had known since childhood had slipped away. I made use of the Hebrew words I had acquired, but they couldn't help me to complete a sentence, either. In great embarrassment, I cut the visit short.

The next day, I was told that his condition was more serious, and the British had transferred him to a hospital outside the camp.

"And does he feel better now?" I asked the nurse.

"Let's pray together," she said without looking at me.

I stood in the empty courtyard in front of the infirmary without moving. I now realized that Dr. Weingarten had connected me to my true world with many fine threads. Had I been smarter and less confused, I would have listened not only to his words but also to the way he uttered them.

When I returned to our shed, my friends greeted me with a shout of joy. Soon, very soon, they would free us. That joy only increased my sadness.

Every day I went to the infirmary to ask about Dr. Weingarten.

"We don't know a thing," the nurse told me. "We have no contact with the hospitals here. Are you a relative of his?" she asked and looked at me. I didn't know how to explain my closeness to him, so I said, "He's my beloved uncle."

We spent the next days running and reciting poems as we ran. It seemed we had to complete a specific number of runs and poems, and only then would they free us. The constant effort made my heart forget Dr. Weingarten. At night I would collapse onto my bed like a sack.

Our group was now in top shape, with agile bodies that were capable of climbing over any wall or up any steep hill. But when it came down to it, the "young people," as we were sometimes called, didn't maintain proper standards of behavior when we were tested.

A fight broke out in the refugee camp, a bitter fight, in which men, women, and children took part. It wasn't clear what the fight was about or who the opposing sides were. Boards and iron bars flew on all sides, and shouts deafened the ears.

During all the weeks we had been at Atlit, there had been no evident threat of an eruption. Because no one forced them to work, the refugees seemed content to us. They could lie down quietly, drink coffee, and play cards.

All the trainees were conscripted to calm the quarrel down. The instructions were to separate the adversaries, pacify them, and appeal for quiet. But, unfortunately, the refugees saw us as an alien force and began to hit us. We got an order to protect ourselves and strike back.

The quarrel grew fiercer. The wounded shouted for help, but no one paid attention to them. Finally, the British Army intervened and did what we hadn't known how to do. In that first battle we had five wounded, including my friend Mark, whose wound, luckily, was slight.

"What happened? What was the fight about?" No one had an answer. The quarrel was groundless, like a dream. Some of our fellows were still angry, even after the storm died down. They grumbled and called the refugees parasites. The refugees holed up in their dark sheds. Their hostility to us, we who were exercising every day, was well concealed, but it was clear that they hadn't forgiven us.

Our liberation from the camp rescued us from this shame. Suddenly, and without any advance notice, we were all freed and dispatched by bus to every corner of the Land. They sent my group to Kibbutz Misgav Yitzhak.

15

Misgav Yitzhak lay in the very heart of the Judean Hills. There was abundant light. The few tall cypress trees cast no shadow. The sky was soaring and cloudless. One's body wanted to lean on a wall, so as not to be the target of the great light, but there was no wall. We stood, exposed, in the courtyard.

At our first meeting, the secretary of the kibbutz, a tall, bald man, spoke in a soft voice and used practical terms that we already knew.

"Article One," he said (it was a new word in our vocabulary). "Misgav Yitzhak isn't a permanent place but a transit spot. From here, we'll go on to more advanced training.

"Article Two: Everything we'll learn here is of equal importance. The work, the studies, the training. You mustn't get lazy and neglectful. The staff will discuss personal problems every week.

"Article Three: Three per room, and the rooms have to be tidied before you go out to work.

"Article Four: Lights out at ten-thirty."

Strangely, these simple, clear words didn't gladden the heart. Life at the previous way stations—in Naples, on the ship, in Atlit— seemed soft compared to the life we could expect here.

We weren't wrong. We worked in the orchard. Alongside the orchard, they were building a new terrace, and we would make that stony earth into fertile soil. Dynamite had already uprooted the boulders, and now we would be breaking up the large rocks, which would be used in the retaining wall of the terrace, and we would be filling the pits with loose brown soil, which we would bring up from the wadi in rubber buckets.

The hammers were heavy, and it was hard to break the rocks. Ephraim didn't make a fuss about scratches and wounds. There were bandages in his pocket, and he promised us that in a month or two our hands would know what to do.

Ephraim lifted the hammer easily, and his blows were strong and precise. Our blows didn't break the rocks; they just scattered chips all over. Ephraim had learned from the Arabs how to split and dress stones and how to lay them. He spoke of the Arabs with admiration. They knew the earth like their own bodies and guarded it. Building terraces was their great secret. Their terraces withstood all the ferocious rainstorms.

Ephraim spoke about the earth and its virtues in Hebrew mixed with Arabic. For us everything was foreign, adopted, and forced. We remembered with nostalgia the running and the training on the shore near Naples. They shaped our muscles and prepared us to absorb Hebrew words. Despite the hardships, there was happiness there. Here, breaking the rocks and carrying buckets up from the wadi was exhausting and joyless.

Were it not for Ephraim, the chilly reception would have wiped out our hidden hopes. Ephraim knew that the journey from one point to another wasn't a trivial matter. You had to admit that it wasn't easy for hands to grasp the hammers and swing them.

Ephraim was a great expert in manual labor, but he wasn't arrogant. He spoke to us simply, the way you talk to a friend. Sometimes it seemed as if he was a member of a secret, ascetic order and what he was teaching us now was a mere smattering of what we would be learning later.

"And the next stop?" one of the comrades asked.

"Still far away," Ephraim replied, laughing.

In the afternoon, we studied the Bible and Ethics of the Fathers. Our teacher, Slobotsky, promised that if we made good progress, we would start reading passages from modern Hebrew literature. But what could we do? During that hot hour, as though in spite, fatigue overcame us, our concentration weakened, and our eyes closed by themselves. The roots of the words floated before our eyes and weren't absorbed.

Our new life here was intense, and it overpowered us.

But sleep at night was deep, like the sleep after the war, and I felt that the walls of the tunnel of sleep were only slightly distant from my body. As it turned out, that was only the opening of the tunnel. Every night the opening widened and brought to my eyes clear visions of my childhood, accompanied by the moist fragrance that follows the rain.

Mother and I were walking without speaking. Mother's silences were among the wonders of her self-expression. When she was quiet, her face displayed a singular purity, and it seemed to me that she had been planted in a world that was entirely her own. I did not dare disturb her. Once, however, I couldn't control myself.

"What are you thinking about?" I asked.

Mother turned to me, and I felt that I had caused her pain.

Now it was different. Mother was sitting by my side, as she did when I was sick. I told her that splitting rocks wasn't trivial work.

When she heard this, she narrowed her eyes and said, "You're using incomprehensible words."

"Me?"

"You appear to be using a secret language."

I became confused and didn't know how to reply. Finally, I realized that I was mixing words from home with new words, so I tried to separate them. I wanted to tell her about all my adventures since I had been parted from her. I knew I had a lot to tell her, but it seemed beyond my power, like a pile of broken stones that I had to load onto my back.

"Mother," I said, "I can't right now."

"No matter," she said. Her short reply implied that we had a lot of time. If I couldn't tell her now, certainly I could do so later on. Mother never pressured me, but this time her patience seemed excessive.

"Mother," I said, "in a little while the bell will ring, and I'll have to go to work. I promise to return as soon as possible."

"Work?" She was surprised. "At your age, studies are your work."

I wanted to tell her more, but the words stuck in my mouth. Or, actually, they clung to one another, and I couldn't pull them apart.

Then Dr. Weingarten appeared, pale but not without some irony. I was afraid he would scold me for not going out to look for him. I was wrong. He was glad to see me.

"Every generation has its passions," he said. "We wanted to reform the world from the foundations to the roof, and you smash rocks to build terraces. Let's pray that your passion will come out better than ours."

I wanted to apologize, but the bell rang and cut off my sleep. It was six o'clock, and we headed toward the orchard. No worry: after two hours of work, we would go to the dining hall, where a splendid breakfast would await us.

16

Construction of the terrace progressed. Ephraim built the retaining wall, and we prepared the stones and handed them to him. Ephraim weighed each stone in his hands and studied it from all sides before placing it in its intended place. This careful placement of one stone next to the other was a skill we had to learn. For the time being, we could only be impressed by the work of his hands.

During those weeks, we learned the words needed for the job: cornerstone, foundation stone, a stone left unturned. But more remarkable than those was the expression "loose soil"; this was the brown earth that crumbled between our fingers when we brought it up from the wadi in rubber buckets.

On another subject: at that point not all the comrades had changed their names. The name-changing began, to tell the truth, on the shore near Naples, but only two of us had agreed to change our names then. One night at the campfire Ephraim announced that Benno had changed his name to Baruch, that Robert would be called Reuven, and that from now on we were to use their new names. This was an unsettling announcement, as though their original names had been uprooted from their bodies and new names planted in their stead. We were all so ill at ease that we laughed.

Ephraim now spoke with each of us separately about changing our names, and a consensus was reached that the name-changing ceremony would take place at the end of the month. Some of the fellows wouldn't agree to it. They couldn't explain their refusal, but it was clear that something in them strongly opposed this difficult act. Persuasion was applied personally, adding an unpleasant secrecy to the whole process.

The name-changing ceremony kept being put off from week to week. No one asked when it would take place. Ephraim understood that the collective renaming would be unsettling and might pain some of us. The secretary of the kibbutz was less sensitive. He spoke of the need to change our names as a national requirement.

"Foreign languages will be our undoing," he said.

But what talk didn't do, life did. Our names began to change without our being aware of it. Benno was called Boni. Every time he heard the new nickname, Benno would purse his lips and smile awkwardly.

My given name is Erwin. Mother chose it from all the names that were fashionable at the time. She liked it. Father also liked my name, but he pronounced it differently. The thought that my name would be erased and that in its place I would bear another one seemed like a betrayal.

"Think of appropriate names for yourselves," Ephraim would pleasantly urge us. But then Mark broke through the whispered persuasion and announced, unceremoniously and with a certain rudeness, that he would not change his name. Thus he removed the veil of secrecy that had enveloped the name-changing. Back in Naples, certain opinions had offended him, and he had more than once expressed his opposition to them. Ephraim would speak to him softly, as though to a rebellious creature that had to be appeased.

In my heart I knew that changing my name was bound up with changing my language. I repeated to myself the explanations that Ephraim had presented to us and tried to justify them. But one night I dreamed I was at home. Father heard the explanations, and his response was unequivocal: "A person shouldn't change his name any more than he changes his mother tongue. Your name is your soul. A person who changes his name is ridiculous." For him the word "ridiculous" meant not only inappropriate but also foolish. Father didn't speak angrily but with a restrained seriousness. I was amazed that the war years hadn't altered him. He was wearing a bright gray suit that lit up his face.

Ephraim met me one evening and asked whether I had found a suitable name. I was about to tell him of my dream, but I realized that it was a secret between me and Father, one that I wasn't permitted to reveal to others.

"I suggest that you change your name to Aharon," Ephraim said. "There is something of Erwin in Aharon. Aharon is a name of the first order. Aharon was Moses' spokesman."

I didn't want to be Moses' spokesman. I was my mother's and father's son. They chose my name, and I was content with their choice. I liked names in which you hear the parents' love. *I can't clothe myself in a name with historical pretensions,* I wanted to say, but of course I didn't say it.

Then it occurred to me to ask him, "What was your original name, Ephraim?"

Ephraim was stunned. He hadn't expected me to ask him that.

He turned away from me, then looked back, and with his head lowered, he said, "My name was always Ephraim."

You're lucky. You didn't have to change your name, I was about to say to him. Ephraim apparently knew what I was thinking and said, "I'm doing this for those still to join us, so that we'll be a solid group." The word "solid" offended my ears, and I almost said, *The individual comes before the group*. Ephraim guessed that thought, too, but he didn't react.

I noticed that, unlike the kibbutz secretary, Ephraim knew how to keep his words from invading places and causing complications or pain. He had a considerable degree of sensitivity. Every time I asked for a sleep day, he authorized it with a nod, without asking, *Why now?* My friends were also not surprised by my need for sleep. Every one of us carried a secret within him.

17

My mother tongue was in constant retreat, and I was suffused with Hebrew words. They expanded my world and connected me to the land and the trees. I no longer had any doubt: my earlier life would dissolve, and I would be bound to the soil and the plants. I would have my own horses, plow, and harrow. I would build terraces and plant trees.

During that time, nothing was as good for my soul as tilling the soil and learning Hebrew and the Bible. But something within me, whose full meaning I couldn't grasp, undermined that complete world. It was mainly the feeling of betrayal. It had begun to bother me in Naples, and then I felt it later, in the camp in Atlit. It kept growing stronger in Misgav Yitzhak, and its essence was my aversion toward my brothers, the refugees. I didn't talk about it with anyone. Our lives were filled with the feeling that we were attacking and conquering new realms. The new language didn't yet serve all the soul's needs, but for practical matters it was a wonderful tool, especially the agricultural vocabulary and the language of military training and weapons.

But what could I do? Sleep overcame me with clear and penetrating visions; not horrors from the war but pictures from home: all the pleasantness that surrounded me in my early years as my parents' only child. These sights were linked in sequence, one after another, night after night. I was pleased by them, but at the same time they clouded my day, as though saying repeatedly: *We are your true life. All your new activity is merely a semblance, not to say an illusion. You belong to Father and Mother, and you will always be theirs. There is no region of truth beyond their borders.*

One night I saw Father dressed in his white suit. The suit gave him a young and festive look. I often heard Mother say, "Why don't you wear your white suit? You look good in it." Father was sitting at a chessboard and told me that he had found a new opening that took his fellow players in the café by surprise.

Father was addicted to chess. In the evening, on his way home from work, he would sometimes go to the Cézanne Café and play two or three games. I loved the way he sat at the board with intense concentration, enveloped in cigarette smoke, in high spirits. People liked him because of his relaxed temperament. Mother would sometimes get angry at him when he was late for dinner, but she forgave him easily. You couldn't stay angry at him. He always greeted you with a radiant face.

That night I went into the Cézanne Café and found him sitting in his favorite corner, deep into the chessboard. Suddenly, he looked up at me.

"Where have you been?" he asked.

His question terrified me. I didn't know how to tie together everything that had happened to me since we parted, so I said, "In lots of places."

"That's strange," he said with a look of surprise.

"What's strange?" I was surprised in turn.

"We were always together, right?"

"Since we parted, we haven't been together," I said, and I immediately knew that wasn't the truth.

"I never felt any parting," said Father, and his kind laugh lit his face.

It occurred to me that Father never saw evil, even when it raised its head from every corner. He always saw the good, even when the good no longer existed. Because of that characteristic, some people called him naive, and they always tried to show him that he was. At such times, he would smile benevolently, as if to say, *What can I do? That's me.*

Father was a businessman, but he ran his business in a pleasant manner. He would sometimes say, "There's enough for everyone." He was cheated from time to time, but he knew how to distinguish between the essential and the trivial. He would forgive deceit easily, but whenever anyone tried to undermine his factory, he defended himself with all his might, like at the chessboard, and he would defeat the schemer. Afterward, he didn't gloat. He used irony—not venomous irony—and showed definitively that trying to harm people wasn't worthwhile. In the end, the wicked fell into the pit they had dug for their adversaries.

Not everyone accepted that opinion. Some people said he was a bit blind. Some said he was willfully blind. Father heard them, but he didn't change his views. He would just repeat, "Not everyone is evil."

Now, too, the light in Father's face was unextinguished. He sat at the chessboard, with the pieces arranged for play, but the Cézanne Café was empty and wrapped in thin darkness; only Father's face and the chessboard appeared above the shadows.

"Where have you been, Father?" I asked, struggling to breathe.

"Here," he said in a voice I knew in all its timbres.

"But they drove us out and scattered us."

"You're mistaken, my dear. We were together, we were always together, even when we were momentarily parted. The camps existed and then disappeared, but we remained together."

That was Father. Time had not stained his face. His pleasantness and benevolence were the same as ever. Only his white suit was a little rumpled. Aside from that, there was no change.

"Were we together?" I repeated in wonder.

"Don't you see? Don't you feel it? Soon Mother will arrive. True, the circumstances have changed, but we always remained together. You're right. They tried to separate us. They sent us to different, strange places, but in the end we stayed together. Is there any need to prove that?"

Just as he said that last sentence, Mother appeared and stood next to me, young, wearing a summer dress, as if she was about to go on vacation in the mountains.

Then the bell rang, and I woke up. I remembered every word that was said in my sleep. I even remembered the saying from the Bible that Father used to murmur while playing chess, "One who puts on his armor should not boast like one who takes it off," which meant *Don't forget that your defenses aren't properly fortified. There are many gaps in them.* His opponent would reply with a verse of his own, "The conclusion of an event is better than its commencement."

18

Our lives in the training program kept broadening. Our team performed our work duties and daily chores, and the tallest and strongest of us joined the guards, for which we trained at night in a basement. We learned how to take apart and put together a Sten submachine gun, and we would soon learn how to use hand grenades.

This blending in worried me. It seemed that with every day I was drawing farther away from my parents' house, forgetting my experiences in the war, and building an illusory shelter for myself. Mother didn't scold me, but Father's ironic tongue grew sharper each night, and one time he called me a new Jew.

"What's new about me?" I asked, looking at him directly.

"It seems to me that you're changing and growing distant from us."

"You're wrong, Father. Since I lost you, I've been connected to you with all my might. External conditions don't have the power to change me. What was is what will be. You will always be with me. And so will Grandfather and all the tall trees on his farm, which live in me now even more."

"Pardon me if I insulted you," Father said, lowering his head.

. . .

One night my friend Mark took his own life. Aside from his first name, I didn't know a thing about him. The bitter news spread through the training group, and people stood in shock in the area in front of the dining hall.

"How old was he?" asked a passerby.

"Our age," one of us answered.

"Did he have problems?" the man added in a strident and toneless voice.

"No," came the answer, in the same tone.

It was hard for the people in charge of our training to accept exceptional people. They called them "self-serving."

"We're in the service of the nation" was the iron sentence they kept repeating. But now they were also stunned, as though they had been slapped in the face by reality.

Mark was tall and broad, and he had passed through the physical training and language instruction in Naples and Atlit splendidly. He stood out because of his light leaps and high jumps. But with all that, he refused to change his name. Ephraim, to his credit, was considerate of Mark's refusal and didn't impose his opinion upon him.

Death, which had only been waiting for us in the thicket, had pounced again. How little we knew of Mark. In Naples I shared a tent with him, and at Misgav Yitzhak we were both in room 32. He hardly spoke, and I was afraid to talk to him. At night he would lie in bed with his eyes open and not say a word. When I sometimes woke up in the middle of the night, he would be awake. His concentrated gaze seemed to pierce the darkness. Once in Italy he woke up in the middle of the night and stood next to the tent, not moving until dawn.

Meanwhile, the local kibbutz members gathered in the yard.

"He is no more," they said. "He has gone from us. Why did he do it? Why was there no one to stop him? He was apparently attracted to death."

And so their words rolled by, as though they would be able to banish the twinges of conscience that threatened to strike them.

Everyone expected us to tell them something about Mark, but we didn't know anything, either. Because we stood in silence, they pointed an accusing finger at us.

That afternoon the coffin was placed in the yard in front of the culture hall. We surrounded it with guilty eyes. The kibbutz secretary apologized and said, "We know nothing about Mark, not even his family name. He was with us for months; how is it that we didn't sense his intention?"

The sun was low in the sky, shining on us and revealing our transience. From the time that we were separated from our parents, we had been wandering from place to place. Ephraim tried to plant the feeling in us that this soil was our true home. His success, I must say, was only partial.

Benno, as usual, didn't hold his tongue. After the kibbutz secretary spoke, he said, "Why speak? Better to be silent. When will we learn to be silent?" We seemed like a frightened herd compared to him. He always knew how to separate the essential from the trivial.

A woman, not very young, read a poem, and then a young man stood on a crate and played the flute. For a moment it seemed as if someone would come from far away, stand there, and recite an elegy for the handsome young man who had taken his own life. No one came. A weighty bewilderment spread across people's faces, as though enveloping them in a dreadful secret. The secret grew from moment to moment.

At the graveside a man with thin gray hair spoke about the survivors, that not all of them were capable of withstanding this long struggle. But we mustn't accuse them of weakness of will. They had been in the ghettos and the camps and had seen horrible sights. Despite his considerate words, I felt that his speech was laden with anger. He concluded by saying, "The Jewish settlers here are about to face great trials. No one must act on his own accord."

After the grave was covered, the young man with the flute played a sad song, and that was the end of the ceremony.

Everyone dispersed. We didn't know what to do, so we gathered in Mark's and my room and sat on the beds. Ephraim now stood out in his silence. He wanted to say a few words, but they were stuck in his throat. Finally, he suggested making coffee.

Where did Mark go? the silence asked. Now I clearly saw his sculpted movements: his high jumps, his rope jumping, his rhythmic running along the shore in Naples. All of his movements had a natural elegance. He never said, *That's mine!* Or, *Who took my blanket?* He spoke little, asked few questions. His inner world guided his expressions, and in his expressions there was the beauty of a young man whose outward appearance corresponded to his inner self.

Mark strove like the rest of us, but he had a different goal. His refusal to change his name was not ideological but aesthetic. "It isn't right to change the name given to you by your parents," he once declared.

His whole being expressed a quiet meticulousness—the way he rolled up his sleeves, for example. Little things like that bestowed on him a grace that cannot be imitated.

Toward midnight one of the quieter fellows, someone whose voice we hardly knew, stirred. He spoke in a quavering, restrained voice, mixing Hebrew, Yiddish, and Polish words that trembled in his mouth. *Let Mark, who has just left us, rest in peace. Don't disturb his repose,* we understood him to say. You could tell that he had caught the unspoken claims and accusations, and now he wanted to defend his friend.

"Let him have his death the way he wanted it," he said, raising his voice. Strangely, his were the words that made us weep.

I once again saw the distant shore near Naples, and Mark: different from the rest of us but not conspicuously so. Only after you had been in his company did you learn that you couldn't get close to him. He closed himself off behind locks and bolts. His silence was a kind of intense, frozen speech. I tried to get close to him, but I didn't know how. I had hoped he would open his mouth and speak to me as to a friend, but that didn't happen. If someone came too close or tried to deprive him of what he regarded as his privacy, he would glare at that person and protest, as when they asked him to change his name or to sing at the campfire. His speech was always brief: one or two sentences, and the words were sharp blades. It was impossible to like him. When he heard a compliment he would grimace, as though he had been served tasteless food.

Now his death had come, as sudden as a bolt of lightning.

19

Mark's death stirred things up everywhere, but no one talked about him or expressed an opinion. Caution was evident in the movements of the training course staff, as if they had just now realized that in these boys, usually quiet and introverted, a dangerous restlessness roiled. It was clear that words did not have the power to lay bare their dark secrets. It was better to concentrate on work.

The winter rain began, and we stopped building terraces. Ephraim taught us to prune. Pruning is not a simple job. You have to keep the balance between the shoots and the fruit-bearing branches, and let the light reach the leaves. It was possible to prop up young trees with stakes. Branches that grew out of the trunk were called "pigs" in Hebrew, and they had to be removed, too. In summary, this was the science of pruning. We would learn a lot more about growing deciduous trees.

"Did you ever talk with Mark?" Yechiel asked me one day. He was a boy who did all his duties diligently and brought us a wheelbarrow full of snacks every day at ten and four.

"Not much," I answered.

"I didn't talk to him, either. How is it that we didn't speak with him?" he asked.

"It was hard to speak with him."

"I should have talked with him." Yechiel blamed himself.

"There was no sign he was in distress," I said, immediately regretting my superficiality.

Yechiel concentrated on his work. You couldn't say he was smart or exceptional. He just did what he was told to with diligence. The thin sandwiches that he made for our snacks were tasty; they were wrapped in white paper that was pleasant to touch. He had actually been transferred to the kitchen, where he prepared the snacks.

Yechiel was careful about the words that left his mouth. He never exaggerated or claimed to have done something he hadn't done or been part of. His character was already evident in Naples. True, he didn't stand out in running or calisthenics, but he did what was asked of him and was enthusiastic about the boys who were outstanding. "A colorless young man," he was called behind his back.

Work and the activities after work distracted us from Mark's death, but not Yechiel. After Mark's death, his concentration deepened. From time to time he raised his head and expressed surprise that we had stopped asking about Mark. Once I heard him say to himself, "Mark is gone."

Yechiel was a bit older than most of us, but the child in him sometimes surfaced and filled his face.

"Tonight I dreamed that Mark came back to life," he told me.

"How did he look?" I was drawn in by his voice.

"Exactly the way he was. He was wearing the green sweater. Do you believe in the resurrection of the dead?" He surprised me, and I didn't know what to answer.

"I don't have a clear opinion," I said.

Without looking at me, he said, "My mother used to tell me that the day would come when the dead would come back to life."

I didn't know how to respond to this revelation, so I kept silent.

Yechiel noticed my embarrassment and said, "I try to believe what my mother believed. I don't always manage." His face was pure, as though he hadn't been in the ghetto and the camps but instead had sat in his mother's house and absorbed her beliefs.

I felt unclean and stepped aside.

Meanwhile, we turned a new page. At night we went out to learn the mountain trails and wadis around us. Ephraim called that walk "scouting." In my imagination, he intended to take us to Mark's hidden cave, where he was now living alone. The night was dark, and very few stars were visible in the sky.

The months of training in Naples, Atlit, and Misgav Yitzhak had left their mark on us. Our step was taut and agile. We easily managed to climb up and pass over obstacles. We were light and fleet on our feet.

Ephraim proved to be not only an expert in building terraces but also an excellent scout who knew the trails perfectly. The stars in the sky also showed him the way. I can still hear him call out, "Raise your eyes to the heavens and use the stars."

On the way back Yechiel told me that he spoke with his mother and brothers every night.

"What do they say to you?" I asked sharply, without considering his feelings.

"They are interested in my new place."

"What do you tell them?"

"I tell them everything I do."

"Have they changed?"

"No."

The honesty of his words pinched me. I was ashamed to be fishing around in his soul without revealing a thing about myself.

Sometime earlier, when they had asked for a volunteer to prepare sandwiches for the ten o'clock and four o'clock snacks, Yechiel rose to his feet and said, "Me." Any job would have suited him, but that job was most fitting of all. He always made more food than was necessary and served it all with a bright face. Because of his modesty, he wasn't seen as a worker who did an efficient job but as a servant, someone not strong enough for the building of terraces. Most likely, he sensed that contempt, but I never heard him complain.

In time, when I came to think about the nature of religiosity and about the self-abnegation and innocence needed for it, Yechiel appeared before my eyes. I doubt that he regarded himself as a believer, but every time he recalled his mother, his face changed, as though he was merging with her.

20

After Mark's death, the illusory silence in which we had wrapped ourselves dissolved. Our instruction—calisthenics and field training at night—was intense. We could take apart and put together the Sten with our eyes closed. This firearm was now a part of our body. Soon we would study the Bren light machine gun.

On some nights we were fired at, and the training course staff took up positions and returned fire. But the daytime was quiet and clear. We worked in the orchard and planted plum seedlings on the terrace.

I saw Robert looking around with wonder.

"What amazes you?" I asked cautiously.

"The light." He surprised me.

"Is the light here different from what we knew?"

"Absolutely."

I noticed that he didn't look only at the light. A few days earlier he had found a small fossil among the rocks. He showed it to me and said, "This is a different perspective on life."

"I don't understand." I wasn't ashamed to admit it.

"A chance reminder that we're transitory."

His words astonished me. There was a sense of detachment

in them that I myself had not yet been able to express. Like all of us, Robert worked diligently, but sometimes a delicate wonderment touched his face, showing me that he had his own way of seeing.

Robert noticed that the Judean Hills were rounded and covered with thin scrub. Unlike the Carpathians, the mountains of our youth, in the Judean Hills, horizontal areas were more common than verticals. He saw the world in geometrical terms: vertical, horizontal, or curved lines. His father had been an artist, and he had inherited that way of seeing.

"Do you want to be an artist?" I invaded his privacy.

"I hope to," he said.

During the war, Robert was sheltered by a friend of his father's, a Polish nobleman who had lost his fortune. Despite his bitterness, he stayed loyal to his Jewish friend. There were precious things in his village home—textiles, carpets, and many paintings. Most of the paintings were done by Robert's father, in return for sheltering Robert.

So Robert was surrounded by his father's paintings during the war. His father had done many paintings of the members of the nobleman's family, of his house, and of the landscape around the house. Robert did not go hungry, and he wasn't beaten. This was evident in his conduct at Misgav Yitzhak: He was quiet and not overeager. His contemplations were soft and pleasant.

"What's your mother tongue, if I may ask?"

"German. But during the war, with Stash, I spoke Polish."

"And what's easier for you?"

"Polish."

There was no need to worry about Robert. He had his own language, the language of line and color.

I liked his quietness, the few words that would leave his

mouth, his gaze when it rested on an object or looked out onto the landscape.

"Was Stash kind to you?"

"He was introverted, and nothing outside himself interested him. He was afraid that his daughter would come one day and get her hands on his property."

I wanted to ask him more about that marvelous hiding place, but I didn't.

That was the way my friends emerged from their hiding places and were revealed. But slumber tried once again to capture me at midday. I felt it approaching, and only with great effort did I manage not to collapse. Finally, I asked Ephraim for a sleep day. He agreed, but this time he asked, "Is it necessary?"

Without taking off my clothes, I laid my head on the pillow and was borne on waves of darkness. I slept for two days straight. If it weren't for the noise of tractors returning to the garage, it's doubtful that I would have awakened then. My strange sleep habits were already well known, and when I woke up, everyone's eyes were upon me.

In my sleep I ran after Mark, but he quickly sailed by, going around obstacles and climbing walls. I eventually caught up with him. He looked at me angrily and then tried to ignore me.

"Mark." I stopped, out of breath. "Where are you running?"

"From you," he replied.

"What harm did I do you?"

"Why are you following me?"

"Your death gives me no peace."

"Go back to your place, and don't run after me," he said and disappeared. I kept going, but now it was a voyage with no destination. There were many dangers in my path. Somehow I overcame them, and when I woke up, I was tired, as if I hadn't slept at all.

I was glad that no one asked me anything. I went back to the terrace to water the seedlings we had planted. Very gradually, the slumber dissipated and wakefulness returned.

21

Winter. The work outside stopped, and we sat in the class-room and studied the book of Samuel. Slobotsky, the teacher, read slowly and softly, and his voice hovered over the pages. I saw Elkanah, the prophet Samuel's father, as a tall, restrained man, whose movements were imbued with silence. I also saw his two wives, Peninah and Hannah. Peninah was broad and angry, and Hannah was thin and trembling. Elkanah spoke to Hannah's heart with soft words, but the words only increased the trembling of her shoulders. She did not dare raise her head.

The words of the story were simple, but their melody was new to me. This was the language of these hills, absent all decoration and radiating silence.

Benno noticed that there were few adjectives. Slobotsky treated that comment with respect and wondered whether they were necessary. When Slobotsky read, it was almost like singing, and he planted the melody in us. Some of the words were not understandable, and Slobotsky explained them with his hands or facial expressions. Sometimes it seemed he was trying to con-vey the meaning of the sentences to us without the mediation of explanations.

"Hannah spoke in her heart; only her lips moved, but her voice was not heard." There was voiced prayer and voiceless prayer. Eli the priest was old and blind and no longer distinguished between voiced and voiceless prayer. Voiceless prayer seemed to him like the mutterings of a drunk, like meaningless words. No wonder he didn't understand what his two sons, Hofni and Pinhas, were doing.

What those words showed me was strange. Every word was a picture. In the filth where Hofni and Pinhas wallowed, Hannah and her son seemed like ministering angels. Interestingly, Hannah did not see the corruption; she saw only God. She prayed and swore an oath, and later she was to leave her only son in that polluted temple, as if it were a place where God dwelled.

Slobotsky read. Not everyone was as enthralled by his reading as I was. But each in his own way, Robert and Benno, who was always as sharp as a razor, were listening intently. Benno found the following verses to be light in the darkness: "And Samuel ministered before the Lord, a young boy girded with a linen priestly vest. And his mother would make him a little vest and bring it up to him from year to year, when she came up with her husband to offer the yearly sacrifice." Slobotsky also commented that only a child whose thoughts were pure and who was distant from the corruption could wear a child's priestly vest. On the day of judgment, no priestly vest could protect Hofni and Pinhas.

"Why are we studying the Bible and not biology?" shouted one of the boys. Slobotsky didn't respond to that remark, but that first chapter of the book of Samuel made my body tremble as it had not for a long time. It seemed that the words Slobotsky presented to us were carved out, each word individually, and laden with secret content. I felt something similar when I saw for the first time the blue of the inner Carpathians. I was so astonished that I wept. Mother didn't know what to do and enfolded me in her arms.

Robert responded differently. A thin smile hovered over his lips all morning, as though Slobotsky's reading had revealed to him combinations of forms whose beauty he had not imagined. Later he commented that Hofni and Pinhas, because of the similar sound of their names, became one; togetherness made their actions even darker.

"Now the sons of Eli were sons of Bihlee'al." Here, too, the sounds link their parentage with their sin. Not only were Robert's eyes wide open but his ears, too.

Slobotsky wore khaki clothes, like all of us. He was about fifty, but when he spoke, he seemed younger and like a musician or orchestra conductor. He repeated every verse several times, examining its musicality. Sometimes he repeated a single word. When he was enthusiastic, he did not seem like a local, but like someone who had come from far away. Indeed, he had come from far away. He was born in Shedlitz and studied in Berlin.

Slobotsky's teaching style drove some of the boys mad. They called it hypnosis. But most of us were woven into his magic and listened to the details that he drew out of every verse.

"The Bible must be read attentively," he sometimes said. "Many secrets are hidden in it. Too bad that my colleagues, the researchers, refuse to listen to its melodies. History and geography have their place, but the secrets are more important than they are."

Sometime after that, I saw a man in the yard, scouting with his eyes. At first I didn't recognize him, but when I approached him, I saw right away: it was none other than Dr. Weingarten.

"Where did you disappear to? I've been looking for you," he said and walked toward me with open arms.

I didn't know what to say except "They brought me here." But

I realized that this didn't excuse me from my responsibility. I was ashamed that I hadn't gone out to look for him.

He was wearing the same coat he had worn in Atlit. He was pale, and he walked cautiously, like a man who had been struck repeatedly. He had been in the hospital for about a month, and now he was living in a transit camp. His latest circumstances hadn't erased the irony from his lips. Twice a week he guarded a building site. Up to now thieves hadn't attacked him.

I brought him to the dining hall and asked for a late lunch for my uncle, who had come to visit me. I received a full tray. Dr. Weingarten ate, and I saw him sitting in our home with Father and felt the delicate silence that enveloped their chess games. I knew I ought to ask him many questions because only he remained to tell me everything that had happened to my father and mother. But that very necessity stopped my tongue. I sat next to him in silence. Finally, I began to speak.

"I didn't know that Father had a strong voice."

"He had a voice that touched every one of us," Dr. Weingarten replied, "even those who didn't understand the text he was telling us about. Sometimes it sounded like a voice calling from the depths, and sometimes like prayer. The tempo was uniform. Every word was well pronounced. That was the vital energy he gave us night after night, for many months."

"They used to return the manuscripts that Father sent out." The words tumbled from my mouth.

"They didn't understand your father. Nor did I, after reading two of his books. I sensed that he had great talent, but it seemed tangled up; I hoped that someday he would emerge from this entanglement. I didn't absorb the logic of his sentences. Only when he was telling us stories at night did I feel he was conveying his brilliant depths to us. After the war, I went back to our city and hoped to find at least one of his books, at least a few pages. I didn't find a thing."

I didn't ask any more. I was afraid.

I accompanied Dr. Weingarten to the road leading to the tran-sit camp, and I promised to come and visit him. I also told him I had a new Bible teacher named Slobotsky, a teacher of great stature.

"I know him," he said. "We both studied in Berlin. How is he?"

"He's teaching us the book of Samuel."

"Give him my regards," Dr. Weingarten said, and went on his way.

22

That night I felt very lonely. It seemed that the separation from my parents and their language, which began during the war and continued after the liberation and on the way to Palestine, had now come to its bitter conclusion. I knew it was my fault. I hadn't tried to preserve the warmth of their speech. It occurred to me that Mark certainly felt something similar when he took his life.

I saw before my eyes the many feet that had trudged alongside me, heavy feet, swollen with too much walking. I knew those feet had found it hard to walk in that arduous way, but they carried me from place to place, as though they had sworn to bring me to safety. For some reason, the dining hall emptied fast. I took my notebook out of my folder and wrote:

> My mother's name: Bunia.
>
> My father's name: Michael.
>
> My grandfather's name: Meir Yoseph.
>
> The city of my birth: Czernowitz.
>
> The street where I lived: Masaryk.
>
> My grandparents' villages: Dratzintz and Zhadova.

The name of our housekeeper: Victoria.

The kind of coach that took us from the city to the country and back was called a fiacre.

My nickname: Ervinko.

For the first time I saw the names of my family, my city, and my grandparents' villages in Hebrew letters. The names gleamed in my notebook, as though garbed in clothing that wasn't theirs. For a moment I was sorry I had clothed my dear ones in strange garments, and I was about to erase the list.

After that I went outside and felt better. I met Benno. Benno didn't usually reveal his emotions. No one knew where or how he had passed the war years. He caught on quickly. Before you even began to think, he had taken two steps forward. His thinking was logical and dazzling, but not without feeling. I didn't restrain myself and told him that a short time earlier I had been struck by a feeling of deep loneliness.

Benno didn't respond to that but spoke about Mark, who had prepared his body and mind for his daring act. I was surprised by the word "daring," but I didn't question it.

"There are people who can't live with contradictions," he said.

I knew every aspect of the word "contradictions." Since the liberation, I had been living with it day after day, had been scorched by it at night, and had carried it with me everywhere. But for some reason I had never articulated it. Father didn't like the word, but he occasionally used it.

"What contradictions are we talking about?" I wanted to hear Benno's opinion. He lowered his head, as though he was going to draw the correct words out from within it. Then he raised his head and said, "All during the war, and even more so after the liberation,

I prepared myself for life, not for death. My whole family—my parents, my brothers and sisters, my grandparents, my uncles and aunts, my cousins—all of them died, and only I remained. Why did I remain? What is the meaning of my survival? I still remember all of them by name, but I can't prevent forgetfulness. Every day of training, every day of planting in the orchard, even every day of learning Hebrew makes me forget them. Change. Renewal. Didn't we adopt those words in order to break loose and forget them? I and those like me do everything we can to live fulfilling lives in good health on this land. Is there no ugliness in this? Is there no arrogance? I don't want to speak for everyone, but I don't know how to live with their deaths. Maybe it's impossible. Weren't those Mark's thoughts, which bore him to that great darkness?"

After a few moments of silence, he said, "Sorry," and went on his way.

I stayed where I was. Benno's clear words struck me. I was sorry I had missed the opportunity to get close to him but, on the other hand, perhaps I had done well by not asking more. One does not ask about deep wounds. I now sensed that his thoughts were teetering on the abyss. I was gripped with fear that he might do what Mark had done. I went to look for him. It turned out that he was looking for me, too.

We sat in the dining hall, spread jam on slices of bread, and drank tea. We spoke about the terraces and about life without books. A person rises in the morning and goes out to the hills, works for seven or eight hours, and returns home sodden with labor. He takes a shower, prepares a meal for himself, sits at the table with his wife, and sleeps the sleep of the righteous. But Benno's parents were teachers in a secondary school, and their whole life was books.

"My father and mother, too," I said, revealing just a bit.

23

That night I also returned to my city, and to the long avenue that led to my home in its outskirts. The house was empty, as happened sometimes when I returned from school early. I went from room to room. Everything was in its place, silent and with no discernible smell. The objects in my room were also in place, just as I left them: the bookcase, the briefcase, and the photograph of the Carpathians, which Mother had enlarged and hung on the wall. It was two o'clock.

"Father!" I called out. The sound lingered in the air for a second and then faded. I realized that Father wasn't home at that hour, but Mother, if she had no special errands, was usually in the living room, waiting for me.

I touched my briefcase, which lay on the dresser, and it occurred to me that I had not gone to school for many years. Sweat covered my body. What would I tell Mother when we met? Mother didn't appear, but the housemaid, Victoria, opened the back door and stood on the threshold. Upon seeing me, she called out in alarm, "He's here. How did he get here?"

"I came home," I said.

"There's no one in the house," she said, showing her tobacco-stained front teeth.

"Where are they?" I asked in my ordinary voice.

"Why are you asking?"

"I want to know."

She frowned at me and said, "Go away. Go back to your place."

"What place?"

"The place you came from."

"This is my place," I said, not moving.

"If you don't go, I'll throw you out." The anger in her face grew more intense.

I gathered all my strength. "Victoria, don't you recognize me?"

"Certainly I recognize you. But you don't belong to this house anymore. Your home is in another place."

"Where?"

"I don't know. You'd better clear out of here before I call the yardman."

"Mr. Vilitsky will recognize me and won't throw me out of my house." I spoke in a conciliatory way.

"You're wrong. He'll sweep you out."

"I don't understand your behavior, Victoria. We were friends. When Father and Mother went out together, we would sit on the floor and play dominoes or hide-and-seek. You would tell me about the village where you were born. What's changed since then?"

She contained her anger for a moment and then said, "You must understand; your place is no longer here. I don't know where you live, but it's not here. You haven't been here in years. Apparently, you got lost and ended up here."

"But everything here is as it was."

"You're mistaken."

"Isn't this my school briefcase?"

"If you open it, you'll see that it's not yours anymore."

"Whose is it?"

"My nephew's."

Then the true face of the house was revealed to me. Everything was in its place—or, rather, most things were in their places—but the light wasn't the same. The bedspreads were covered in blue, a color the peasants loved.

What is this? I was about to ask. But there was no one to ask. Victoria had disappeared. Most likely, I said to myself, she's gone to bring our yardman, Mr. Vilitsky. No more than a few minutes passed before I heard his voice, hoarse from cigarettes.

"I'm coming."

Soon Victoria's voice was heard. "We have to get rid of him right away."

It occurred to me to go out and look at the back stairs that led to the basement. It was dark, and the familiar smell of mildew, not unpleasant, filled the air.

"Where is he?" I heard the yardman's voice.

"He was here, I swear."

I knew that soon the door would open, and Mr. Vilitsky would grab me by my shirt and throw me into the air shaft. My body froze, but I did manage to say out loud:

"This is my house, my eternal house. No one can deprive me of it. You can grab me and throw me down the dark air shaft, but you can't take this house from me. It's planted in my body." I wanted to add something else, but my voice was stuck in my throat.

The bell in the exercise yard woke me up and saved me. Everyone got up, and so did I.

In the afternoon, I received permission to visit Dr. Weingarten. The transit camp wasn't far off, just a half hour's walk. Dr. Weingarten was pleased to see me and hugged me. To avoid asking him what my parents' fate had been, I told him about my work in the orchard and about the Bible studies with Slobotsky. He told me right away that Slobotsky was known as a genius in Berlin and had been appointed as a teaching assistant at an early age, and Martin Buber constantly praised him. He was well liked by Jews and non-Jews.

"How strange that he's teaching Bible in a training course now."

We sat on Dr. Weingarten's bed in silence. His companions in the shed also sat on their beds, smoking and sipping coffee from thick cups.

"And Mother?" The question slipped out.

"She, too, was a wonder. She worked in the kitchen, and from the scanty supplies available to her, she made tasty, nourishing meals. She got thin, like all of us, but her beauty didn't fade. She was the nourishing angel of the entire camp."

I heard this, and shivers passed through my body, as though I had only now learned how my parents had left this world. I didn't ask anything else. The images before my eyes made me shiver again. Dr. Weingarten sensed my emotions.

"I won't rest until I find your father's manuscripts," he said.

"Where are they, in your opinion?"

"With non-Jewish acquaintances to whom he gave them to read. I regret that I was tempted into emigrating prematurely. I should have stayed and gone from place to place to look. If I don't manage to do so, you'll do it, right?"

"You'll manage," I replied, in Hebrew for some reason.

Dr. Weingarten wasn't surprised. He knew Hebrew. It was too bad he was in the immigrants' settlement and had no one to converse with.

"I can't forgive myself," he said, "for not realizing until we were in the camp, when I heard his voice and his stories, the greatness of your father's soul. Your father and mother were superior people," he said, and fell silent.

I was also mute.

Then he rose to his feet and said, "Return to the training course, dear boy. They're certainly expecting you. And I'll go to the building site, to guard it." I felt that he did not now wish to remain in the company of loved ones.

I hugged him and promised to come back. I realized that Dr. Weingarten had conveyed to me not only these scenes but also something of himself, and my heart ached.

24

We resumed building terraces. Yechiel improved the quality of the ten o'clock and four o'clock snacks beyond recognition. Each food had a new taste. Sometimes he made me think of young Samuel wearing the priestly vest, perhaps because of the checkered sweater he wore.

Some of the fellows picked on him. I reprimanded them. I usually didn't comment, but when injustice cried out, it was hard for me to restrain myself. I inherited that trait from my father. Father was a pleasant man, but I observed him raise his voice more than once.

True, Yechiel wasn't quick during our training and weapons exercises. Nor did he stand out in our studies. But he saw things that we didn't see. He told me about his dreams with simplicity, as though there was no difference between nighttime visions and reality. Sometime earlier he'd asked me whether I also dreamed. I didn't conceal the truth from him. He didn't ask anything else. He was satisfied with what people told him and didn't ask too many questions. I wouldn't have been surprised if, like young Samuel, he told me that one evening he had heard an unidentified voice that had shocked him.

. . .

I opened my notebook and once again saw my mother's and father's names in Hebrew letters. This time, too, they seemed strange in their new clothing.

Grandfather, I assumed, would have been glad that I wrote his name in Hebrew. For years he was worried about my Judaism. He didn't express his fear explicitly, but his arms communicated it when he hugged me. Father, I assumed, would have responded with reservations to my efforts to acquire the language. He would be afraid that I would lose my mother tongue. *A person without a mother tongue can't hear his own voice. His language will be spoiled forever. There's no substitute for a mother tongue.* I'd already heard him say that in Naples and in Atlit, but not as clearly as in Misgav Yitzhak.

By this time, we had been in Misgav Yitzhak for eight months. Some of the boys did change. They grew taller, their shoulders broadened, and they looked like the local boys. Robert, however, did not change. His light touch was evident in everything he did. He was tall and lanky, and his fingers were delicate. Despite the manual labor, his fingers hadn't thickened. They remained bony and vulnerable. He touched objects with caution, looked at them, and put them down without making a sound. He kept discovering surprising new colors, forms, and poses. He lived in constant amazement. His life during the war and after it didn't spoil his visions. He walked among us like a prince. Unlike Benno, he didn't try to organize or articulate his thoughts. I was afraid for his fingers whenever he rolled a chunk of rock or picked up a heavy stone.

Every time they called him by his new name, something in me became alarmed, as if Robert had been called upon to do something against his nature.

I returned to the empty dining hall, took out my notebook with the list I had made, and read it out loud. Suddenly I realized something I had known in the depths of my soul but hadn't dared express: I had parents and a home, and now I would be preparing myself to return to them. That discovery made me so happy that I started to hum the song "Land, My Land," which Ephraim had taught us.

Slobotsky's Bible lessons were put off until after work hours. We were all tired, and our eyes would close. Slobotsky read, and his reading flowed over my fatigue; I could take in only partial images. Still, I listened. When the Ark of the Lord was captured by the Philistines, it declared: "Better to be among strangers than among people of the Covenant who violate the Ten Commandments every day."

"It's magic!" one of the boys shouted. "A wooden cabinet has no feelings or speech."

This time Slobotsky stopped reading and said, "A person doesn't have to believe in the anger of the tablets of the Covenant that were given on Mount Sinai, but can we remain indifferent to the profanation and corruption of that sanctified place?"

We were all tired, the words and images intermingled, and only Slobotsky's fine voice could be heard. Sometimes it seemed that Slobotsky wasn't teaching so much as sowing the words of the Bible for the days to come.

25

⚬❧⚬

Time carried me along quickly, as though on a raft without oars. The day began at six and ended at eleven at night. I fell onto my bed and plunged into deep sleep. Sometimes a dream or, rather, a scrap of a dream invaded my sleep and terrified me. But my exhaustion was so leaden that it crushed even the nightmares.

More than eight months had passed since Mark's death, and Ephraim decided to hold a memorial. The thought that in a little while we would be standing in the cemetery next to Mark's little tombstone wrenched me out of what we were doing and made me confront that dreadful day when they discovered Mark's body hanging from a window bar.

Ephraim wanted to bring the young flute player who had played at the funeral to the memorial. But it turned out that the boy had already been drafted. Finally, the administrator of the training course agreed to play. Once again the question arose of who would speak. How strange that Mark's death was so recent but at the same time so far away and inconceivable. It occurred to me that if he had left behind a list, like my list, one of us could have read it, brought to life his place of birth, and reconnected Mark to us.

Before my eyes, I saw his sharp leaps, his high jumps, and his graceful and noble stride. It turned out that during his time in Naples and Atlit, he was preparing himself not for life but for his death, and in Misgav Yitzhak he did what he thought was right.

That night my father appeared to me as I had not seen him for many days: leaning over his desk, withdrawn and in deep concentration. I didn't see him much when he was writing. He wrote mainly at night. He wrote for years, and every time he finished a book, he would send it to a publisher. The reply came quickly and immediately darkened his face. Mother would stand next to him, as though reprimanded.

Father noticed that I was observing him. He turned to me and said, "I can't do it anymore. I'm passing the pen to you. You'll do what I couldn't."

I was astonished by these words and said, "What should I do?"

"Do what I was unable to do," he repeated.

"I can't write, Father. I've lost my language, and I can't write in the new one."

"A person doesn't lose his mother tongue." He cut me off sharply.

"I've lost it. Believe me."

"This is beyond my understanding," he said.

I wanted to cry, but the tears wouldn't come. But I was able to string some words together and said, "It's not my fault, Father, if I may express an opinion about myself."

"And what about the survival of our souls? Mother and I pinned great hopes on you. I've reached the end of my strength. All these years, I've tried with all my might to find a new form, but without success. I had hoped you would continue what I began. If you can't, either, what is the meaning of our lives?"

"It's a burden beyond my power, Father."

"So it seems to you."

I overcame the choking in my throat.

"I'm here, Father, in the heart of the bare Judean Hills. These hills can't tolerate a language that isn't theirs."

"And what is their language?"

"Silence and more silence. In that silence we're building terraces, planting trees, and every day we acquire a handful of Hebrew words. The book of Samuel is marvelous but parsimonious with words. That is the language of these hills—fewer and fewer words."

"And you speak that language?"

"Every day."

"So we won't be able to speak the way we used to anymore?"

I told him I had made a list of all the people who had filled my life and would soon add to it. This was my dam against oblivion. I conceded that working the soil was overwhelming me and didn't leave space for my former life.

"Your mother and I are your former life?"

"Father, you and Mother are planted in me, and I am with you even when conditions don't permit it. One day, when the vicissitudes of my life become known to you, you'll understand that I'm attached to you and, through you, to my grandparents and the Carpathians. My latest incarnation is strange and full of contradictions. But I haven't forgotten for a moment that you and Mother are my soul. I have no other. I haven't betrayed you, and I never will. As for the language, even if I forget all the words that connected us, you will be with me always, and we'll always speak the way we did."

Tears welled up in Father's eyes, as though he understood my situation.

26

The memorial for Mark was held toward evening. The light was low and pleasant, in total contrast to the event for which we had gathered.

"We have come here to remember our comrade Mark," Ephraim said. "The office investigated and checked with the Jewish Agency, and we discovered that Mark's family name was Stolz. Other details—his father's and mother's names and his place of birth—have not yet come to light. But at least they managed to rescue one detail from the jaws of oblivion."

We have come here to remember. I silently repeated Ephraim's words. *How and with what will we remember him?* I asked myself. The new detail that had just been made known to me spoiled the figure that had taken shape in my mind. "Stolz" means "proud" in German. Mark was not a proud young man. Proud implies he was pleased with himself and his achievements. He did what we all did, and with more success, but he wasn't proud. He didn't try to stand out. He was free, and his freedom was more important to him than pride.

The administrator of the training course played the flute, and we sang "The Partisans' Song." I recalled my list, and for a moment I was sorry I hadn't brought the notebook with me. But I immediately realized this was an idle thought.

Everything proceeded at a leaden pace, with long pauses. And like most newly created ceremonies, it was without taste.

Benno's face showed his displeasure. It was clear that this ceremony was not to his liking. When we were about to disperse, Yechiel walked up to Mark's grave, covered his forehead with his left hand, closed his eyes, and in a soft voice recited the Kaddish in the Ashkenazic pronunciation. When he finished, he took a few steps backward and returned to his place.

Astonishment reigned. Everyone expected Ephraim to protest Yechiel's action. But Ephraim, to everyone's surprise, stood still and said nothing. His lips curved into a smile, which made all of us stare at him.

In any case, Yechiel's unexpected act made an impression. We didn't foresee independent action from him. He always did as he was told. Although the skill of his fingers was evident in the kitchen and in preparing snacks for us, no one saw that as an expression of his own will.

"He has something that we don't." That was Benno's reaction.

"What is it?"

"Faith that he inherited from his parents."

"We're already beyond that." That harsh response came quickly from someone standing behind us.

That night I sat in the dining hall. I took out the notebook in which I had written my list and added the names of my uncles Arthur and Isidor, and Mount Strelitz, at whose foot we would sit for many hours—Father, Mother, and I—listening to its summer music.

How strange that during the years of separation from Father, I hadn't remembered his writing at night. I was sure that he placed his greatest efforts in the chess games.

I looked up and saw Yechiel. The way he stood showed that he was embarrassed. I didn't know what to say to him. Eventually, I overcame what was blocking my speech and said, "It's good that we parted from Mark with a prayer, thanks to you, Yechiel." My words apparently touched him, and he burst into tears.

"Yechiel," I said, "you rescued us from the shame of muteness."

His weeping grew stronger and his body shook. I went over to him and gave him a hug. After a few minutes he stopped crying and went into the kitchen, his place of work.

27

One evening a refugee came by the training camp, looking for his nephew. His dress, his appearance, and, most of all, his posture showed how out of place he was in our silent surroundings. He was momentarily pleased when he heard my German; it turned out he was from my region. He had been wandering for weeks, and he had already been to quite a few kibbutzim, farms, cooperative villages, and training courses, pursuing idle rumors. He had resolved to do whatever he could to find his nephew and not to skip over any place where young people were being sent.

I wanted to show him the orchard and the new terraces, but he thanked me and hurried away. As we stood at the gate, I recognized in him several features of my grandfather Meir Yoseph.

From time to time, strangers drifted in. Once, a Jew in traditional European dress arrived, bringing spices for the kitchen. After selling his wares, he stood in the yard for a long time, looking at the landscape and the people, and then, without asking about anything, left.

That night, for the first time, we went out for night patrol armed with guns. A few nights earlier, the tall, well-trained guards of the training camp had gone out, lain in wait for infiltrators, and toward dawn caught five of them. The infiltrators were brought, bound, to the dining hall, and once they were questioned, they were given coffee and cigarettes. After promising that they would no longer attack Jewish settlements, they were finally released, without their five rifles—spoils for Misgav Yitzhak.

For us, happiness mingled with giddy tension. We had been training for months, but our armed patrol had been delayed several times. Now came the moment to feel the danger.

We entered the dark hills walking lightly and crouching correctly and spread out in ambush formation. We lay on the cold, hard ground for about six hours, and before first light, we rose and stood, bent over, on numb legs. Then we returned to the camp, stooped and tired, and slept until noon.

In that sleep I had a long dream that I remembered very well. I was in Atlit, after physical training and language drill, drinking a glass of lemonade and then slaking my thirst with a second glass. Suddenly the walls separating us from the refugees fell down, and an entire congregation stood there, wrapped in prayer shawls, praying silently. I rose to my feet and stepped back. It seemed to me that if I hadn't done so, they would have approached me and knocked me over. I was wrong. Their prayer became softer, and their bodies hardly moved.

"What's this?" The words slipped out. My voice was loud and tore through their silent prayer.

All at once they removed their prayer shawls and glared at me. The arrows shooting from their eyes became stuck in my flesh and immobilized me. In vain I tried to gather all my strength to run away from them. But I was tied down, the target of their hostile looks. One of them, tall and sturdy, turned to me and said, "What did you do to us?"

"I didn't mean to do anything," I apologized.

"You put a stop to our prayer. We can't go back to it."

"It seemed to me you were about to trample me. I was wrong. Pardon my error."

I woke up to the noise of the tractors returning to the garage, but those images from the dream didn't fade. They stayed before my eyes for a long time.

Toward evening I went to visit Dr. Weingarten in the immigrants' settlement. I didn't find him. He had gone out to guard a building site, the men in his shed told me.

While I was standing there wondering where to go, a short refugee came over, fixed his eyes on me, and asked, "Aren't you the sleepy boy?"

"That's me," I said.

"You've gotten a lot taller," he said. "You're suntanned. I almost didn't recognize you. I'll tell you the truth. We were sure you wouldn't make it and that you'd return your soul to your Creator in one of the camps. We were very tempted to leave you behind. But there were some among us who argued strongly that we had to bring you to safety. You owe your life to them. They, the few, the stubborn, carried you. A lot of people will tell you that they carried you, but don't believe them. Only a handful did. I wasn't one of them."

He paused for a moment and then asked, "When did you wake up?"

"In Naples," I told him.

"All at once? After all, you didn't move during the weeks we were wandering, except when you smelled the water in streams. You would crawl in order to drink from them. How did you emerge from your slumber?"

"It happened," I said, just to be rid of him.

"And now are you awake?"

"As you see," I replied, trying to go.

But the man wouldn't leave me alone.

"You have to find the people who carried you and thank them," he said. "Some of them are here. I'll point them out."

"I'll come back in a few days," I said, and turned my back to him.

"Don't put off that obligation, and don't be an ingrate," he said, running after me.

"I won't put it off," I said, and walked faster.

"We tend to put off paying our great debts. That's our weakness. Don't do it. There are things we can't run away from, and the sooner we do them, the better it is for us. We have to learn to say thank you and not deny those who were good to us."

"I promise," I said, to escape his clutches. I ran all the way back to the training camp, and I was out of breath when I reached the gate.

28

The shooting directed at our training camp didn't let up, even in daylight. We received reinforcements from the nearby settlements and we dug trenches, fortified existing positions, and built new ones.

One night, while I was on watch at one of the posts, I felt sorry for myself; soon they would attack us, I would die, and I then wouldn't see my parents anymore. I asked Robert, my partner on watch, if he also heard noises.

"No," he answered. That single word, devoid of doubt, sounded like a reproach to me, and I was ashamed that noises made me afraid.

Slobotsky was not recruited for guard duty. Along with Yechiel, he brought coffee and sandwiches to each of the posts. In fact, they were more exposed than we were, especially Slobotsky, who hadn't learned to bend his tall body down.

Eventually, the order was given to fire, and we did so, along with those in nearby positions. The darkness was thick, and we could see only the sparks of light flashing from the barrels of our guns. After a few minutes we stopped shooting. Silence reigned. We waited for a response, but the response was slow in coming. It was clear the infiltrators were crawling toward our positions. The two ambushes the officers had set up didn't stop them. Luckily for us, the silence lasted until dawn.

We lived in the trenches and at our posts. We didn't work or study, and we hardly washed. The image of Yechiel, hunched over when he came with our meals, was that of a youth who had seen a lot of suffering in his life and who now wanted only to be devoted to people who were in danger. Because he wasn't bearing arms, Yechiel felt inferior in ability to his friends, and he always scurried to satisfy us. His devotion didn't make him the object of mockery, but neither did he receive special thanks. Slobotsky, who poured coffee for us with trembling hands, also failed to receive a warm welcome. But some of us, like Benno and Robert, didn't forget that he was nearly fifty and a graduate of the University of Berlin. It was proper to respect his sensitivity, not to mention his erudition.

So the days passed. If we had been permitted to take a break temporarily from our patrols and ambush positions, we would have stretched our muscles and overcome our fears. Lying on the ground for a long period stultified the mind. It would have been better to expose us to some risks.

Robert told me that he had seen Stash, the man who had sheltered him, in a dream, selling the paintings his father had given him. He recognized the portraits of his mother, his sister, and himself.

"I begged him in vain not to sell the paintings, but Stash stood by his decision. 'I'll sell them no matter what,' he said. Since my pleading was of no use, I knelt down and said, 'Please, by your mercy, don't sell the eternal life of my father's soul.' Upon hearing that emotional appeal, he tightened his lips into an ironic smile and said, 'Since when do the new Jews believe in the immortality of the soul? After all, they threw away their ancestors' faith long ago.' I rose to my feet and protested. 'My father was a believing man,' I said. 'What did he believe in? In art that brings balm to the soul.' 'I beg your pardon, my young friend,' Stash replied. 'Modern art isn't a faith, it's a disturbance.' 'And won't his soul live eternally?' I asked. 'Not unless he repents from the sin of his new beliefs,' Stash said, and then disappeared into the darkness."

The dream unsettled Robert. Throughout his time with Stash, he had never conversed with him. Occasionally, Stash would express his opinion about the Jews and their way of life, but he had never voiced such an explicit judgment. Once, though, he told Robert he should accept the Catholic religion. A man without faith is like a driven leaf, he said. Robert, who was dependent on Stash's kindness, was afraid he would eventually force him to convert, but in the end, he left him alone.

Our lives at our posts, with no changing of the watches, was one long, gray day. In daylight we alternated: one of us would remain on guard while the other slept curled up on an old mattress. At night both of us would be awake.

Robert was certain a great war was on its way and that we would have to live at our posts not just for weeks but for months. That prediction was hard for me to bear. Something had to happen, I hoped, that would release us from this tedious lying down. Robert told me that the length of time he had spent in hiding with Stash had diminished his ability to concentrate. He had hoped that the training and the work in the fields would cure this, but now here we were dug into position and lying in place.

Ephraim came to visit us with the news that we would soon leave our posts and join the regular soldiers. The high command had decided that the village across the way, which was firing on us day and night, had to be attacked. They had not yet decided what our task would be in the mission but, in any event, we had to be prepared.

That night Robert turned to me and said, "I don't know what will happen to us in the war. If my parents come to look for me, tell them that I thought about them all the time. Not only in hiding with Stash, but also when we were liberated. I love them a lot."

"We'll get out of this the way we got out of earlier troubles," I said, and was embarrassed by the shallow words that had come from my mouth.

29

⌒⌒

The order to go into action was given. We had been preparing for this hour since Naples; now our bodies would speak in their full, strong language. I had often forgotten what we had been training for and had been mired in images and visions. Now the veil was lifted, and we were standing in the yard in front of the culture hall.

Ephraim was delayed. We stepped in place and stamped our feet. I remembered the memorial ceremony for Mark, which had been held there. It seemed he was now observing us with a clear-eyed gaze, as if to say, *I chose my death at a time and place that I found right. I couldn't bear the thought that someone might shoot me.*

Yechiel went out with us, too. He had trained like the rest of us, but he still didn't seem like a soldier. The cartridge belt was loose on his thin body, as though about to slip down. Ephraim, or who knows who, had decided to include him. Yechiel hadn't objected. On the contrary, he was obviously pleased.

The real soldiers had begun racing about in the early evening. For the first time, I saw them up close. They weren't sturdy or tall, like the soldiers of our training course. But they moved with agility, and the rifles in their hands seemed to be tailored to fit them. They laughed and joked, imperceptibly soothing the fears that were lodged within us.

Finally, Ephraim arrived, and he immediately quieted and reassured us. We wouldn't attack or conquer positions this time. Instead, we would dig in at a distance from the battlefield, and if the enemy tried to flee or call in reinforcements, we would strike them with all our power.

This was a task without glory, but it was still our first combat mission. Ephraim asked whether anyone had questions. There were two questions, which he answered at length. From his answers, we understood that the target this time was the village across the way, which was full of troublemakers and arms caches. Their positions were fortified, and it was important to surprise them and block their escape routes.

The trained units, experienced in combat, would attack first, and we would wait. If there were surprises—and there were always surprises—and the attacking forces had to withdraw, we would have to cover them. Everything sounded clear, but was nevertheless wrapped in secrecy.

Edward, one of the boys, asked me if by chance I had an extra bandage. I had one and gave it to him. He was glad and put it into one of the pouches of his cartridge belt. I asked him if he was nervous. He made a gesture with his hand, as if to say that ambushes didn't fall within the scope of danger.

Edward was one of those people you like at first sight, similar to the rest of us in every way, but still different. He was more than six feet tall and not outstanding in training or brilliant in studies, but the goodness of his heart was boundless. Because of that quality, everyone liked him.

Edward's mother tongue was Hungarian, and it would probably stay Hungarian forever, because every Hebrew word that came from his mouth was stamped with a Hungarian pronunciation and accent.

"All of you will speak Hebrew with a decent accent some-day," he once acknowledged, "and only I will always speak Hungarian."

Pay attention and be careful, I wanted to tell him. Your height places you in constant danger. You have to be sure to walk hunched over. But I didn't say it. Edward seemed calm and content that we had left our posts. Lying in those positions, especially because of his height, had shrunk him.

"Now that torture is over," he said. "Now my legs aren't con-fined in a cast. Those gangs won't dare leave their holes. If they come out, we'll beat them hip over thigh," he said, and we both laughed. In his last lesson, Slobotsky had spoken about the expres-sion "hip over thigh" in the Samson story in the book of Judges and explained its meaning.

We went out after midnight. Darkness and silence were melded together. I walked behind Yechiel, and I could see that it was hard for him to wear the loaded cartridge belt. It occurred to me that they hadn't done well by subjecting him to this test. If, perish the thought, he was shot, we would all bear the guilt for the rest of our lives.

We proceeded according to the rules of advancing by night. The way forward seemed long, as if we wouldn't reach the appointed place until much later. I was wrong.

When we advanced a bit farther, we began to be pelted by a heavy rain of bullets. Whoever wasn't hit clung to the ground and returned fire. But the ones who were hit groaned from pain and shouted, "Medic! Medic!" Fortunately for us, our ambush group came to our aid and eliminated the enemy unit. Everything began to quiet down within minutes, but for the ones who were hit—

including me—our lives were cut in two: the seventeen and a half years before the shots and then the life after them.

I apparently lost consciousness. My comrades carried me in their arms back to the kibbutz and from there to the hospital. The big operation, for which we had prepared ourselves for many days and with great thoroughness, had failed.

30

I was unconscious for two days, and when I woke up, I didn't remember a thing. The place looked like the white storeroom where I hid during the last days of the war. I was sure then that I had reached the final stop of my escape, and I awaited my death. Fortune smiled upon me: the German Army was preoccupied with retreat and had stopped looking for people in hiding places.

A young nurse approached me and asked my name. I told her. She looked at me and said quietly, "That's a nice name." I didn't feel any pain. I closed my eyes, and it seemed to me that my friends' names were being called out and that my name had been omitted from the list. I wanted to get up and ask to have my name restored, but my voice was stuck in my throat, and I sank back into the pillow.

The nurse gave me spoonfuls of water, which I sipped. Then I saw for the first time the doctors and nurses standing around me, and I wanted to tell them, *Don't worry. I'm just tired. In an hour or two I'll get to my feet and join my friends.*

The next day the nurses returned and looked at me with concern. I told them that in a little while I'd get my strength back and stand on my feet. I was pleased that the Hebrew words came easily to my lips. In the haziness of sleep, it had seemed to me that all the

Hebrew words I had acquired in Naples, in Atlit, and at the training course had fallen away and that I would have to relearn what I had already learned. I was sorry for that loss.

"I feel better," I said. The doctors and nurses looked at me questioningly, but they didn't ask me anything. I didn't know at that time the seriousness of my injuries. Months of training had shaped my body and planted within me the feeling that I could withstand all required efforts, and even a serious injury. I didn't know if my friends felt as I did. But I, in any event, was a mass of muscles, prepared to lift any load.

Only that evening did I realize that I couldn't move my legs. It seemed that my legs had fallen asleep, as happened to me sometimes. If I rubbed them, they would hurt me a bit, but then I'd feel them as before. That night I felt pain, and the nurse didn't keep from me that I had wounds in both legs. But I didn't believe her. I told her that my father had also been wounded on the front, in the First World War, and that the doctors hadn't believed he would recover from his injuries, either.

Benno came to visit me, and I was glad to see him, as though he had come from a familiar world. He knew things about my wounds that I didn't know. I asked him about our friends, and he replied that everyone was all right. I sensed he was hiding things from me, but then I dismissed that suspicion. Benno was a man of truth. I had often heard him correct a friend who hadn't told the truth. When he heard a lie, he would stamp his feet.

The next day I learned that two of my friends had been wounded and that Ephraim himself had been shot in the right arm. Now I knew that Benno hadn't wanted to add to my pain.

That night the head of the department, Dr. Winter, came to speak with me. He promised me that the medical staff would do everything they could to save my legs. That promise, which sounded like an oath, did not soothe me. I looked at him, a tall man who spoke in decisive sentences, and asked him in my mother tongue whether there were miracles in medicine.

"There are," he said. "But we don't call them miracles."

"And what is their medical name?" I challenged him.

"Lack of knowledge that will be clarified in the future."

His speech in my mother tongue was soft, but at the same time it strove for precision. He explained things to me at length and in a leisurely way, as though speaking to a relative, and he demonstrated with his fingers what the surgeons had done and what they were going to do in the future. While he was talking, I noticed that he resembled my uncle Arthur. But he had a deep cleft in his chin.

"Where are you from?" he asked.

"From Czernowitz," I didn't hesitate to tell him.

"I knew it," he said. "Your German gave it away."

That night I had a long dream. In my dream I was sitting with Mother in the kitchen, a place we both loved, and I was drinking cocoa. On such occasions Mother liked to describe a bit of her life to me. Usually, it was some detail of her daily goings-on, but in her telling, it sounded like something that she had brought up from the depths, wrapped in thrilling fragrances and colors.

The hours in the kitchen were often laden with silence, with no loud laughter or lofty speech; they passed as though we were submerged underwater, with both of us swimming and enjoying every movement. At the time, of course, I didn't know exactly what Mother was conveying to me.

This time she sat and stared at me in wonder, without saying anything. I wanted to say to her, *Mother, why are you quiet?* But I didn't dare. Her wonder was complete and intense, as when she

told me about celebrating the bright and fragrant holiday of Sha-
vuot with my grandparents.

"Let me tell you everything that has happened to me since we
were parted," I said. I expected my words would attract her attention, but to my surprise she responded to them with a thin smile
that made me fall entirely silent.

"I won't hide anything from you," I added.

When she heard that, she hugged me and kissed my forehead,
and then the smile returned and parted her lips.

"Don't you believe me?"

Her smile broadened, and she said, "So many things have happened to both of us, that if we came together to tell them, the
nights at our disposal wouldn't be enough."

"Everything here is in its place, Mother. That means that we
didn't hope for this in vain."

"You're right, my dear. The kitchen is in its place, the house is
in its place, Father is in the next room listening to music. But I'm
a bit tired. Can't you see that on me?"

"It's visible."

"And now I'll tell you something that might surprise you: you
don't need to tell me. I know everything. We were never parted. I
was always in every place you were. And now, at last, we've come
back to our home."

31

The next day I still refused to accept that my injury was almost fatal. The pain was intense, and the injections didn't lessen it. But in my heart I believed that the diagnosis would soon turn out to be mistaken. In my sleep I saw Mother again. Her smile showed no worry. She did indeed know that I had been wounded but, like me, she also believed that it was a superficial wound and that I would soon rise to my feet.

My friends came to visit me and brought me fruit and chocolate. They seemed worried. I asked them not to worry about me. My request didn't erase the fear from their faces.

My bed was rolled out to the glassed-in balcony. The lawn around it looked well cared for, and the flowers and bushes reminded me of the public park in the city of my birth.

"How long will the treatment last?" I asked the nurse.

She looked at me with alarm and said, "I don't know. You must ask Dr. Winter."

The pain tormented me at night as well, but my instincts kept whispering to me that in a day or two I would surprise everyone and stand on my own. In my childhood they had taken out my tonsils, and I lay in bed for a week. Every day I gobbled up two portions of ice cream, as a cure. Now the taste of that pink ice cream returned to my mouth. Suddenly, I saw Mother sitting next to me and looking at me. Her look contained everything that was buried within her: her endless love for Father and me.

For as long as I could remember, Father wrote at night. He had many ways of sitting at his desk. Sometimes his expression, or rather his pose, resembled that of someone who was blaming his father for not letting him study at the university.

A fierce dispute had developed between those two sensitive men. I didn't know all the details. Father never forgave his father, and his father, who tried several times to appease him, merely rekindled his anger.

Father wrote incessantly. But when the packages came back from the publishers to whom he had sent his manuscripts, his face would fall and darken. Mother would quickly kneel at his side and reassure him that all the gates weren't locked. Father's face would close up, and Mother, in great despair, would run to the kitchen and make blintzes with cheese and raisins—a dish all three of us loved.

Mother liked my father's writing, and she kept saying that the day would arrive, and would not be long in coming, when the editors would admit their error and book after book would be published. Father was doubtful, and every time a good word was said about his writing, he would lower his head and blush.

That night I dreamed we were riding on a train. The train moved slowly, and I could look at the dappled landscapes of autumn. For a moment it seemed we were entering the railroad station of my city. But that was an error. We drew close to a bridge suspended over a deep chasm. We were about to cross the river below, and for the first time in my life I dared to look into the steep abyss. I saw the damp rock walls and the churning water and the foamy whiteness. I knew why in previous years I had been too frightened to lower my eyes and look down.

The train increased its speed. To my surprise, low houses topped with thatched roofs emerged from a fog, brindled cows grazed in broad fields, and thin smoke spiraled up from the chimneys of the houses. Now I knew that the train was returning me to the station of my city.

The pain yanked me out of my sleep, and the nurse rushed to give me an injection to ease it. They would operate on me at sunrise. I didn't understand why they operated so early in the morning. They hang murderers at dawn. Patients should be operated on in daylight. I looked at the nurse and didn't say anything to her. Dr. Winter was already dressed in his white gown, and his three assistants were also prepared. The clacking of the train still sounded in my ears, and before my eyes, the chasm opened up again.

Dr. Winter told me that in a little while they would put me to sleep, and he and his assistants would try to do everything to save my legs. The word "save" should have awakened me from my illusions, but it didn't. On the contrary, I clung to my belief that in a little while they would announce that a mistake had been made in the diagnosis; my legs would once again belong to my body, and if I was allowed to sleep for two or three days, they would heal completely.

While those thoughts were racing around my head, they placed the anesthesia mask over my face. It felt deeply suffocating. I plunged into the abyss.

When I opened my eyes, I saw Dr. Winter, and he told me

right away that the operation had been a success. But this was only the beginning. Further operations lay ahead of me in the coming months.

"Thank you," I said.

"We don't deserve it yet."

"Will I be able to walk?"

"Let's hope so."

Dr. Winter was a cautious man, and whatever he let out of his mouth was weighed and measured.

"This is only the beginning," he repeated, meaning that the journey to recuperation had just begun. Didn't Dr. Winter see that I was pressed for time? I urgently needed to continue in Father's path; this thought flashed through my mind.

"What did your father do?" asked Dr. Winter.

"He was an author."

"And what was his name?"

"His name was like mine," I said, and was glad that I came up with an answer to his question.

32

Benno came to visit me. I told him that, in contrast to the prognosis of the doctors, I felt the day was not far off when I would stand on my own two feet. Benno didn't ask me what my feeling was based on, and we talked instead about classical music. I was glad I had the strength to distance myself from myself and draw close to him. My father and mother didn't play any musical instruments, but they loved classical music. Sometime before the war, they bought a record player and records, and we used to sit and listen for hours.

Benno and I began speaking in Hebrew, but at a certain point we switched over to our mother tongue. Unlike in the training program, linguistic discipline was lax here. Homey words were heard in every corridor.

Benno excused our deviation. "A person recovering from an operation is permitted to speak his mother tongue." Robert, too, when he came to visit me, ignored the prohibitions and spoke to me in our mother tongue. In the training program, these prohibitions were self-explanatory, and we barely noticed them. But here, among the patients and the white beds, a person returns to his home, and not only in his sleep.

One of the male nurses, a gray-haired man, asked Robert whether I'd been wounded at the front.

"Correct," Robert confirmed.

"It's wrong to send boys to the front who aren't yet eighteen," he said reproachfully.

"He did it of his own free will."

"Undergrounds and armies don't know what free will is," he replied, and left.

After a few minutes, he returned and said, "It's wrong to send boys who survived the Holocaust to the front. Even in the Red Army they didn't draft boys of his age. They trained them, and only after training, which lasted for about a year, did they send them to the front."

I didn't pity myself. I was certain that my injury was just one episode in my training and that when I recovered, they would send me to officers' school. My injury wasn't a handicap, I repeated to myself. Important officers were wounded and continued to command.

Robert sat at a distance and sketched me. When he finished, he showed me the drawing.

"It's a good drawing," I said, and was pleased by it. Robert responded to my comment with a smile. I liked his smile, a mixture of softness and awareness of his own value; this also came through in the drawing.

After breakfast, the nurse took me out to the balcony and told me what was going on in the country: about the assaults on the roads and the settlements that were being attacked day and night. I was sorry that instead of fighting at the front I was lying in bed, and a nurse was taking me out to the balcony every day like an infant.

"You did your part, beyond what was demanded," the nurse told me.

"I didn't do a thing."

"You fought."

"You're wrong. I didn't manage to fight."

"You were wounded at the front, right?"

I tried to remember the names of my friends who had been wounded, who were now lying in a hospital like me, but I couldn't. Because of their new Hebrew names and the confusion this caused, I couldn't picture them.

I asked the nurse's name, and she answered simply, "Sabina."

"You didn't change your name?" I was surprised.

"No," she said, smiling.

"Didn't they tell you to change it?"

"They did," she said, and her smile filled her face.

Unlike me, Sabina had stood her ground and had not changed her name, a sign that I should have done the same. A person doesn't abandon the name that his father and mother gave him. I was angry at myself.

Sabina was two and a half years older than I, but her face was that of a grown-up. For the moment, she was a practical nurse, but she wanted to study for a diploma and become a registered nurse. The word "diploma" reminded me of my uncle, my father's brother, Stefan, whom I hadn't seen for years. Suddenly, I saw him. He had finished all the requirements at the university, but one of the professors had it in for him, so he hadn't received a diploma.

That night I saw Father sitting at his desk and writing. It seemed to me that his efforts and my efforts to rejoin my legs to my body were shared. I wanted to call out to him, *We'll both do it*, but I realized that this was erroneous. There was no connection between his writing and my injury.

"Will my legs be reattached to my body?" I asked Father fearfully.

"I have no doubt," he replied as he raised his big eyes to mine.

"But the doctors . . . ," I said, and the words stuck in my throat.

"We are commanded to make the effort, and salvation will come in the blink of an eye." That didn't come from his treasury of sayings. Because of his many humiliations, he had lost faith in himself and was now pinning the rest of his hopes on a miracle from heaven. I was sorry that he had lost his faith in himself and in his way of thinking and had adopted once again the old faith that he had abandoned in his youth.

33

The days passed. Except for Dr. Winter, all the doctors said the paralysis of my legs was irreversible. Their whisperings gnawed at my hopes, but I didn't despair. I swallowed the drugs they gave me, and when the pain grew more intense, the nurse gave me an injection.

My comrades were sent into action two or three times a week. They stopped building terraces, clearing land, and planting trees. I alone was sprawled out in bed, groaning in great pain and not doing anything useful. My friends weren't coming to see me as often as they had in the first weeks after I was wounded, but they came at least once every two weeks. Each time, I saw how they had changed. They were tanner, they had developed their muscles, and they lived their lives wreathed with danger.

Occasionally, I asked the doctors if my condition had improved. The answer was always prompt, concise, repetitive. One of the hospital volunteers took the trouble to visit me once a week. She asked me how I felt and expected me to reply at length. I answered her briefly. She appeared to believe I was in despair and tried to encourage me. I kept telling her that I wasn't discouraged, that I saw my future as a working man. I didn't speak with her about my innermost feelings because she might think I was a prisoner of illusions.

Then one day, Dr. Winter informed me that they were going to operate on me again, at dawn on the following day. He sat on my bed and explained to me the importance of this third operation. I looked hard at him and saw that he worried about me like a father.

My recovery, he said, would move forward in stages. At every stage, my chances would improve somewhat. I observed his lips and the movements of his hands.

"How many years will it take?" I asked.

"Indeed, my friend, not in a day, but you must not lose hope. Hope is our most important asset."

I noticed that Dr. Winter resembled my uncle Stefan, my father's brother. He was also an easygoing man who always tried to help people.

That night I slept restlessly. Pictures of the war and of the time after the war passed before me. Nothing significant bound them together. I asked myself what they were showing me and why, and I had no answer.

Finally, I managed to tell myself, *Connecting the parts and giving meaning to it all are my tasks.* I was glad I had parted from the dream without depressing thoughts.

When I awoke from the operation, Dr. Winter was standing next to me. He asked how I was.

"While you were attaching my legs to my body, I was trying to put together what I saw at night into a single picture."

"And did you manage?" Dr. Winter wondered.

"Partially."

"I see that you're walking in your father's path."

"Also my mother's."

I was surprised that my mind was clear, because after the second operation I felt blurred and didn't recognize where I was.

. . .

I heard that one of my comrades had been wounded in action and was in the adjacent building. I asked the nurse to take me to his room. To my surprise, it was none other than Edward.

"What happened?" I asked as I approached his bed.

"I was wounded," he said softly.

I saw that one of Edward's arms was wrapped in a thick bandage.

Edward was a head taller than the rest of us, well over six feet. We looked like dwarfs next to him. He was also well formed. But he displayed an astonishing innocence. In Naples, the smugglers, thieves, and cheats would exploit this. They made him work like a dog and then gave him only a few bills. He would go out right away and buy pizza for the group. He never worried about himself. His clothes were too small and ragged, but he still looked handsome. The girls liked his height and his strength but not his innocence. A short, ugly refugee whose business was doing well captured their hearts faster than Edward did. Once, a woman refugee, a few years older than Edward, attached herself to him and wanted to live with him. If our group hadn't opposed it strongly, he would probably have been caught up in her net.

I didn't ask about his wound, but I could see the pain in his face. The injections were not working.

Edward eventually told me that two fingers of his right hand had been shot off. This wonderful fellow, whose tall good looks we had all admired, was lying in bed like a trapped deer. Unlike the other wounded men, he didn't blame his comrades or his commanding officer. If you go to war and go on the attack, he explained to me simply, you will encounter danger. It was best not to think about it, because if you did, the attack wouldn't take place.

"Victory is more important than my two fingers," he concluded.

Edward then fell silent. I saw that his wound had carved thick lines into his face and neck, and the head on the pillow no longer resembled the handsome one that I remembered. I asked the nurse to take me out to the corridor. I was flooded with sorrow, but, as though in spite, tears would not come.

34

I went back to see Edward later that afternoon. He was lying on a wide pillow that a volunteer had brought for him. I told him that for now there had been no change in my condition, and they would soon transfer me to a convalescent home.

"I can't go back into battle, either," he said, and a pained smile filled his face. The new lines that had been stamped onto it stood out even more.

The friends who came to visit us toward evening stayed longer with Edward. Clearly, he was a new casualty, and they were already used to my injury.

That night I saw Father again, sitting at his desk. This time, his way of sitting was different, not bent over. He had apparently been encouraged by Mother's words, and maybe by the writing itself.

"What are you struggling with, Father?" I dared to ask him.

Father raised his head from the papers. It seemed that he was about to scold me for pulling him out of his work. I was wrong. He looked at me with fatherly compassion and said, "Give me a moment to think."

I now saw his face as it had never before been revealed to me.

Surprise and disappointment stirred about on it. For years, he would return home each evening and rush to his desk. Mother would wait for him to finish his tangled efforts before sitting down to eat, but the struggle would usually last a long time. The meal she had prepared would get cold, and she would desperately try to improvise a new one.

"I'm struggling with the words," Father answered objectively, without resentment.

I didn't understand what he was talking about. His answer seemed like a riddle for me to solve. Mother didn't quite understand his complexities, either. He never gave a full answer to her many questions about what he was struggling with, but she completely identified with his efforts. Her lack of understanding didn't prevent her from following him.

"Why struggle with words?" I asked.

"Because they are easily falsified," he promptly replied.

"How can we know what is true and what is counterfeit?"

"An example," he said, "would be the word 'I.' It would seem that there is nothing simpler, but it holds many dangers within it. The 'I' loves to raise its head arrogantly. An arrogant 'I' is a grave flaw. An 'I' without modesty is a blemished 'I.' Even worse is the word 'we.' 'We' is a pretentious word, and you have to be cautious with it, too. 'We' without 'I' is a hollow word."

"Thank you, Father," I said, though I didn't fully grasp his intention.

He turned toward me and said, "Son, I did what I could. I didn't do a lot. In fact, very little. My fate didn't bear me along the right paths. I don't know what will happen to me and where time will take me. I see that God gave you an understanding heart, and you will do what I didn't manage to do."

"Father, I can't take that burden upon myself."

"It isn't a burden; it's holy work, if I may for once use that por-
tentous expression."

"Father," I implored him, "I was wounded, and I don't know
whether I'll be able to stand on my feet."

"Son, unlike me, you inherited some of your grandparents'
faith, and they will instruct you in what to do."

"I don't know what you mean, Father."

"The meaning will become clear to you as you work."

I wanted to say to him, *Father, don't forget that I don't have a language. My mother tongue, though I understand it, has been lost, and it's
doubtful that the new language has taken root in me.*

I couldn't hear his answer, but his trembling hand said to me,
You have to gird yourself with patience, and God will watch over you. I
was surprised by the word "God." He was always careful about
using it and had often scolded Mother for saying, "Thank God."

35

In the hospital I was able to sink back into the thick slumber that took hold of me after the war. Blood tests early in the morning, meals, and doctors' visits did indeed awaken me, but, amazingly, the flood of sleep wasn't halted. And I didn't have to ask Ephraim for a sleep day and be ashamed of my request.

When I closed my eyes and plunged into sleep, I was reconnected with the first, fresh images of my childhood. After the war, I was able to touch these images, but then I was disturbed by the refugees carrying me on their shoulders and could no longer see them.

Summer vacations with my grandparents were always a pilgrimage, with the expectation of new sights. Unlike Father, Mother was not at odds with her parents, and every return to her first home was full of great excitement.

Grandfather would come out to greet us with his face aglow. He was always close to God, whether he was sitting at the table or standing alongside one of His sacred implements: the bottle of dark cherry brandy, the tall wax candles, the brass basin for washing hands.

Grandfather was present but also a bit distant from us. Our arrival would bring a bit of commotion to his sanctuary. Objects that had stood in place for months without being exposed to a stranger's eyes suddenly seemed to be shrinking in their corners.

Mother didn't worship God the way Grandfather did, but she knew the house and all its hidden places. In Grandfather's house, prayer would return to her, and she would pray with her eyes shut. Father kept his distance from ceremonies and prayers, and at the Friday night welcoming of the Sabbath, he would sit next to Mother in silence. Grandfather was fond of him and accepted him as a son.

Marvels surrounded Grandfather's sanctuary. Tall trees rose toward heaven, cliffs loomed between the trees, and animals would peek out from the shrubbery: a hare as white as snow, an astonished deer, a shiny brown colt. Down below, a stream burbled softly.

The summer nights in the Carpathian Mountains were long and bright and did not belong to either day or night. They were entities unto themselves. We would sit outside on mats, and Father would slice into a watermelon. He tended to keep a distance from the excitement, but on the white nights of summer, he, too, would emerge from his shell and take part in the festivities. Grandfather didn't sit on a mat. He would sit in his room, perusing a book or praying. He appeared only when coffee was being served and would then sit with us for a short while.

Our abrupt departure from the Carpathians was like being plucked from a pleasant sleep. The coach appeared early in the morning, having come from the city to our door. My heart wept, but I didn't allow any tears to flow. Grandfather enfolded my head in his two large hands and blessed me. Grandmother cried and wiped her tears away with a white peasant kerchief.

All of this I saw again in my deep slumber, and I knew that none of it had been permanently snatched away. On the contrary, I now saw it even more clearly. The years had not spoiled these images. There was nothing temporary about them. There were no newspapers or radios in the Carpathians, no theater or cinema. After a month's stay in Grandfather's sanctuary, the city seemed foul, and its places of entertainment graceless.

36

As promised, they transferred me to a convalescent home.
Benno got a day off and kept me company. Before leaving,
I had a short conversation with Dr. Winter. I asked him whether
there had been any improvement in my condition.

"Your condition is definitely encouraging," he answered, emphasizing every word. When I went on to ask whether there was
hope that I might stand on my own again, he lowered his head
for a moment, then raised it and said, "You must be patient. We
will do our part, and your body will do its part." For a moment I
wondered about the statement "Your body will do its part," but
I didn't pursue it.

Dr. Winter spoke very objectively, but I felt that he hadn't
told me the entire truth. Of course he didn't wish to sow any illusions, but I had the feeling that in his heart he knew that one day I
would rise to my feet. When I asked what would be done with my
belongings at Misgav Yitzhak, I was told they would wait for me
in my room, and when I returned, I would find them in their place.
That answer also told me that my banishment was temporary. I
took my Bible with me, and my notebooks. The transfer was done
in great haste, and I barely had time to be moved by the flowers
that the nurses gave me.

. . .

The convalescent home distanced me from my friends, but it didn't distance my thoughts from them. They were still training and going out on missions, and from time to time, they came to visit me. They had changed since I was wounded. In the first days after I was wounded, they whispered in my presence and waited for me to speak. Now as they stood next to me, they spoke about their dangerous deeds and laughed out loud. They took my injury for granted.

They were my friends. Through all my recent changes, I was still with them. I remembered their old names and I was familiar with their reactions, but in recent weeks I sensed they were drawing away from me. At first they believed, perhaps under my influence, that my rehabilitation would be rapid and that I would return to them. But when it became clear that my recovery would be long and I was unlikely to return, their attitude toward me changed. It wasn't rejection, but withdrawal, as though they were distancing themselves from a sick friend whose fate had shunted him onto another path. Now it was clear to me: they would go their way, and I would remain here or in a similar institution.

Only Benno and Robert came every week. Benno doubted that he would be able to play the violin again. The war years and the time that had passed since then had kept him away from the instrument. Benno marvelously combined an agile mind with deep sensitivity, and I wondered why he doubted his ability.

"The violin loves flexible, trained fingers," he told me. "The music is hidden in my fingers. For years, they haven't touched strings."

I noticed that he was speaking about the practical side of playing. In the small city of his birth, he had been a soloist with the local orchestra from the age of eleven, and many people admired him. Everyone—not just his parents—was sure he had a bright future. All during the war years, music enveloped him and protected him. But at the end of the war, Benno discovered that music didn't flow in his fingers as before. I wanted to shout with all my might, *You're worthy of it!* But I was gripped with the fear that he might take my exclamation in the wrong way, so I kept my mouth shut.

Before coming to see me, Benno had been with Edward. Edward had sunk into a depression, and the nurses were trying to pull him out of it. He spent most of the day turned inward, not saying a word, and toward evening he would start sobbing.

"Mama, mama," he would call out in a choked voice. So it was, every day. The staff was helpless.

"Did you talk to him?" I asked, stupidly.

"It's hard to talk with him," Benno replied. "He doesn't answer."

It seemed that Edward's melancholy was clinging to Benno, too. I raised myself up on my arms and said, "We've gotten out of worse situations. You mustn't despair." Benno hadn't expected that response. His face changed, as though he was about to burst into tears. He didn't cry, but a cold gloom enveloped him and tightened his face. He covered it with his hands.

For the moment we were joined in sorrow, and we didn't speak until sunset. After a while, Benno tried to recover, to talk with me and cheer me up, but the words that came out of his mouth were fractured and said nothing.

"Excuse me," he said and left. He appeared to realize only now that the gates to playing the violin had been locked.

37

The schedule in the convalescent home was different from that of the hospital. It was quieter there and not as strict. If I wasn't seized with pain, I would get up and drag myself to the dining hall on crutches. How strange that walking on crutches wasn't humiliating. But when I was pushed in a wheelchair, I felt submission and shame.

Just a few months earlier, I could stand, and I was a member of Ephraim's unit. Never, not even in the darkest moments of the war, did I see myself lying helpless in bed. Even in my gloomiest imaginings, death refused to show itself to me. The war hadn't harmed my body. My friends, who also got no exercise during the war years, regained their strength rapidly, and we came together as a unit within a short time. When we went out to do our exercises early in the morning or returned at night covered with dust, the crowd of refugees would cheer for us. We were their pride.

"Look how handsome they are, how muscular," everyone would say. "This is the army of our future. From now on, we won't go like sheep to the slaughter." But truth to tell, this was ultimately just lip service and superficial enthusiasm. The refugees were busy with commerce, with smuggling, with money changing, and with theft. At night, around the kerosene stoves, they would argue using the old expressions, each accusing the other and repeating, "We can't stay together. Jewish togetherness has always been our downfall. We have to disperse, to shed every vestige of Jewishness that has clung to us, and sail to Australia or New Zealand. The new ingathering to Palestine is just another one of the illusions of Jewish history." Their conversation was a mixture of well-known facts, bitter words, and fears.

Once, an older refugee grabbed my coat and whispered to me, "Don't be seduced into going to Palestine. Our enemies haven't died. They have gone underground, and when the day comes, they'll rear their heads." I didn't know how to answer him, and I went on my way. But his face and his bald head clung to me for many days.

Other patients who were recovering from their operations came to see me and ask how I was. They wanted to know where I came from, who my parents were, and how I had been saved during the war. It was hard for me to talk about myself. I was afraid they would pity me. I had already noticed that people adopted a didactic tone toward the survivors. But the nurses didn't ask about my earlier life. They took care of me with dedication and not a word about my injury.

One night I dreamed about Mark. He looked exactly as he used to.

"Hello, Mark. What are you doing here?" I allowed myself to speak to him in my mother tongue.

"I'm walking through the farm. I didn't manage to see the vegetable garden," he answered, also in my mother tongue.

"Strange." The word slipped from my mouth.

"What's strange?" Mark looked at me in surprise.

"Just a few months ago they bore you to your final rest. Am I mistaken?" I couldn't help but say that to him.

"You're mistaken." Mark's reply was swift.

"Sorry." I retreated.

"You're not to blame. Most people think that death separates us forever. That's an error. There's no greater error than that. Death is another facet of our lives."

"Marvelous!" I couldn't restrain myself.

"Don't be too impressed before you understand the whole deal," he said, and turned his back to me.

"Mark, don't be angry with me," I managed to call out before I woke up.

Robert was standing next to my bed. I couldn't keep from him that I had just dreamed about Mark.

"What did he say to you?" asked Robert, leaning toward me.

"He denied his death."

"Exactly what did he say?"

"He said, with marvelous directness, that death is a facet of our lives."

Robert didn't respond, and we were silent.

Robert had brought some sketches, and he showed them to me. At first glance, they looked excellent, but the more I looked at them, the more I saw they had no inner essence. I set aside that impression and said, "They're good."

"I'm not sure." He surprised me.

"Why are you in doubt?" For a moment it seemed to me that my critical thoughts had made him say, "I'm not sure."

"They're good," I repeated.

"I always ask myself, 'What would Father say?'" Again Robert surprised me.

"What would he say?"

"He would never say, 'Good,' but 'There's something more to do.'"

"Is there always something more to do?" I wondered.

"For Father, it was endless. In other words, we'll never get to the right level."

"Is that discouraging?"

"That's how he worked all those years."

That evening Robert didn't tell me anything about our friends. I felt that I hadn't behaved truthfully with him, but I didn't know how to make amends. He, for his part, cut his visit short. I, to add insult to injury, said, "Bring more drawings."

38

I tried to cleave to the Hebrew letters, and the effort cost me deeply. It was hard for me to make them part of my thoughts, and without that close connection, everything was chaotic, falling into the depths of darkness. I felt that the Bible was calling on me to get to know its sentences, but I didn't dare. Everything there was crowned with ancient splendor. I read, understood the words, but this was the thin air of high altitudes, and those who dwell there are far above us.

I remembered the teacher Slobotsky, and I was flooded with longing for Misgav Yitzhak. Slobotsky tried to connect us to the Hebrew sentence, but I wasn't ready for it then. Now, I was far from my friends and from Slobotsky's voice.

In my childhood Mother loved to read to me. Her way of reading was quiet, with no mimicry. When I got older and read by myself, Mother's voice would accompany my reading, and I would read at her pace. By the age of ten, I was already addicted to books. Sometimes Mother would pull me out of the fervor that swept me away and serve me a cup of cocoa. She understood my spirit and didn't rebuke me, even when I read until late at night.

"What are you reading?" Father would sometimes surprise me. I would tell him the name of the book. If it pleased him, he would say "Fine," and smile. Father was sparing with speech, not to mention explanations. I didn't understand his inner struggles or his moods. But it was impossible not to love him.

Once, I entered his room and saw a card on the table. "We are returning the manuscript, 'Wild Roses,' which you sent to us," it read. "The book is interesting, but it does not suit our publishing program." At that time, I of course couldn't know what damage that card had done. Mother had to muster her entire soul to calm the tremor in Father's fingers.

"You don't write for the masses," she said. That was the sentence she kept repeating.

Suddenly, an image of our house rose up before me. It wasn't a big house, but it was covered with carpets and embroidery and full of good smells. Mother made sure that pleasant-looking curtains hung at my window and at Father's. She believed that pretty accessories enlarged a person's vision.

One of the patients, a quiet one, approached my table.

"Where were you during the war?" he asked cautiously. I was alarmed, as though he had pulled off the thick blanket in which I'd been wrapped for a long time and exposed my shame.

I didn't know how to answer, so I just said, "Like everyone."

"But *you*, what place were *you* in?"

"In a cellar."

"In what cellar, where?" He wouldn't leave me alone.

It was strange: outwardly, the man didn't look too pedantic or insistent, but his questions left no room for doubt. He wouldn't let me off easily.

"I committed no crime," I protested.

"I wasn't talking about a crime—perish the thought—but I wish to know."

I hadn't spoken about those dark years, neither to myself nor with my friends. Nor did my friends tell me anything. Once, I asked Mark where he was during the war. He pierced through me with his gaze and silenced me completely. From then on, I knew the boundaries of conversation between us.

Now this strange patient was standing next to me, demanding to know my secret.

I looked at him again. He didn't seem like someone who was plotting to harm me. But his face didn't display any softness or a desire to compromise.

"In Vaska's cellar," I said

He smiled at my words, as though he understood that I didn't intend to reveal any more.

I remembered Vaska from my earliest childhood. He frequented our house. We would buy from him fruit and vegetables, which he would deliver to us in his wide wagon and store in our basement. Father liked peasants, their way of thinking and their way of life. He would pour a drink for Vaska and himself and sink into conversation with him. Vaska was among those he was fond of.

A few days before we were driven out of the ghetto, Father brought me to Vaska. He agreed to take me in, and Father paid him, on the spot, with gold and silver coins. Vaska laid his hand on his heart and swore that he would watch over me like the apple of his eye.

"How long were you with Vaska?" the patient asked me with a smile. He understood that I wouldn't reveal what had really happened to me. War stories, even simple ones, don't emerge from hiding easily.

At Vaska's, I learned very quickly what imprisonment was and what darkness was. Images and thoughts tormented me day and night, but I didn't open my mouth and I never asked for anything.

Twice a day, Vaska would bring me a cup of milk and a piece of bread, and at night—not before tying my hands—he would take me to use the latrine. Sometimes he would forget me for a day or two, and I would be tortured with hunger until I could hardly breathe.

After two months of imprisonment, it occurred to Vaska that his wife could teach me to knit socks and gloves. I knitted for most of the day. If I didn't fill my quota, Vaska would threaten to hand me over to the police, and if he was in a foul mood, he would beat me.

I plotted to run away and die. Vaska, who always feared I would flee, secured the cellar with two locks. That's how I lived for almost two years.

Once, about a year before the end of the war, Vaska forgot to lock the door, and I ran away to the forest. Long after the war ended, my fingers moved by themselves to the rhythm of knitting. Even when I lay in bed, my fingers would tense up, anxious to fill the quota.

The patient wouldn't let me alone. He stared at me intently, following my thoughts. Finally, he said, "In any event, I expected you to tell me."

I didn't know what to answer.

"There are things one mustn't talk about," I said.

The patient bowed his head and didn't bother me anymore. He returned to his room.

39

That night I dreamed I was traveling on a train. The train moved slowly and paused at small stations. I remembered those stations from my childhood. They were made of gray wood. A thin barrenness woven from gray threads covered them. Not even the locomotive, breathing with great force, could tear that barrenness from the stations. The passengers on the platform were few. They were wearing long, thick garments, which made them look short. The stationmaster wore a red hat. He stood at some distance from the locomotive, rubbing his hands together. Then, with the sweep of a flag, he sent the train on its way.

Once again, I was in a green, mountainous landscape dotted with horses, colts, and cows. I was very moved, because in a short time I would be in the city of my birth, at my home, with its broad garden that extended across the front and the back.

One of the passengers turned to me. "Where are you going?" he asked.

The question upset me, but I didn't conceal the truth from him.

"I'm going home."

"Where is your home?"

I told him.

He looked at me with great wonder.

"I'm from this region," he said, "but the place—at least, the way you pronounce it—is unknown to me."

I repeated the name of my neighborhood, which was on the outskirts of the city.

"Perhaps it isn't widely known," I quickly added.

"It's known, very well known," he replied. "You're getting over-wrought." He changed his tone of voice.

"'Overwrought' isn't the appropriate word. I haven't yet found the correct words for what I am feeling." I spoke in a burst that surprised me.

He agreed with me. "We all lack words when it comes to speaking about ourselves."

"I'm glad you understand me," I said.

"What's your family name, if I may ask?"

I told him.

He raised his head in surprise and said, "I know your fam-ily, my young friend, maybe better than you do." He recited the names of my great-grandfather, my grandfather, my father, and my uncles and aunts. "Your father is an impressive man. He's an author. Before the war, we used to see each other and talk about literature and philosophy. The war cut me off from most of my friends. I'm a solitary man. As the Jews say, as solitary as a stone."

"Are you a Jew, sir?" I dared to ask.

He apparently expected that question and answered with a smile.

"One-quarter Jew, to be mathematical. The Christian in me saved me from death. Now the quarter-Jew in me lies mired in depression. I hid him so well that he shrank. I'm sorry for him. But what could I do? Even that quarter endangered me."

I was pleased to be with him, and I wanted to say, *You talk like a Jew, like my father and like my uncles.* He caught what I wanted to say to him and said, "There are things that can't be uprooted. To tell you the truth, without that quarter-Jew in me, my life wouldn't be worth living."

I looked closely at him. He was about fifty, and he was wearing a checked suit with a matching tie, and gold-framed glasses. My uncle Isidor used to wear a suit exactly like that. His appearance was always elegant, and women were attracted to him.

"Did you know my uncle Isidor?" I asked.

"Certainly I knew him. Who didn't? He was handsome and intelligent, and conversation with him nourished the Jew in me. Here everything is barren, and since the Jews departed, the wasteland has spread; it infests every corner. I mourn their disappearance every day. I also remember you, my friend. You were an observant boy. You're like your mother. Your mother was the most sensitive of women. She didn't talk a lot, but what came out of her mouth penetrated the heart. Why are you going home? What do you want to find there?"

"Everyone."

He bowed his head and said, "My young friend, I don't know what to tell you. The war devastated us. Everything has changed, changed for the worse. Without Jews, life has no meaning, and it's ugly."

"What do you advise me to do?" I asked him in great despair.

"Don't tarry here for too long. This land devours its inhabitants. A country that didn't know how to protect its Jews is a country without God. If I were in your place, I would take the first train out of here."

"And not go home?"

"Only for a short glance, and no more. I, in any case, was glad to see you. You brought life to my soul. I regret that I have to get off here. This is my place in this wasteland. Take care of yourself, my friend. I don't know if God will bring us together again."

"Thank you."

"Don't thank me. I'm not worthy of thanks. I didn't help my brothers in their hour of sorrow. If I had gone with them, my life would have been different, believe me."

I tried to detain him. "Don't get off," I said.

He must have sensed my helplessness.

"I would gladly accompany you," he replied, "but I must go to the doctor. I'm struggling with two serious illnesses. I don't know whether the doctor will be able to help me. I don't trust the local doctors. I doubt they can even be veterinarians."

The word "veterinarians" struck me as funny, and I laughed.

"Don't laugh, my friend. I spoke cautiously so as not to make things hard for you. My situation is worse than the way I described it."

The train slowed down, and I was afraid to be left alone.

"God knows where this train will take me," I said.

"Don't be afraid. The next stop is the Pine Tree neighborhood; may it be remembered for good. Your house is about two hundred meters from the station."

"That's exactly the place I'm meaning to get to."

"Don't be afraid," he said, already standing on the platform. "Someone like you, who's been through the seven levels of hell, won't be scared by a little goblin."

When I heard those clear words, I woke up.

40

When I awoke, the sunlight was already streaming into the room. Everything was in its place. My crutches were propped up against the dresser. The green shirt that I'd been given by the convalescent home was on the wheelchair. Only my body was still moving with the rhythm of the train. That stranger, who looked amazingly like my uncle Isidor, still appeared before my eyes, as though refusing to part from me.

For a moment I forgot that my legs were injured. I tried to pull myself up the way I used to, and I hurt myself.

In the dining hall the other patients greeted me cordially and invited me to join them at their tables. I was still puzzled by the dream and by the patients who didn't belong to it. Right away, they started asking me about the circumstances of my injury.

"The time hasn't come to talk about it." The sentence popped out of my mouth.

The other patients mistakenly believed that I was in pain or depressed. In fact, I was still immersed in sleep and didn't want to leave it.

"How long have you been in this country?" One of them couldn't keep himself from asking.

I told him.

A woman raised her eyes to mine and said, "We don't want to make things hard for you. But we want you to know that you're one of us, flesh of our flesh. You're not alone in the world."

I wanted to thank her, but I couldn't find the right words.

"If you need something," she continued, "don't hesitate to tell us. We're not rich, but we have enough to make things easy for you."

"I don't need anything."

"We're like a family, and we watch over one another."

"At this time, I want to be by myself." I spoke bluntly.

"And you don't need anything?"

"You don't have to worry about me. My injury is temporary. I'll soon manage to get up and walk."

My words surprised them, and they looked at me with a pity that hurt me.

I was sorry that the clear images from my dream were fading, that even the rhythmical rocking of the train had stopped. The powerful feeling that had throbbed within me and had borne me on its wings—that I was getting closer to my home, to my parents, and to my room—dissolved in the light of day, as if it had never been.

I went back to my room. Depression plunged its claws into me. I could go out and totter around on my crutches, but I know that they couldn't take me away from here. Again I would be exposed, and again everyone would stare at me. If I'd had a book to read, I would have sunk into reading. The last book I read at home was *Siddhartha* by Hermann Hesse. All the years I was imprisoned in the cellar, images from that book appeared before my eyes.

It occurred to me that if I could find the book, it would connect me to my home and my parents and make my legs move. The feeling was strong and urgent, and I went out into the corridor.

"If you really want to help me," I said to one of the patients, "please find me a copy of *Siddhartha* by Hermann Hesse. I need that book now the way I need air to breathe."

He looked at me in surprise and said, "I'll check in the library."

"If you mean the library of the convalescent home, they don't have books in German."

"But there are a lot of books in Hebrew."

"At this time, I need *Siddhartha* in the original." I didn't relent.

"I'll look. I promise."

He didn't seem to understand my request, but he didn't argue with me. Instead, he looked at me cautiously, as though seeing a side of me that hadn't been visible before.

"Just *Siddhartha*," I repeated.

"I understand," he said, and stepped back a little.

"That was the last book I read at home," I said. I thought he would be moved by that, but it actually made no impression on him. After a short pause, he said, as though doing his duty, "I'll be in the municipal library in the afternoon." He then walked away, terminating the conversation.

I went back to my room and sank into a deep sleep. I felt that the darkness was bandaging and healing my legs with powerful forces. I didn't know if this should make me happy, because the feeling might have been deceptive. I wanted to stand up, but it was beyond my ability.

The pain didn't die down. From minute to minute, it grew more intense. *On the day that I stand up on my feet, I said to myself, I won't forget this feeling of grace. And if I can find the words in my mouth— I will pray.*

41

I waited for the man to bring me *Siddhartha*, but for some reason
he ignored me. I didn't ask him about it, and he didn't apologize. He apparently believed I had spoken from my roaring pain
and not from an inner need. I didn't know how to extricate myself
from this entanglement, so I kept silent.

I asked the nurse to look for *Siddhartha* in the library of her
moshav. She promised to do so, and a few days later she told me
that the moshav library had no books in foreign languages. On
the day the moshav was established, its members swore that they
would neither speak nor read in any foreign language.

My friends came to visit me, and I was pleased to see them. With
all the ardor of youth, they were doing what I was unable to do.
Since I'd last seen them, they'd grown taller and more suntanned.
The dangers they were facing didn't diminish their joy in life. On
the contrary, they were merrier.

Benno told me that all his efforts to obtain a violin and music
books had so far failed.

"Music stirs strongly within me. There are days when it fills
me from head to toe, but because I have no instrument to play, it

poisons me instead." He asked whether I understood him, and I said I did. I tried to console him.

"Soon the war will be over here."

His answer came immediately. "And I will remain a spiritual cripple."

Dr. Winter came to examine me.

"Patience, my friend," he said softly. "Your fractures are knitting." I noticed that he didn't say "*the* fractures" but, rather, "*your* fractures," implying there was a reciprocal relationship between me and the fractures, though I couldn't see what it was. I could only feel the pain they caused me.

The next day, without first asking for Benno's permission, I spoke about him to the patients around the dining table.

"I have a friend who's a fine musician," I said, "a member of my training group and a soldier. He's looking for a violin to play in his spare time. If you have a violin, perhaps you can lend it to him."

"We aren't musicians," one of the patients said, "and we don't have violins, but we'll look around. What's the fellow's name?"

I told him.

"I haven't heard of him."

I didn't hold back. "You will," I replied.

The patient looked at me with a practical expression.

"A few days ago you asked for a book in German," he said, "and now you're asking for a violin for your friend. We're simple people. We never went to concerts. For many years we were pioneers. We worked in the fields and orchards. We've gotten old, and now we're spending our days in hospitals and convalescent homes. We can't help you with things we don't have connections to." His face was open and expressed exactly what he thought. His friends followed his words with intense eyes.

"Thank you," I said.

"Don't be angry at us. We love you the way we love our own sons. I myself am a bereaved father, and since my son died in battle, every soldier is dear to me. A wounded soldier ever the more so."

"Thank you," I said again.

"This is a hard country that has no mercy on the people who live in it. A person dedicates his soul to the soil, but the soil doesn't reward him with kindness. All the years we have lived here, we tilled the earth, and at night we stood watch. Our sons, who joined the Palmach, were even more dedicated than we were. But their dedication didn't save them on the battlefield."

I went back to my room and thought about the man's sunken cheeks. I felt sorry for him because all his labor on the land hadn't brought him a blessing. And now he was battling a harsh illness.

That night I saw Benno in my sleep, holding a violin in his hand. A member of Misgav Yitzhak had given him the instrument. But instead of being happy, Benno said, "Thank you. It's too late."

"Why?" the man wondered.

"During all the years of the war, I didn't practice or play. Music once flowed from my fingers. Now there's nothing in them, just stiffness. Stiffness at my age can't be corrected."

"You're a young man."

"The age of seven is the cutoff for a violinist."

"You can play in an orchestra."

"I prepared myself to be a soloist from the age of four. I kept to a rigid schedule, and I practiced every day. Mother made certain always to remind me of my duty. What can I do? The war cut my life in two."

"Too bad," said the man, taking the violin from Benno's hands. "If you change your mind, I'll gladly lend it to you."

"Thank you, thank you, from the depths of my heart." Benno spoke in a submissive tone of voice.

"I don't play it," the man said. "My late mother used to encourage me. Rather, she forced me. My desire to play, to be honest, was quite small."

"Thank you," Benno repeated.

"You're very welcome," said the man, and he walked away.

I noticed that in my sleep I saw people with more clarity. They appeared to be carved out of the darkness, and their inner essence lit up their faces. I hadn't seen Mark in my sleep for some time, so I didn't know what was stirring in his soul. But since Benno told me that music was imprisoned in him and was poisoning him, I saw him as a person who had given up on the great hopes his parents had pinned on him. He was now only marking time on a gray plain, without climbing or achieving. Benno didn't speak about it, but it was what his face and his hands told me.

Father asked me again, "What are you doing to prepare yourself to be an author?"

"I'm doing things," I told him. "But my legs are shattered, and it's hard to lift myself up. Broken legs block forward motion. I pray that God will bring my legs back to life."

"From whom did you learn to pray?" Father was surprised.

"From Grandfather."

"As far as I remember, Grandfather didn't teach you to pray."

"I observed him while he was standing in silent prayer."

"Prayer is speech, not standing in silence."

"Haven't I heard people say that it's possible to be silent and pray?"

"It's beyond my understanding," said Father in a voice whose every nuance I recognized.

"When God gives my legs back to me, Father, I'll set out to find the right way to express everything that happened to us."

His voice softened. "Where will you go?"

"To all the awful places where we were."

"Why are you speaking in the plural?"

"Because you, Mother, and I are covered by the same heavenly canopy."

"I knew you were courageous," said Father, and his eyes filled with tears.

42

I saw Father again, leaning over his desk and writing. He was so immersed in his work that he didn't notice I had entered the house. I stood at the door without uttering a word. Finally, I could no longer control my excitement.

"Father!" I called out.

He made a gesture with his right hand, one I had never seen him make. It was as though he was saying, *Leave me alone. Why are you bothering me?* I went outside and stood on the front steps. It was evening, and the sky was dark blue, without a cloud. Thin smoke curled up from the distant houses.

I expected our dog Miro to notice me and come over. All around me a thick silence prevailed, such as I hadn't experienced for many years. It occurred to me that Mother might be sitting behind the house, reading a book. I tried to move my legs, but my legs did not move. I remembered that I'd been wounded, and that the fractures hadn't yet healed. I said to myself, *If Mother comes, I won't tell her what happened to me.*

I saw the gardener down on his knees, planting new flowers. His quiet, focused kneeling made me think of some ancient ceremony where people don't talk but are connected to inanimate things. I left him and didn't call him by name.

Strange, I said to myself, *I returned home, and no one is paying attention to me. Father is so immersed in his writing that he won't pause to ask how I am.*

I waited for Mother. I was about to call out, *Mother,* as I used to when I came home from school. But there was no need for that. She appeared, and her appearance astonished me: she was so different—shorter, and her hair had turned gray. Her eyes were cast down, not meeting mine. *Mother,* I wanted to call out. But I held my tongue.

Mother knew everything. Not a detail escaped her. She had heard about my wound the day it happened. She had also heard about Dr. Winter's desperate operations.

"How did the news reach you?"

"A mother knows everything, and what she doesn't know, she guesses," she said, and the soft smile returned to her face. "You look better than I imagined," she quickly added. "Thank God we're seeing each other again."

"How is Father?"

"He's completely immersed in writing. He hardly eats, hardly drinks. I have to stand there and beg him. He's always depriving himself. I don't understand why or what for."

"Do you read what he writes?"

"His writing now is beyond me. I understand the words and the sentences, but the contexts are not comprehensible to me. I'm afraid that publishers will return his manuscript again. I don't understand why he's been torturing himself all these years. There's some hidden reason for his torments. What it is, I don't know."

"Where's our Miro?" I asked.

"Of course you remember that time when we questioned whether dogs also have souls. Father wouldn't take a position, but you and I believed—actually, we were certain—that dogs, espe-

cially our Miro, have souls. I had plenty of proof. I don't remember
them all now, but I do remember when you were six and they took
out your tonsils. You were in bed sick in the hospital, and all that
time, Miro lay mourning in his corner, not eating and not drinking. It wasn't until you came home that Miro got up, came over to
you, and ate from your hand. Do you remember?"

"Certainly I remember."

"Only a creature with a soul can sense something that is at a
distance and understand it."

"I'm reading the Bible and am becoming attached to the words,"
I told her.

"Are you religious?" She was alarmed.

"Don't worry. My faith is like yours and like Father's."

"I'm glad," she said, her eyes brightening. "But don't torment
yourself like Father. For Father, writing is a totally ascetic experience. He doesn't move from his desk. He's always tense, as though
planning some miraculous escape. I hope you won't take his path."

"I'm recovering from my fractures. The recuperation is slow
and long. But in the meantime, I'm getting to know my body and
my soul, if I may say so. By the way, do we have *Siddhartha* at home?"

"A wonderful book. I'll send it to you. But where? I don't have
your address."

"It's very simple, Kibbutz Misgav Yitzhak, Palestine. That's my
home now. Any mail you send will get to me, but I need *Siddhartha*
like I need air to breathe."

"I'll send it right away," she said and disappeared.

43

In about two months, on February sixteenth, I would turn eighteen. My years seemed long to me. Life before the war, in the ghetto, in the hiding place, wandering after the war, in Naples, sailing to Palestine, at Atlit, at work on the terrace and the orchards, at the advanced training—eighteen years couldn't hold it all. Benno had a similar feeling. With him, the world was divided differently: the years when he played his music, practicing day and night and performing, and the years that followed, which stretched ahead like a yellow wasteland.

I had read the Hebrew Bible that the hospital rabbi gave me when I was still in pain and half asleep. His untidy appearance and the way he muttered as he handed the book to me clouded my spirit. It appeared to be the way one gave this type of book to a dying man, so that he would say his confessions before he died.

At the convalescent home, I read the Bible with my own eyes, and I was glad that I understood most of the words. The Binding of Isaac: the story was dreadful but was told with restraint, in a few words, perhaps so that we could hear the silence between them. I felt a closeness to those measured sentences, and it didn't seem to be a story with a moral, because what was the moral? Rather, it was intended to seep into one's cells, and there it would wait patiently until it was deciphered.

Mother didn't like to interpret stories. She would read softly and say, "Now let's put down the book and close our eyes." Father liked to read whole chapters of his books to Mother. Mother had various expressions of attention: bending her head or lowering it entirely or cradling it in her hand.

I found myself back at home almost every night. Father received a letter from a well-known publishing house, saying they were willing to publish his books. Mother's face brightened. Her hair regained its blackness She spoke in her happy voice. Father sat in his study, his face expressionless. Mother stood alongside him, reading the letter over and over, but the good news didn't make an impression on Father. Sadness spread across his face and covered it.

"Dear, it's wonderful news, believe me!" Mother implored as she knelt down beside him. Father turned to her but didn't utter a word. With great sadness, Mother burst into tears. Father emerged from his silence.

"I hope you're right," he said. "But why not allow me to keep a pinch of doubt for myself. Disappointment has always been my lot. It's hard for me to believe that the world has changed."

Robert came to visit me and brought a bundle of oranges. Misgav Yitzhak had been mobilized for the harvest. The fragrance of the oranges reminded me of the smell of our pantry at home, where apples and pears lay in big wicker baskets, and there were always a few oranges in a net bag for an emergency, if one of us got sick.

Robert also brought some sketches. I saw right away that they were better than the earlier ones. This time I was careful and didn't say they were excellent. Although the outlines remained unfinished, patches of light had been added around each of them, brightening the entire drawing.

Unlike most of our friends, Robert hadn't changed. The work and the training hadn't altered him. His body was well formed, but not exaggeratedly so. There was a balance between his inner self and his outward appearance. Now his inner self would be expressed through fine lines and tints, and I was pleased for him.

Robert asked me what I wanted to do. The question embarrassed me, and I was about to tell him, *I don't know,* but instead I said something that I hadn't even yet said to myself.

"I want to be an author."

"When did that wish take shape?" he asked cautiously.

"Apparently, it was inside me."

"I hope you'll succeed."

"All his life, my father wanted to be an author," I said, and immediately realized that I wasn't allowed to reveal my father's pain.

"And what happened?"

"He didn't manage to fulfill his destiny in writing," I said, but then quickly added, "His talent was actually expressed in speech."

"What language do you want to write in?" Robert's question pained me without meaning to.

"In Hebrew, I assume. I feel that this language, whose outer shell is all that I'm touching now, will bind me to what I brought with me."

"They say that you can express yourself well only in your mother tongue."

"For years, I haven't been connected to my mother tongue. Now I expect that the Hebrew letters will link me to what's hidden inside me."

"When did this become clear to you?"

"Just recently."

Robert parted from me as though retreating, and I didn't ask him to stay as I used to. I was ashamed of what had occurred to me about my father, and of the way I had given voice to it. I remembered that Mother used to say that the right things arrive unnoticed, when we don't expect them. That idea amazed me, but I hadn't understood it till now.

How could I be an author, when it was hard for me even to read a daily paper, not to mention the Bible, the Mishnah, and the many other books I had to read?

Benno came to visit me that evening.

"If you see Robert," I said, "tell him to forgive me. Everything I said was totally stupid."

Winter came. The rain didn't stop, and it evoked images of the forests where I had been. I would have liked to spend more time looking at them, but the nurses and the volunteer women didn't leave me alone with their questions.

I stopped asking the doctor at the convalescent home about my medical condition. When I asked him once, he gave me a look so full of pity that it shocked me. I was waiting for Dr. Winter to visit. He had operated on me, and he would rescue me from my pain.

I would spend half of each day in bed. Lying there nourished my imagination. The days carried me along. Sometimes I was rushing on a train, and sometimes in a military truck. One night I dreamed I was sailing with Mother on a raft that carried logs.

"Where are we sailing?" I asked Mother.

"Home, my dear," she answered with a bright smile.

"And where will we stop?"

"That depends on the pilot of the raft. He knows the currents of the river and where to stop. He'll stop at one of the nearby docks, and we'll get off." Her voice was quiet and full of comforting patience, as when we went on trips to the mountains together with Father.

I tried to control my excitement. "Are we far from home?"

"In my estimation, we're very close. I hope the currents will allow us to stop at the next dock. I'm not worried."

But I was afraid. The pilot's oars seemed weak and about to break. The water surged and licked at the beams of the raft.

"Mother, is everything all right?"

"One hundred percent." This time she spoke colloquially. "What are you worried about?"

"The currents."

"No need to worry, my dear. We've been through worse. These currents are child's play in comparison. I'm sure we'll reach home at the end of the journey," she said, and hugged me.

"And where's Father?" I belatedly noticed his absence.

"He's waiting for us at home, my dear." But that reply, which was meant to calm me, actually increased my dread.

"He never left us alone before," I said.

"This time he allowed himself," said Mother, laughing in an unfamiliar way.

These frenzied dream journeys, during which I was tossed about, showed me clearly that many obstacles still stood in my path before I could reach my home. But what could be done? My lower body, in which I tried to inspire movement, refused to move, and I was stuck in place.

A new patient arrived, a boy my age whose right arm had been amputated. He raised a commotion right away. He had arrived from Hungary a few months earlier, was conscripted into the Palmach, and like me was wounded in his first battle. He blamed the army for sending him to the front without training. He was speaking volubly in Hungarian and spreading fear.

The day after his arrival, two sturdy men came and spoke with him in Hungarian. The boy was demanding to be sent back to Hungary. *This isn't a country of decent people,* he said. *The Hungarians are better.*

The two men spoke to him earnestly, but he was boiling with rage, listing one after another all the injustices that had been done to him from the time he boarded the ship until he was sent to the front.

"Now I'm stuck without an arm," he said. "What can I do in life without an arm? Who'll hire me? Let me get out of here. This isn't a convalescent home, it's a prison."

"It's raining. Where will you go in the rain?" one of the men said, pointing at the window.

"The rain won't hurt me." The boy spoke stubbornly.

"You'll catch cold."

"You don't die from a cold."

In the end the boy stood up and headed toward the exit. The two men didn't stop him. They followed him without touching him. Then he started to run. They ran after him until all three of them disappeared in the fog.

That night I read the end of the story of the Binding of Isaac again. I was amazed by the objectivity with which that dreadful trial ends. But, on the other hand, where was the morality of obedience to an inhuman command? What could Abraham say to himself? *I've succeeded. I've obeyed the command of God. I stifled the compassion within me. I have served as an example to future generations.*

What could he say to his son? *Thank you for standing with me. You did so with great daring. Your courage is greater than mine.* The episode was a dark tangle that led to another tangle, so it was better for Abraham just to go to Beersheba with the donkeys and not say anything. Any talk about a test like that would be stupid. Abraham obeyed the command and did what he did. There was no doubt that he would be tormented by it all his life. And so the story falls silent there.

44

The fellow with the amputated arm didn't come back.

For several days I sat and copied from the Bible. Once, I heard Mother say that beginning artists copy the paintings of famous artists to learn from them. Father didn't agree with that method. He claimed that imitation brought no benefit.

I copied slowly and tried to form each letter clearly and separately. I felt the strength inherent in the Hebrew words and was glad to have close contact with them. Every day I copied out two or three passages.

Benno saw my copies and was astounded by the precision. He asked what it meant. I didn't know how to put what I was thinking into words. Finally, I said, "Hebrew letters have an ancient beauty that moves me."

Benno told me that a member of Misgav Yitzhak had lent him a violin, and he had played it for two hours.

"How's your playing?" I asked cautiously.

"Far from what you could call playing. My fingers won't do what they're supposed to. They forgot they were once agile."

"Can't you wake them up?"

"I tried, and I'll try again."

I wanted to tell Benno that my daily copying brought me close not only to the shape of the letters but also to the rhythm of the sentences.

"Are you training yourself to be an author?"

"Maybe. To tell the truth, I don't know what I'm headed for."

I had already told Benno that my father wrote for many years without success. Now I added, "He didn't manage to publish even a single book. But it turns out that the war didn't weaken him. Prisoners who were with him in the camp told me that even under the darkest conditions, he continued to write complete sentences on slips of cardboard."

The moment those words left my mouth, the narrow cupboard in Father's study, where his manuscripts were kept, appeared before my eyes. Mother saved every sheet of his writing, and after every rejection, she used to say, "I'm waiting for a wise publisher, who will reveal to the world the beauty hidden in Father's writings."

"Did you read what he wrote?" Benno asked cautiously.

"Not even a single line. Mother used to say, *It's not for someone your age. One day you'll sit and read it. Everything is arranged in this cupboard. If Father doesn't succeed in publishing the books, you'll do it. I'm sure you'll do it.*"

"Did your mother want you to follow in your father's footsteps?"

"I'm not sure. Father was very tormented by his writing. His torments brought him neither recognition nor joy."

"I have no idea how to write," said Benno with a bashful smile. "Violinists are awkward speakers."

That night I dreamed that the Hebrew letters were racing around on a blank sheet of paper. I tried to arrange them into sentences, but they slipped away from me. At first that amused me. Finally, I spoke to my fingers.

"Fingers, fingers, you have to practice," I said. "Without practice, there are no sentences." At that moment, I saw Benno and his embarrassment, and I woke up soaked in sweat.

45

Patients came and went, but I remained in my room. Friends who came to visit me brought me the bits of my possessions that I had left in the training program. Memories of the days I had spent at Misgav Yitzhak secretly stirred within me. In my sleep I continued to fill the pit on the terrace with loose earth and to plant Santa Rosa plum seedlings.

One day, Edward came to visit and told me he planned to leave Misgav Yitzhak and settle in Tel Aviv.

"Why?" I carelessly asked.

He hesitated for a moment and said, "Because I want to feel closer to my parents. In Tel Aviv the houses resemble the ones in the city of my birth." He added bashfully, "My friends aren't encouraging me."

"What do they say?"

"They say that it's good to stay together."

"And what have you decided?" I was drawn to his voice.

"I'm leaving tomorrow, and I came to say goodbye to you."

I held my breath. Edward was one of those people you like being with from the moment you meet them. His goodness of heart was visible on his face. He always volunteered to take the middle watch, the hardest one, but because of his naïveté, he didn't gain the friendships he deserved. The wise and the clever ones outshined him.

Edward's right hand was wrapped in a brown bandage. The bandage called attention to the place where two of his fingers had been shorn off. His handsomeness hadn't been damaged, but his face had become downcast, which made his wrinkled forehead more prominent. It was clear to me that leaving the kibbutz was full of risks, but who was I to advise him to stay? I turned my thoughts elsewhere.

"In what city were you born?" I asked.

"In Cracow," he said, and his face shone. After a short pause, he added, "Some streets in Tel Aviv remind me of it."

What will you do in Tel Aviv? I wanted to ask him. *Who will give you a place to live and feed you?*

Edward apparently read my mind.

"Someone certainly needs a worker in a bakery," he said, "or in a shoe-repair shop, or cleaning the stairs of their building. I'm not choosy. Whatever I'm offered, I'll take."

I showed him some pages that I'd copied from the book of Genesis.

"What's that?" he wondered.

"I'm copying from the Bible."

"Interesting," he said, still looking surprised. I expected him to ask why I was doing it, but I forgot that it wasn't Edward's way to raise questions.

"The letters are pretty," he said. "You'll surely hang the pages on the wall."

"Why?" I asked in turn.

"It will decorate the room," he said. The wonder didn't leave his face.

"I copy slowly," I said.

"I was never any good at penmanship," Edward said. "I thought that in Hebrew my writing would be nicer. I was wrong: the Hebrew letters were misshapen, too. Now I'll have to teach my left hand to write. I'm leaving soon. I'll come back to visit you. Meanwhile, be strong and brave, the way Ephraim taught us."

All of Edward's naïveté was evident even in his back when he turned it to me. The thought that he was going to Tel Aviv because some of its streets were like the ones in the city of his birth stuck in my mind only after he went away.

The practical nurse came over to me. She was a tall woman, carelessly dressed, and with a look of perpetual wonderment. Her face reminded me of the tall women on the coast of Naples. We used to sneak over to them whenever we had some spare change. Some of them were quiet and submissive, offering their bodies without complaining or rushing. But others were angry, and they would scream and pinch whenever you made a careless move. Those secret pleasures didn't go well with the moral purity that was being demanded of us, but they did cultivate the manliness that was bursting out of us so strongly. We were afraid to talk about those experiences and kept them secret. Ephraim spoke to us quite often about moral purity, decent behavior, and untainted love. It was clear that if we were caught, we would face a trial before our comrades. That fear spoiled the pleasure of the sin.

The nurse brought me plum compote.

"How do you feel today?" she asked.

"Well," I said.

"A guy like you should feel great."

"Why 'great' in particular?"

"Because you're young and handsome," she said, winking at me.

I caught the hint, but I ignored it.

"Give me your hand," she said, putting out hers.

I reached out.

"A nice hand," she said, kissing it.

She apparently had far-reaching intentions, but luckily for me the doctor came in to talk with me, and she scurried away.

46

The new patients wouldn't leave me alone. They were impressed by my spoken Hebrew. I of course didn't tell them about the three to four hours every day that I spent copying from the book of Genesis. That activity bound me not only to the words but also to their form.

The patients didn't ask me where I was from or what my mother tongue was. Instead, they were worried about my future. The past wasn't important to them. In their youth they had been pioneers, and since then they thought only about the future.

"What are you going to do?" one of the patients startled me one day by asking.

"I'm training myself to be an author." I tried to emerge from my misery for a moment.

He pierced through me with his gaze. "How are you training yourself?"

"I'm studying the Bible," I said, without emphasizing any of the words.

He looked at me in surprise, and then his eyes narrowed.

"We all studied Bible," he said with derision.

"I pray in my heart that the Bible will help me write."

The word "pray" actually got this patient mad, and he confronted me like someone who had been insulted to the depths of his soul.

"You pray?" he said. "What are you praying for, and who to?"

"I pray in my heart," I repeated.

He didn't let up. "You're a young man. You shouldn't give yourself over to false visions. We came to the Land to live in reality, in this reality. Remove the word 'pray' from your head. The Jews have prayed more than enough."

I didn't know how to answer, so I just said, "So be it." But that one wasn't satisfied with this retreat.

"We came to this country to work the soil. To bring forth bread from the earth and not to give ourselves over to imaginary things. You're allowed to study the Bible—to learn botany from it, geography, history—but not to sink into worthless beliefs that we had been given for generations."

Only later, on my bed in my room, did I feel those angry words seeping into me.

Words spoken with conviction work upon you in secret and uproot the tender sprouts that come up in your secret garden without your being aware of it. *I have to keep away from those patients,* I said to myself, though I knew that in this shared space, I couldn't escape their prying eyes.

The sharp pains reappeared. I didn't give up on my copying. The more I copied, the more I felt the power of the exposed sentences. I didn't deceive myself into believing that I could make use of them. They were carved out of a whole world, and I had only fragments. In my sleep I saw the vocalized words in their entirety and in their full splendor, and fear made my body tremble.

. . .

Ephraim came to visit me. His entire right arm was bandaged, and he was sitting in a wheelchair. To my surprise, he hadn't changed. A few lines crisscrossed his face, but except for that, he was the same Ephraim: bashful in an unfamiliar place. He was a master of carrying burdens and smashing rocks, an excellent exercise coach by day and by night. But hospitals and convalescent homes unsettled him.

I told him I was copying from the book of Genesis into my notebook.

"Copying?" he wondered. "Why copy?"

I tried to string together a few words to tell him about my struggles to connect with the Hebrew letters, but some of his inarticulateness had rubbed off on me. I observed his simplicity, his direct engagement with life, his willingness to help, even in his present situation, and I was ashamed of my authorial pretensions. In my embarrassment, I said, "I haven't lost hope."

"Who planted that good feeling in you?"

"It's hard for me to say. I feel that one day I'll stand on my own."

"What do the doctors say?"

"Doctors aren't usually optimistic."

My words seemed exaggerated—or who knows what—to Ephraim. He groped for something to say to me.

"Medicine in our time is advanced."

The cliché pained me.

I asked him about his wound.

He didn't hide the truth from me. "I won't be able to go back to my work," he said. "I'll return to my kibbutz."

I remembered Ephraim's modest way of standing on the pristine coast of Naples, the long runs with him, the big meals after hours of exhausting training. His poetry recitations while we were running made him appear like a spiritual adviser who believed in the power of human speech. He planted within us many poems by Natan Alterman, Avraham Shlonsky, and Leah Goldberg, quite a few verses from the Bible, and even some sayings from Ethics of the Fathers.

I was afraid Ephraim would be angry at me for giving myself over simply to copying from the book of Genesis. As I said, he was the same Ephraim, only more attentive. But some of the beliefs that had guided his life must have slackened within him after he was wounded, or they had been silenced.

"Tomorrow is the fateful operation," he said as he was leaving. "I've already gotten used to the thought that they're going to amputate some of my arm."

"No!" The word leaped from my mouth.

"Being without an arm isn't shameful. You can do a lot even without an arm." The voice from the old days returned to him.

For a moment it seemed that Ephraim wasn't talking about himself but had come to tell me that even on shaky legs a person can do what's required.

47

The woman at the defense ministry who was responsible for the war-wounded visited me. It was hard when people spoke to me as though to a cripple whose needs must be taken care of. My youthful energy still flowed within me, and the desire to once again stand on my own hadn't been extinguished. While I had known pain and despair in the past months, I also knew how to shake off these feelings and return to my desk and copy whole passages with more energy.

"Do you understand what you're copying?" the woman asked me arrogantly. *I'm copying not only to train my right hand,* I wanted to tell her, *but also to connect with the hidden meanings of the ancient letters.* But I restrained myself and said, "I understand."

She didn't let up. "I'm interested in what you understand."

I couldn't restrain myself.

"In secondary school I started to learn Latin," I said. "True, my studies were interrupted, but ancient texts are no strangers to me."

My words appeared to stun her.

"I believe you," she said.

It's not a matter of belief, I wanted to say.

After that, she changed her tone and addressed practical matters. She asked me if I wished to live in a kibbutz or a city.

"In a city," I answered without hesitation.

"Do you have relatives who live in a city?"

"No." I was brief.

She looked at me, half doubting and half pitying.

"It won't be easy," she said.

With that, our meeting ended.

At every turn, people asked me about personal matters. Or they tried to be helpful. I was confined to a wheelchair, but my thoughts were as free as ever. In my imagination I ran along the beach, lifted hammers, smashed stones, and built a wall for the terrace.

Dr. Winter examined me and found that my condition had improved immeasurably. But another operation was needed, a relatively simple one, to connect what hadn't yet been connected. Even though he showed me the X-rays, I couldn't get a clear picture of my situation from his explanations. To my obstinately repeated question of whether I would be able to stand on my own, he answered, "I hope so." Sometimes he added, "A doctor isn't a prophet or a prophet's son. He watches what he does and hopes in his heart for success."

Dr. Winter heard about my interview with the woman who was responsible for the war-wounded. He immediately listed for me the advantages of the kibbutz: society, mutual assistance, and, of course, medical supervision. He didn't take into account that I needed solitude, hours of quiet, and uninterrupted sleep. When I told him this, he narrowed his eyes and said, "Man is a social creature, and solitude brings despair."

"It brings inspiration to me," I informed him.

He was stunned by my answer, shrugged his shoulders in a way that showed he wasn't pleased with my words, and then went back to the treatment room.

·   ·   ·

That night I dreamed I was sitting at a table and trying to put together broken Hebrew letters. I invested all my efforts, but I couldn't manage it: the broken pieces wouldn't fit together. But amazingly, another effort, from deeper within me, not only connected the pieces, but also enabled me to construct my own Hebrew sentence: "Mother, don't despair. I'm on my way to you." I felt that the written message expressed what I hadn't been able to say out loud.

Not long before this, I sometimes asked Ephraim for a sleep day. At first he accepted my request with some understanding, but eventually he began to ask, "Is this necessary?" What could I tell him? That I needed it like I need air to breathe? Once, when I did let that expression slip out, he looked baffled.

At the convalescent home, I would plunge easily and without guilt feelings into slumber. I quickly reached the bottom, reconnecting with everyone I had been connected to. I had plenty of time, and no one was pressuring me. The threat that the morning bell in the courtyard of the training program would uproot me from the foundation of my life had faded. The moment I plunged in, I was totally in my own world.

48

Everyone in the Land was enlisted in the struggle, even old people. I still saw myself returning to Ephraim's team, and it was hard for me to accept that I would not be regaining my youth, that I was sentenced to observe and not take part. I imagined myself walking on my own, awestruck by the pinkish-red peach blossoms in the orchard.

One night I saw Father, and he was pale from some significant effort. I asked him whether he had succeeded in finding a publisher. He looked at me with great intensity.

"One mustn't despair," he said. "I have been in places that could have discouraged men even stronger than I, but I, as you see, am alive and well." It was hard to know whether he was talking about his experience in the camps or about his writing, with which he had struggled for years.

I went back to copying. Sometimes I had the feeling that I wasn't copying but revealing ancient finds, removing the earth that clung to them, and suddenly—as in a magic trick—an urn decorated with Hebrew letters stood before me.

Every day brought new discoveries. I dreamed that in an excavation I found ancient coins. I tried to read what was written on them. In the end I managed to read the name of Eli the priest on one of them. I was glad that the old priest, who fell from his chair and met his death on the stone floor, had come to life in a figure on a coin.

Sometimes the formal, printed letters seemed to be angry at me for removing them from their pages and writing them in cursive.

"We're permanent letters, not written letters. You aren't allowed to change our form and move us from place to place. The printed form is our proper resting place."

The copying filled my days. I told Mother that it wasn't an ordinary task, but a slow coming to know and melding of hearts. Letters that weren't revealed to you in childhood require a prolonged period of acquaintance.

"What do you mean by acquaintance?" Mother wondered. "A person can copy and copy, and in the end he acquires only the skeletons of letters, and not the living letters. Only the letters of your mother tongue live inside you."

I knew there was a degree of truth to her words, but nevertheless I refused to accept her argument. The days I spent in copying did connect me to the Hebrew letters. Roman letters became foreign to me.

"That's what people mean by 'neither here nor there,'" said Mother, in a voice not her own.

I couldn't believe my ears. Mother wasn't a pedant, and she didn't intentionally use hurtful words. But she tried to warn me before I reached the edge of the abyss.

I woke up early. The nighttime visions remained before my eyes and made me dizzy. There was no one in the dining hall. The practical nurse accosted me again. This time she wasn't satisfied with kissing my hand, and she also kissed my neck. I knew what she was plotting.

"Not today," I said firmly and slipped out of her hands.

I drank two cups of coffee and went back to my room. I had neither the strength nor the will to sit and copy. The despair that secretly dwelled within me raised its head. I knew that I mustn't close my eyes.

My longing for Dr. Weingarten brought him to me. He went looking for me that morning, and by eleven there he was. I was astonished by the change in his appearance: he was tan all over. He was no longer guarding building sites; now he was working in an orchard.

"Dr. Weingarten!" I called out, raising my upper body.

When he heard my excitement, he said, "What can I do? This is my new incarnation."

I told him about my injury and about Dr. Winter's efforts to restore my legs to me.

I saw his face fill with sorrow. He sat next to me and didn't say a word. Finally, he asked to learn more about my recuperation. My mother tongue no longer flowed easily from my mouth. Still, I managed to depict with words some of what I was feeling. Dr. Weingarten stared at me.

"It's hard for me to decide whether you're more like your father or your mother," he said. "Your face is your mother's, but your expressions are your father's."

I told him more about my struggles with the Hebrew language. He asked whether I had managed to write anything. I said I hadn't.

"Did you try?"

"No."

Once again Dr. Weingarten promised himself that if he had

the strength, he would return to Europe to look for Father's lost manuscripts. I wanted to stop him from leaving, but a great fatigue fell upon me, and I sank into a deep sleep.

In my sleep I saw the refugee camp, the rumbling kerosene stoves, and the tense faces of the people staring at me. I had the powerful feeling that they were all my relatives and that they had distanced themselves from me—or that I had distanced myself from them. That bitter estrangement hurt me.

I wanted to call out in a loud voice, *I didn't betray you. I'll always be with you. You are inside me.* But my voice was blocked and stifled. I woke up out of breath.

49

I couldn't sleep that night. The pains wouldn't let up. Dr. Winter kept promising me that the next operation would give me much relief. I wanted to believe him, but the pain discouraged me. After a sleepless night, it was hard for me to copy.

I intended to write a letter to Mother and tell her about the sleepless nights and about my distress with language. I sat at the table for a long time, but I couldn't finish even a single sentence.

In the afternoon, one of the patients brought me a thin booklet containing the story "In the Prime of Her Life," by S. Y. Agnon. I read the first words: "In the prime of her life, my mother died. She was just about one and thirty years of age at her death. Few and bad were the days of the years of her life. She sat at home all day and never left the house. Her friends and neighbors did not come to visit her, nor did my father welcome guests. Our house stood silent in its grief. Its doors did not open for the stranger."

I read, and my hands trembled. What stillness, like at the entrance to a sanctuary. And every word specifically chosen, simple and unique. "In the prime of her life." I didn't know the source of that expression. The sound of "prime" was echoed in the sound of "life," emphasizing that unusual word. The entire passage stood on its own, but at the same time, it was related to the Bible: "about one and thirty years," "few and bad." I read it over and over, and it was hard for me to part with that passage, full of silence and grief.

I dragged myself out of my room, but I didn't see anyone I could tell about my discovery. I was glad that the passage had been revealed only to me; from now on, I had a pillar of fire in whose light I could walk. I kept repeating to myself: not *"about thirty-one years old,"* but *"about one and thirty years of age."* A subtle and marvelous innovation.

I was afraid to keep reading. I stood at the threshold of the story. *It would be best to absorb that passage before I continue,* I said. *I assume that there is much treasure hidden in this story. I ought to prepare myself for it.*

Robert came and brought me some sketches and a drawing. The sketches were better than the drawing. I concealed my opinion from him. The sketches were of a landscape that was not from here. The trees were bathed in moist darkness, and sadness dripped from them. Robert liked to draw the local cypresses, but what could he do? The charcoal tricked him and wrapped them in the darkness of another place.

I told him that this darkness wasn't local. Robert didn't agree with me and claimed he was trying to be precise in the amounts of light and shade and to make his sketch faithful to what his eyes saw.

"Do we know what our eyes show us?" I said.

"I don't understand," he said, as though he had caught me saying something inexact. I didn't have the right words within me to explain it to him.

"It's not important," I said.

But Robert kept claiming that he was drawing exactly what his eyes saw—in order to mingle with this soil, among other things. He said he liked these landscapes better than the ones we came from. They were more spiritual.

. . .

No one to whom God has granted the ability to do something is miserable. Benno couldn't do what he wanted to do, and he was burdened with restlessness. Restlessness makes a person bitter and critical. Benno mocked my copying and called it a useless activity. It would have been easier for me if he had refrained from visiting, but he insisted on coming once a week, bringing me some fruit or a chocolate bar. Apparently, I was the only one with whom he could talk about his problems. Unfortunately, he was a bitter person and cast his bitterness onto me.

And so each of us climbed his own path up the steep mountain. Instead of helping one another, we made each other fail. I was sorry for Benno because his talent was frozen, and he wasn't even trying to thaw it out.

Again I read the beginning of "In the Prime of Her Life." Only an artist who knows his way achieves such clarity and restraint. *I don't have that stillness*, I said to myself, *and for now I don't have the ability to choose my words.* Sleep is what takes me by storm and sweeps me on its waves, and when I emerge from the darkness, the light doesn't help me. It blinds me.

One of the patients, a talkative one, asked me if I was writing.

"No," I answered decisively.

"How do you expect to become a writer if you don't write?"

"I'm waiting for better days."

"If you're talking about quiet, you should know that a great war is on its way."

Stupidly, I told him that I was reading "In the Prime of Her Life" by Agnon.

"You have to read current literature and not moldy stories about the shtetl."

"Are you referring to S. Yizhar and Moshe Shamir?" I asked.

"Both of them."

I didn't know what to say. Practical people silenced me. In the end I wanted to tell them, *You're right. There's no doubt that you're right.* But what could I do? The great sleep directed me. I lived in its seasons. The other seasons didn't influence me.

The man couldn't understand my way of thinking.

"You have to train yourself for secretarial work," he persisted. "People are considerate of war invalids, and the employment agency sends them to offices."

"No," I blurted out.

"Why not?"

"Invalids also have ambitions. It's wrong to stifle their ambitions."

He cut me off. "Work comes before everything," he said.

"I worked in an orchard," I said, raising my voice, "and I'll continue working there. With my friends I built a big terrace, and I planted the first seedlings there. I hate office work. I'll continue training and going out on missions at night. My legs will return to me, and they will be at my disposal. It's wrong to send injured people to gray offices."

The man didn't expect to hear a protest like that and retreated somewhat. But I refused to listen to his apologies and stood up on my crutches.

"Office work destroys the soul," I said. "I'm connected to the orchard, and every day I will get up early to see the buds and flowers. That is my eternal inheritance."

I went back to my room.

50

Dr. Winter showed me the X-rays and assured me that the upcoming operation would greatly improve my walking. I wanted to believe him, but I was hobbled by doubt. Every day I would copy a chapter from the book of Samuel and two or three passages from "In the Prime of Her Life." Sometimes I felt that copying was like a prayer whose content is not understood, and sometimes it seemed that I wasn't copying of my own free will but that somebody was forcing the task on me.

I was hoping for the day when I would place my pen on the paper and my own words would flow in measured abundance, word after word.

I had a long conversation with one of the patients, who stunned me with his insights. When I told him I was copying the book of Samuel and the story "In the Prime of Her Life," he looked me in the eye, without a hint of arrogance, and said that was the correct way to acquire the Hebrew letters.

"Who instructed you to do that?"

"I myself."

"The Hebrew language has many secrets, and we must approach it modestly, as we approach the holy scriptures. Do you feel the secrets?" he whispered in wonderment.

"I feel that copying brings me nearer to the letters," I said.

"You're doing it the right way." Again, he encouraged me. This man didn't speak the way other people at the convalescent home spoke.

"Where are you from, sir?" I asked him cautiously.

"From a little village in the Carpathians," he told me. "I learned Hebrew from the prayers. I used to pray three times a day. Once, I knew the whole prayer book by heart. Years of work in the orange groves have driven quite a few prayers from my heart, but now they're slowly returning to me. What you learned in childhood isn't easily erased."

"In my house they didn't pray." I didn't conceal it from him.

"I also didn't know how to value prayer. I believed that working the soil would cure my bodily and spiritual pains, and, like everyone, I sang, 'We've come to the Land to build and be rebuilt by it.' I was glad to call the tools by their Hebrew names, as if they were holy vessels: hoe, pick, spade, rake. Unfortunately, people aren't careful in their speech. They've uprooted words from ancient books and thrown them into an open field and onto a noisy street. Words that have been stored in books are accustomed to a different environment. One mustn't pluck them out high-handedly."

"How are you allowed to use them?" I was drawn to his voice.

"With great caution." He spoke in a whisper.

I didn't understand him fully, but I sensed that his words hit on what I had merely guessed at, without knowing how to express it.

"What do you want to write?" he asked after a brief silence.

"About my parents' life and mine." The words, to which I hadn't given much thought, popped out.

"But you're a young man. For a young person, there's no past and no future."

"I left my childhood days on the slopes of the Carpathians, and they're waiting for me to return to them."

"So we're from the same area. Where did your family live?"

I told him.

"Many lofty souls walked about in our region, including the Ba'al Shem Tov and his disciples. The disciples reinforced the words of their master by putting them in the Holy Tongue. The time will come when you'll copy them, also. Who were your ancestors?"

I told him.

"Your great-grandfather Rabbi Michael was blind; he was a Torah scholar and a prayer leader. His way of praying was well known throughout the region. Anyone who heard him pray became a new person. He changed people not by talking but by the power of prayer."

"Did you see him?"

"I wasn't privileged. I just heard about him from trustworthy people. I left the Carpathians and went to a Zionist training farm. I was sure that agricultural training was more important than prayer. I was a boy, about your age. I went to the training camp, and it seemed like I was breaking a siege. I ran away without saying goodbye to my parents. Now they are up there, and I'm here, the last remnant. All these years I've worked in the orchard, and I was sure that the work would heal me. Then I got sick, and now I spend my time with doctors and in convalescent homes. That's the punishment for a man who left his elderly parents and sailed to a distant land."

"At the training farm, did you also train your hearts?" I said, glad that I thought to ask.

"I don't know what we did. Sometimes it seemed to me that the orange groves made their owners rich and emptied my soul. If my parents were still alive, I'd go back to them and ask forgiveness."

"Your ancestors have certainly forgiven you," I said, trying to comfort him.

"I haven't forgiven myself. I sometimes dream that I've returned home, to the Carpathian region, and I find everyone just as I left them. In my heart I know that's an illusion and a deception."

"If you bring me a prayer book, I'll copy from it, too." This thought just then occurred to me.

"I'll bring you one. I have two prayer books: one is from home and one is local. It's hard for me to pray. Sometimes I see myself praying, but I haven't achieved actual prayer. At times, I feel that if I returned to the Carpathian Mountains, they would restore prayer to me. I beg your pardon; I've been incessantly talking about myself. Where were you wounded, my friend? In battle?"

"They surprised us."

"Many of my friends were killed in the orange groves. They lay in wait for them. The silence there is a false silence. Suddenly, a human serpent leaps out and kills you. Sometimes it seems to me that I'm still digging shallow trenches around the trees and filling them with water. The end justifies the means, we used to say. That's a false saying. Anyone who abandons his parents can never atone for his sin.

"I'm ashamed that I can't pray for your recovery. In the Carpathian Mountains, a person would open up the prayer book and pray for his friend. Today, when I open the prayer book, it appears to be angry at me. The letters of prayer aren't like regular letters. They look for the right soul so they can rise up with it.

"I'll bring you the prayer book that I brought with me from home. Maybe you, who were tormented from childhood, will find the way to prayer. You should know, prayer isn't speech, but silence. Whoever knows how to be silent can hear God talking to him. Spoken prayer is on a lower level. To be silent with the prayer book demands great strength. I've spoken too much. Forgive me."

"Too little, in my opinion."

"We've forgotten, my friend. We've forgotten what was shown

to us. We ran away to the orange groves to redeem the Jewish people. We were sure that the hoe would bring redemption."

"I love the orange groves." I held nothing back.

"Maybe they sinned without malice, but they sinned."

After the man left, I felt his presence even more strongly. The longer I kept my eyes shut, the more clearly I saw that he had come from another world, and I was sorry I hadn't asked him more about my great-grandfather Rabbi Michael, because only vague rumors about him had reached my ears.

I was suddenly afraid that I would never again see that wonderful man, whom I'd been with for only a short time.

I rose, gripped my crutches, and went outside.

51

I copied diligently, and while doing so, I saw Edward before my eyes. He was wandering in Tel Aviv in search of work. People noticed his handicap right away and refused to employ him. He didn't tell them he had been wounded in action, had left the training course, and had come to Tel Aviv to be close to buildings that looked like those in the city of his birth.

"Everyone will eventually return to his native city." One of the patients surprised me by saying this. As I heard this emerge from his mouth, I understood that he was revealing an innermost thought. But most of the other patients had a different opinion.

I expected that adults would speak about their past with yearning or nostalgia, but that wasn't the case: the present was more important to them.

"We sacrificed our lives for the present," they said. "We cut ourselves off from our parents and homes to build a new present."

It was hard for me to resist that pointed observation. I felt that these people had done something unbelievable. The sharpest of all was a short man whom everyone called Lonek.

"I was right," he said repeatedly. "If I hadn't left my city in time, we wouldn't have had anything."

"What a terrible way to be right." The answer came quickly.

"Even so . . ."

"I'm ashamed not only of your words but also of your tone."

"We didn't do what we did for our own sake."

The arguments went on for hours. There was no lack of insults, of sudden outbursts, of accusations. I didn't understand all of it.

I went back to copying. Copying soothed me. The clear letters, separate from one another, contained everything that was beyond my power to say. I looked forward to the day when the letters would be joined to my body and my voice.

That night I told Mother that Edward had left the kibbutz and was wandering around Tel Aviv, among houses that looked like the ones in his city, Cracow.

Mother's reaction surprised me.

"Edward is flesh of our flesh," she said. "He was tested in that horrible war and was saved. But in the new war he lost two fingers. He's a handsome young man. The wound those evil people inflicted didn't spoil his good looks."

"And I?" I asked.

"You, too, will stand on your own soon. More and more, you resemble your father. I pray that fortune will favor you and that what you write will light the way for people."

"What happened to Father's manuscripts?"

"They're hidden."

"Can we get to them?"

"The ways of God are hidden. But I'm sure that Father hid his soul in yours, and the day will come that you will write."

"Will I write like Father?"

"You'll write in your own voice. Every person has his own voice and tone."

Mother spoke to me often. Her tone of voice was the same, but her movements were different. I felt that she was trying to tell me things that words couldn't convey. The effort was visible on her lips, and it blocked the words in her mouth.

"You're trying too hard," I told her. "There's no reason to hurry. What we don't manage tonight, we'll manage in the coming nights. So long as we're connected, there's nothing to fear." My words brought a smile to her face, and that made me happy.

The seasons changed. Most of the patients returned home, and new ones were expected. Only I stayed where I was.

The practical nurse no longer hid her intentions. She ignored my injury and was planning to surprise me. I was afraid of the size of her body and of her desire. My legs weren't what they had been. Had she been a quiet sort of woman, I would have said to her, *Leave me alone. I'm about to have an operation. If Dr. Winter manages to restore my legs, we'll get drunk and make love.* But for the moment, I was limited in my movements. Pain sucked my blood. I didn't need a woman to embrace but a woman to listen to me.

A patient who came to the convalescent home after an operation recognized me.

"It's the sleepy boy!" he called out in a voice that startled me. I considered denying it, but the man's happiness was so radiant that I didn't dare. He had also been wounded in the war, but his injury appeared to be more serious than mine: in both his arms and his legs.

"The sleepy boy," he called out again. "You were so handsome. We looked at you and asked ourselves, who are you, and what do you bear in your soul? Miracles didn't happen for us during the war, but you, your existence, was a miracle. Your sleep bore witness to your connection to deeper realms, and from there you were drawing your sustenance. We were sure you would sleep forever, and we would carry you from place to place. Who woke you up?"

"I woke myself up."

"We also tried to wake you, but we didn't know how to dive down into where you were. Where were you wounded?"

"They surprised us."

"The same for us as well."

He was about thirty. His thin face was unshaven, but the light hadn't gone out of his eyes. I was glad that I would be near him so he could tell me about himself and about the refugees.

"As soon as we were freed from the camp in Atlit, we were drafted. We were so glad. There was a great surge of enthusiasm among us, and a desire to do great deeds. We didn't imagine that this enthusiasm might be cut off. We didn't realize that here, too, we could be wounded or killed. The doctor told me I was lucky. I'll eventually be walking in the land of the living. The doctor was religious. I never saw a religious doctor before in my life. None of the doctors in our district went to synagogue, not even on Yom Kippur. 'You will walk in the land of the living,' he said simply. Nowadays, only a believer can be optimistic. By the way, where are you from?"

I told him.

"We're from the same area. And what's your name, if I may ask?"

I told him.

"That name rings a bell with me, and I can tell you that somebody with that name was out and about in our village. Let me think about it."

"It's not at all important."

"If it rings, it's for a reason. We'll talk. We'll remember. But now I have to shut my eyes. I got tired from the trip."

The man from the Carpathians who promised to bring me a prayer book kept his word. He brought it to me wrapped in a brown cloth.

"Keep this prayer book, and it will watch over you," he said.

"Thank you."

"You don't thank people for this type of thing," he said, and went away.

52

About a year before the outbreak of the war, Father received a booklet with a story in it by a little-known author named Franz Kafka. Father read it and was overwhelmed. When Mother noticed his excitement, she served him a cup of coffee and a piece of cheesecake. In response to her question about what was so moving about the story, Father didn't cite anything specific.

"That's exactly the way you have to write today," he finally said.

"Do you feel an affinity with his writing?" Mother asked cautiously.

"He's my brother, dear, my big brother, who broke through the barriers by storm. Now we know who we are and what our place is in this world." All that day, the thin book never left Father's hands.

I now recalled Father's shrunken way of walking around in his study, and I felt what I hadn't felt back then: the pain and humiliation of his continued failure.

"You, too, will break through the siege," Mother kept saying.

None of us imagined what the near future held for us. Father was busy with the sawmill. But his hours at home were devoted to his artistic asceticism. I also wanted to make things easier for him, but I didn't know how.

. . .

I asked Dr. Winter whether he had heard of an author named Franz Kafka.

"I've heard of him," he said, "but I've never read anything by him. Why do you ask?"

I told him that Father loved his writing.

Dr. Winter read what people had read before the war: Stefan Zweig, Arthur Schnitzler, and, most beloved of all, Rilke. His time was limited. The operations took up his days and nights.

"My friend, your operation is also approaching," he finally said. "You're no longer afraid, right?"

"I am afraid." I didn't hide it from him.

"Let's hope this one will be your last. If we can improve your walking, that will be our reward." Again he explained what he was going to do. His explanations didn't enlighten me at all, but I did absorb at least one of the things he said: proteins. You have to eat food rich in protein. Proteins are important for building muscle. The food they served us took on a new purpose. The thought that the proteins would knit together my torn muscles encouraged me to ask for seconds.

The last night I was in Naples, I ran along the seashore and was surprised to feel like I was floating. Before long, I collapsed on the ground, like a body struck down just as it hit its stride. I woke up and was happy that my breathing was normal.

The patients continued to take care of me. One of them brought me a long box of oranges.

"Years ago I had my own orange grove," he said. "I prepared the soil and planted each tree in the grove. I believed I would have the grove till the end of my days and then leave it to my son. It wasn't a big orange grove, but it was very well taken care of. Everyone who saw my orange grove couldn't stop raving about it. I lived there for only twelve years. Then I got sick and had to sell it. Now I have five trees in my garden."

Just a few months earlier, these patients used to drive me crazy with their questions. But now they no longer annoyed me. Instead, they told me about their lives, and I felt close to them. They spoke Hebrew, but their tone and their choice of words made my heart recall people I had been close to in my earlier incarnations, at home and in the ghetto. It sometimes seemed that they, too, had been there. The Hebrew they spoke wasn't a local dialect; it stayed with them wherever they were.

"I was young and sure that the earth would redeem us. It did redeem, but not us," the man with the oranges said, and a smile spread across his face. "I'll be able to bear my illness for another month or two, and in the end it will vanquish me."

I pray that you'll be with us for many more days, I was about to say, but I didn't.

"I was young and frivolous, and I went after big ideas. I was certain I was building a better world in this one." He turned to me. "You believe in the world to come," he said with wonder.

I was alarmed. "Yes," I said.

"Until I was fourteen, I believed in the world to come. After that, my prayers became flawed, and my faith became tarnished. I don't know which came first."

I knew this was to be my last meeting with him. *Stay with me a bit longer,* I wanted to say, but I didn't dare. He looked at me fondly and said, "I hope the operation is successful and that you'll be able to stand on your own. You're very young." He rose to his feet and left quickly.

53

I was sent back to the hospital and prepared for my seventh operation. The nurses tried to entertain me. The anesthesiologist—a short man—was devoted to his instruments and looked at me benevolently. In the next room, Dr. Winter was talking earnestly to a wounded man from the Haganah, trying to convince him that sometimes an artificial limb was preferable to a damaged leg that couldn't be fixed.

"Doctor, save my leg," begged the wounded man. "I have no one in the world." His weeping was not loud, but it reached into every fiber of my being. "If you save my leg, I'll thank you all my life. Not only will I thank you, but my mother, who went up to heaven in smoke, will thank you, too. She did everything she could to save me. If I'm left without a leg, what will happen to me? My mother's sorrow will be greater than mine, believe me."

Dr. Winter stopped replying. The wounded man made all sorts of entreaties and finally cried out in a voice that made the walls shake, "If you can't save my leg, kill me. Death is preferable to life without my leg."

The young man kept murmuring and begging, as if Dr. Winter were a man of God who had the power to change the way of the world.

"I'm just a doctor, my friend. I'm neither an angel nor an archangel." He spoke softly to the wounded man.

Those were the last words that filtered into me before the anesthesia separated me from the world of light.

Each time I was anesthetized, I would revisit the trains of my childhood.

In first class they served coffee and cheesecake, and cocoa for the children. The waitresses were young women dressed in red-and-white uniforms; they were full of mischief, quick-witted, and ready to entertain every passenger. Sometimes, to amuse me, they would bring me a small chocolate bar wrapped in shiny colored paper.

This time, it seemed to me, something was different.

"Where are you going, sweetie?" one of the waitresses asked me.

"Home," I told her.

"Where is your home?"

I whispered in her ear.

"And where are your parents?"

"They're waiting for me at the station." I spoke out clearly.

"Aren't you afraid to travel alone?" she asked in sympathy.

"I've already gotten used to it," I said, surprised by what came from my mouth.

The train raced forward with great power. The smells of coffee and tobacco surrounded me. The people next to me were strangers. They looked at me and smiled. Their smiles were unpleasant, but that didn't prevent me from keeping myself happy, because in a little while I would reach the last stop, and my parents would come to greet me with shouts of joy.

At every station a few people got off, and the carriage gradually emptied. The waitresses stopped serving coffee and cake. They had disappeared. Soon I would be left alone.

It seemed to me that this wasn't the first time this train had been emptied of its passengers. Every time I rode in it, it emptied out. What will happen to me when I'm all alone? I wondered, worried. My parents will be steadfastly waiting for me. I mustn't disappoint them.

As fear increasingly took hold of me, Uncle Isidor appeared at the forward door, neatly dressed, pleasantly elegant, just as he used to appear in our house. For a moment I hesitated. Was it really Uncle Isidor? Because several times during the past year, I had seen his silhouette and was sure it was he. He liked to join us on our summer trips, and, not surprisingly, every time we traveled by train, he would appear. This time he stood there at his full height.

"Uncle Isidor!" I called out, trying unsuccessfully to get to my feet. I explained to him that just now they were doing the seventh operation.

"I don't understand you," said Uncle Isidor, his eyes widening.

"The famous Dr. Winter is setting the fractures in my legs so that I will be able to stand on them."

"I'm sorry," he said as he approached me. "What operation are you talking about?"

Finally, I understood that he didn't know a thing about what had happened to me since we parted. I didn't know where to begin.

"Uncle Isidor," I said, "why don't you sit next to me until we get to the last stop, and I'll tell you what it's possible to relate."

"Do you have secrets?" He was puzzled.

"I have no secrets. It's just that the story is very long. It's not my fault."

"I'm ready to hear everything."

"Where shall we start?" Some of his playfulness had rubbed off on me.

"With whatever you wish to start with." His benevolent smile, which I knew so well, lit his face.

While I was groping for a way to begin, the nurse woke me up.

"The operation was a success," Dr. Winter said warmly. My attachment to him was a mixture of awe and love. For a long time I had been placed into his hands and into the hands of his staff—all doctors from abroad. They spoke German to one another, or Romanian, and here and there a word in Yiddish. They had joined together what could be joined. Shattered legs could not be completely restored to what they had been. But they could make some kind of walking possible. You must not be ungrateful. You had to respect Dr. Winter's efforts and not ask the impossible of him. If it weren't for the infections that invaded my wounds, my recovery would have been smoother. It wasn't Dr. Winter's fault that there were unexpected delays, I had to repeat to myself.

I lay in bed, still enveloped in the web of anesthesia, surrounded by flowers and chocolate, presents from the nurses and the patients. I closed my eyes and waited for the train to come pick me up and take me to the station in my city.

That night Dr. Weingarten came to visit me, with one of Father's manuscripts in his hand.

"How did it get to you, Dr. Weingarten?" I held my breath.

"One of the refugees, an educated man, happened to come upon this treasure. He knew he had a treasure and asked a huge sum for it. 'I knew the author,' I told him. 'No publisher was willing to publish his writing.' In the end I bought the manuscript for my gold watch. Now let's read it together."

I recognized Father's handwriting, but I couldn't read it.

Dr. Weingarten read it easily, and he quickly brought Father's voice to life. I didn't understand a lot of the words, but the melody captivated me.

"Thank you, Dr. Weingarten."

"Thank your father, who brought such a marvelous work into the world."

54

After recuperating from the operation, I was sent back to my room in the convalescent home. I went to sleep in the bed I had gotten used to. When I woke up, it seemed to me that bits of feeling had returned to my legs. I got to the dining room on crutches. The effort was great, but I did it to abide by the will of the physiotherapist, whom I liked.

Meanwhile, the Hungarian boy whose arm had been amputated returned to the convalescent home. His friends, who accompanied him, had been trying to convince him that a prosthetic arm would be useful to him. *You mustn't reject the doctors' opinion. You must try.* Although he had come back and registered in the office, the Hungarian boy was not convinced that the "hanging rag," which was what he called the prosthesis, would be useful to him. Better an exposed stump, without any adornment.

His friends continued to speak earnestly to him, saying that a false arm made of stiff leather wasn't a rag. He grimaced at their words.

"I want to be the way I was," he declared. "If the unseen authorities have decided that I must live in this world without my right arm, I won't play hide-and-seek." I was stunned by the phrase "the unseen authorities."

. . .

The pain didn't let up. To overcome it or to distract myself from it, I copied from the book of Psalms: a book full of the correct words for prayer. The act of copying conquered me completely, and I felt the letters clinging to my thoughts.

One of the patients invaded my room and saw that I was copying from the Bible.

"You should copy from the newspaper," he said to me loudly. "The newspaper will teach you everyday language and our new ways of thinking. The Bible is rooted in the ways of the ancient world."

I didn't know how to reply to him. I felt that in one fell swoop he was snatching away the thoughts and feelings that had been inundating me for a long while. If he kept on talking to me in his hammering voice, he would take away the little that I had acquired with such great effort.

I wanted to cry, but I controlled myself.

"Hebrew today isn't what it used to be," he went on. "It has cut itself off from books, and now it's connected to life." I had heard that cliché more than once, but the patient's harsh words were like salt being rubbed into my wounds. *Leave me alone!* I wanted to shout.

He apparently noticed my distress and stopped bothering me.

After that came long days of brightness. I sat in my room and read S. Y. Agnon's *A Guest for the Night*. The librarian kept urging me to read S. Yizhar. She promised that if I read some of his stories, I would feel a connection to the Land.

The Hungarian boy approached me.

"How do you feel after the operation?" he asked.

"It hurts." I felt close to him and told him I was copying from the Bible.

"Painters copy great artists to learn their secrets," he quickly replied.

I considered saying to him, *But the Bible was written by unseen authorities*, using the same expression he had used, but I didn't say it.

The boy spoke German with a heavy Hungarian accent. He hadn't managed to learn Hebrew. He was drafted immediately after immigrating and was wounded in his first action. I wanted to tell him about the joy that copying gave me, but I felt it wasn't proper to mix my slight happiness in with his disaster.

For his part, the boy told me that from the age of five he had trained to be a dancer. "But without an arm, it's impossible to be a dancer," he said, chuckling.

I was embarrassed by my luck. My body wasn't my instrument of expression.

The boy asked if I wanted to be an author.

"I'm preparing myself," I said, "and I look forward with all my heart to the day when I'll be able to find that inner melody." It seemed to me that I hadn't explained myself properly. I told him that I'd lost my mother tongue and that only with my father and mother, whose whereabouts were unknown, did I speak it as I used to. If they were still with me, my mother tongue would be growing along with me.

After a short pause, the boy said, "If it weren't for my wound, I would have gone onstage after getting out of the army. Now I'm like a bird with one broken wing, and without flight, there's no dancing. I'm sorry. I never introduced myself. My name is Paul."

"My name is Erwin," I said. I felt that this was an outstanding young man, and his fate would be so, too.

"Both of us are from the Hapsburg Empire that fell apart," said Paul. "You were born in Bukovina, and I was born in Budapest. But a hint of it remains in us both, right?"

I saw before my eyes the young mothers who used to walk their sons and daughters to the conservatory, one carrying a violin, the other a viola. There was an undercurrent of competition in the air: Who would rise to the top? There was one boy among us, Raul Dienstag, for whom everyone predicted a brilliant future. His mother was always with him. She wouldn't allow him to play dodgeball or soccer, but she let him work out in the gymnasium. He was tall and muscular for his age because a violinist must not only be talented but also sturdy—so his mother claimed.

Raul and his mother were among the first to be deported from the city. Raul carried a heavy backpack and held his violin in his hand, and his thin mother carried two overstuffed bags. I didn't know them well. He was one year below me in school. Some students admired him, but quite a few mocked him and called him the Child Prodigy.

When I was six, Mother asked me if I wanted to study violin. I said no. She didn't pressure me. Father was so immersed in his writing that the matter wasn't discussed with him.

Of course I didn't know then that the violin demands all of your energy, from childhood on, and there was no guarantee that you would excel. My friend Benno was in the midst of his ascent, but the war interrupted it. What good would his fingers do him now that they'd lost their agility?

That night I wrote four lines:

> *Not one word remains*
> *That wasn't refined in the furnace of pain.*

The storm is closed within me
Behind bolted doors.

I revised them again and again, and I knew there was much more to revise. But my hands became fists, and I lay the pen down on the paper.

55

I closed my eyes and was borne on waves of darkness. Sometimes I raced along on railroad tracks and sometimes in a truck. On other days I rode in a wagon loaded with refugees. If it weren't for meals, I wouldn't have gotten up at all. Being detached from the darkness was hard for me. In the darkness, no one asked me what I was going to do with my life, where I was going to live, and so on—questions I had no answers for.

I spent most of the day in bed. But when I lay down for an extended period of time, I was also taken to places I didn't want to return to, such as Vaska's cellar. After I fled from him, I almost never saw him in my imagination. I was imprisoned by him for seven hundred and twenty days. I said to myself then that when the time came, I would make an itemized list of every insult and bruise that he inflicted upon me, and this would serve as the indictment I would file against him.

Dr. Winter was sure that my life would change when I started walking. He always sounded optimistic. Now I felt a slight throbbing of the nerves in my legs.

"A miracle has happened for me." The words slipped out.

Dr. Winter's face tightened strangely every time I used the word "miracle." This time he kept himself from saying what he usually said.

"Your body is doing its job," he said simply, "and in the coming days I expect it to show us what it knows how to do."

That night I dreamed that one of the patients suggested to Dr. Winter that he wrap himself in a prayer shawl.

"You are mistaken, my friend. That's not me," he said. "You were most certainly thinking of someone else." The patient was stunned by that answer and left him alone.

The practical nurse, who always lay in wait for me, appeared in the doorway and shut the door behind her. This time she didn't say, *Let me kiss you*, but she looked at me with her big eyes. She apparently expected me to say something, but I was so astonished by her sudden appearance that I didn't say a word.

"I wanted to tell you, Erwin, that you look a lot like my son Walter," she began by saying. "He's your age and your height. During the war, in the fateful month of May, he broke his leg and was confined to his bed. I nursed him with everything I had. I sold clothing and jewelry to bring him nourishing food. But for some reason his leg didn't heal.

"When we heard in the ghetto about the coming Aktion, everyone whose legs could carry them escaped. My relatives and friends advised me to flee until the danger passed. Everyone thought that the sick people and the elderly wouldn't be harmed. I hesitated. I didn't want to leave Walter unattended. But my sister and brother-in-law urged me, and I ran away with all the young people.

"That very night I regretted it and returned to the ghetto, but Walter was already gone. I looked for him everywhere, and finally

I turned myself in so I could be with him. All trace of him was gone. In all the camps where I was—and I was in a lot of camps—I couldn't find him. He's exactly your age and your height. When the war was over, I traveled from place to place. There was no refugee camp where I didn't look for him. I left messages in all the offices of the Joint Distribution Committee. I told him I was going to Palestine.

"I kept waiting for him here, and when I saw you, my hopes were reborn. You can't imagine how much you resemble him. You're his messenger. He sent you to me to tell me that he's alive and coming to me soon. God has punished me enough. I love you the way I love Walter. You're twin brothers. Do you understand me?" She burst into tears and left the room.

I couldn't sleep that night. I wanted to write her a letter and apologize for my strange behavior, but in the end I wrote only jumbles of words. I tore what I had written to shreds, but doing that didn't calm me down, either. I got up, harnessed myself to the crutches, and walked over to the dark dining hall. I went to the tea corner and made myself a cup of tea. The hot liquid seeped into me, and I shut my eyes and fell asleep in a chair.

56

The pain from the operation wouldn't let up. If Dr. Winter hadn't assured me that I would soon feel true relief, my nights would have been too hard to bear.

The last time I was under anesthesia, or perhaps it was the time before that, I sat at my desk and gathered words. The words proved to be made of metal, but they could be moved. I weighed every word before moving it. This was hard work, and I got cramps in my arms. Still, I tried over and over to combine the words and form a sentence from them. I didn't succeed. The words refused to combine.

Yechiel came to visit me. I tried to open my eyes. His quiet way of standing there brought to mind the days when I was together with my comrades, working in the orchard and training diligently. You remembered Yechiel's thin sandwiches even when you were far from the place where they were served to you.

"How are you?" he asked softly.

"Better," I said to make him happy.

"God will help you," he said, not stressing any of the words.

If another person had said that to me, I wouldn't have felt at ease. But from Yechiel's mouth, the words sounded trustworthy.

Yechiel brought with him not only his person but also his personality. Among the comrades, he didn't stand out, but when he was alone, his face mirrored the light in his soul.

I told him about my wish to become an author and that I was preparing myself for it.

"How are you preparing yourself?" he asked.

"I'm copying from the Bible."

"Wonderful," he quickly replied, and I could tell right away that he was trying to create a closeness between us and to help me. "Is it hard?"

"As I'm copying, I try to bond with the letters."

He appeared not to understand my words, but he didn't continue questioning me. I tried to spare him from embarrassment.

"How are things on the kibbutz?" I asked.

"The same. This year everyone is mobilized for the harvest. The orchard produced plenty of fruit, and everyone gathered to pick it. But I'm doing what I always did."

Just a year and a half earlier, I had worked at building the terrace and brought loose brown earth up from the wadi. Now the training program seemed far off, living a life of its own, and it was as if I'd never been there.

"How's Ephraim?"

He didn't hide the truth. "They amputated his arm. We visited him."

"Good God," I blurted out.

"He spoke to us in his usual voice and asked us not to worry about him," Yechiel told me.

"He's an amazing person," I said and immediately realized that trite adjective didn't suit him.

"He asked me to leave the kitchen and prepare myself for other kinds of work. I didn't know what to say. I'm glad to make sandwiches for the fellows, or pots of coffee and tea. But if the kibbutz asks me to do other work, I'll gladly do it."

I remembered that fateful night when we went out on the ambush. I walked behind Yechiel. It seemed he was limping, perhaps because his cartridge belt was hanging loosely on him and wasn't tightly fastened to his shoulder. I was afraid he would be among the first to be hit.

"Yechiel," I said, "do what you feel you must do."

"Thanks," he said, nodding.

"If you do so, you'll be at peace with yourself."

Yechiel hung his head again, smiled, and took a few steps back, until he reached the doorway. He said goodbye and quickly left.

The silence he left in his wake enveloped me for quite a while.

That night I felt that Dr. Winter's efforts to restore my shattered legs and my attempts to bond with the Hebrew letters were a joint struggle. If the letters bonded with my fingers, my legs would also heal. I tossed that thought around in my head, but I didn't dare reveal it to anyone.

Meanwhile, the story "Tehila" by Agnon came my way. I was pleased by it and copied its opening sentences: "There was an old woman in Jerusalem. A fine-looking woman, like none you have ever seen in your life. She was pious and she was wise and she was charming and she was modest. The light in her eyes was kindness and compassion, and the wrinkles on her face, blessings and peace."

Again I felt a connection to the melody of this story. But in my heart I knew this enchanting melody wasn't mine. The tempests that tossed me had taken away my inner peace. It was impossible to write about the ghetto, the hiding places, and the forests with that kind of moderation.

I heard the groaning of the refugees, and I knew that in their voices were buried all the places I'd been. It was too bad they were far from me now. If they were nearby, I could observe them again and learn from their body language. Without their voices, mine was hesitant, wandering, trying to grab on to voices that weren't mine. Ultimately, I was greatly perplexed.

It had been wrong for me to part from the refugees. I absorbed their music, the music of sorrow mixed with bitter irony, but not enough of it. I should have clung to them and not distanced myself. They would have told me more about my father and mother, and about my grandfather, who had been sent to one of the smaller, lesser-known camps, where he perished. I knew painfully well that without their music, I would have none of my own.

That night I saw my great-grandfather, Rabbi Michael, sitting on a tall chair. His face was white, and his eyelids fluttered. He sensed that I had entered his narrow room.

"Who's there?" he asked.

I told him.

"What are you doing, my dear?"

I didn't know how to begin, so I said, "I came to get a blessing from you."

"You're wrong, my dear. I'm no saint."

"They told me that you pray marvelously. Or am I wrong about that, too?"

"People exaggerate."

"And what will you give me?" I asked, like a beggar at the door.

"I have nothing."

"I'm in great distress." I didn't keep it from him.

"Come and sit next to me," he said and took my hand. "How did you get to me? You've certainly come a long way."

"I wanted to get to you."

He turned to face me with his blind eyes and said, "I thank God that He brought you to me."

I woke up and knew that I had been submerged in a deep sleep and had seen sights that had until then been kept from me. I knew that the touch of my great-grandfather's hand had conveyed precious speech to me, but I didn't know what its nature was. I wanted to thank him, but I hadn't dared. I copied Psalm 102, the one that begins, "The prayer of an afflicted man who has fainted and pours forth his complaints before God."

57

The next day I felt that my legs were gradually connecting to my body. I didn't know whether it was a false feeling or a true one. I wanted to get up and see what was happening to me, but any careless movements hurt me, so I stayed in bed.

Dr. Winter came by in the morning, hugged me, and celebrated with me. On a piece of cardboard, he charted the future stages of my recovery.

"A lot depends on you," he said, "on your willpower and perseverance." I was about to ask him if my effort to bond with the letters was having an effect on my legs. Of course I didn't ask.

Less than two years earlier, I stood on my legs and did everything my friends did; in Naples I even excelled in rowing. Then it all changed. I became dependent on the nurses and doctors, and on my friends' visits. Hope deceived me. The deep slumbers took me to previously unknown regions. I was indeed an obedient patient and did what I was told, and I overheard with dismay the whispered consultations about whether to amputate my left leg or to try to save it. Dr. Winter stood fast in that battle like a lion.

"Patience, my friend, patience," he kept repeating. "Maybe you won't be able to run, but you'll walk."

But my mental efforts didn't bear much fruit. Except for end-less copies and a few feeble poems, I didn't manage to write any-thing of value.

"You'll write yet," said Dr. Winter, as though reading my mind.

"I'm not sure. A person who is limited in his movement finds it hard to develop spiritual drive."

"I see you standing on your own two feet."

"Without crutches?"

"With a wanderer's staff," he said, laughing.

Reality hit me in the face yet again. The next day the woman in charge of the war-wounded arrived and tried to convince me to stay on at the kibbutz training farm. She again listed all the advan-tages and then summed it up: "The doctors, the nurses, the staff of the training farm, not to mention your friends—everyone wants to see you living on the farm."

I knew there was some truth to her words, but what I needed was solitude, a withdrawal from everything, so that no one would see me writhing in pain. Solitude, I was about to cry out loud, is as necessary to me as air to breathe.

She fixed me with her gaze and said, "Don't be in a rush to decide."

"I want to live someplace where people won't notice me and pity me," I said in a voice that apparently sounded like a shout. Dr. Winter was also surprised by my stubbornness.

"Without long stretches of solitude, I can't live the life of a creative person," I told him explicitly.

It was hard for those practical people, however sensitive they were, to understand that need. Solitude for them was a gloomy mood that would depress you in the end.

"What have you written up to now?" Good Dr. Winter tried to probe me.

"Nothing."

"Are you sure that writing is your path in life?"

"No, but I hope it is," I said, to show him I was a well-balanced person.

"A person has to prepare himself for a life of action. Imagination deludes us."

I didn't respond.

The day before, it had seemed to me that I had emerged from my injury. Now it was clear that this was only a stage in my recuperation. I would be bound to my crutches for a long time.

Meanwhile, the country was in turmoil. People said Ben-Gurion was about to declare the establishment of the state. There was tension in every corner. I wanted to rejoice, to throw my crutches away and be together with my soldier comrades.

The patients read the newspapers devoutly and were glued to the radio; there was an argument at every table.

"All the Arab countries will attack us," said one side.

"If we don't declare the state now," the other promptly rejoined, "who knows when history will give us another opportunity like this."

The man who had owned the orange grove, whom the doctors had given two months to live, announced that he wanted to change his name back before he died. When he arrived in Palestine, he changed his name from Shainboim, which means "beautiful tree," to Noy, the Hebrew equivalent. Now he wanted to return to his old name.

"The name Shainboim may not have a grand lineage, but it was the name of my parents and of my ancestors for a few hundred years, and in my great arrogance I changed it. If anyone called me by my old name, I wouldn't answer him. Perhaps they won't lash me in the world to come because I changed my name, but my conscience lashes me every day. So I've decided to return to the name of my ancestors."

"We all changed our names," one of the patients at the table replied.

"I'm returning the name Noy to its beautiful garden and leaving it behind."

"You're throwing away not only a name but also a people's dream."

"The dream, if it's to be fulfilled, will be fulfilled without me. I won't demand my part in fulfilling the dream."

"For us you'll stay Noy."

"I've already put in my will that if I don't manage to change my name while I'm still alive, I want my heirs to do it for me. And on my grave will be written 'Here lies Jacob Shainboim.'"

"You'll be sorry."

"I'm at peace with my soul."

"If everyone changes their names back, we'll be back in the ghetto. We'll be faceless again. People will speak Yiddish in Tel Aviv and on the kibbutzim. Be aware that a man who bears the name Shainboim plants the exile here."

"I'm not ashamed of my ancestors' name."

"You're trampling on the dream of many good people."

"In the end it's a private matter."

"Nothing is private in our society. The private sphere is also public. In these difficult times, when a great war looms at our gate, you're concerned with yourself?"

"I want to leave the world with the name of my ancestors. That's all. I'm not asking for anything more."

"I won't argue with you any longer. Do what you want. I told you my opinion." The other patient wanted to end the discussion, and so he did.

. . .

Toward evening one of the patients brought me a collection of stories by Franz Kafka in Hebrew. I hadn't expected a surprise like that. I immediately saw Father before my eyes, holding the book in his hand and saying, "This is the way you're supposed to write." There was ice in his voice. Mother, who knew his pain, tried to talk sense to him, but he was resolute. "This is the way you're supposed to write." Even I, who didn't understand his struggles, felt that the sentence was cutting into his flesh. After that, he didn't sit at his desk for many days. Mother prepared the food that he loved, but it didn't please him as before. His facial expression changed, and he gained weight.

I didn't dare open the book to read it. Only late at night, I sat and copied the beginning of the story "A Country Doctor":

> I was in great perplexity; I had to start on an urgent journey; a seriously ill patient was waiting for me in a village ten miles off; a thick blizzard of snow filled all the wide spaces between him and me; I had a gig, a light gig with big wheels, exactly right for our country roads; muffled in furs, my bag of instruments in my hand, I was in the courtyard all ready for the journey; but there was no horse to be had, no horse. My own horse had died in the night, worn out by the fatigues of this icy winter.

I read it again and again. I had never heard a story with that rhythm. The facts rushed out upon one another. The punctuation, the tension, built up. Then I heard Father calling out, "Franz Kafka broke through the barriers. His horses gallop, but he knows how to guide them." At that time, I didn't understand that a severe condemnation of himself was hidden in his praise.

58

The country was seething. Everyone was conscripted, and my friends stopped visiting me. The convalescent home was emptying of its patients. Only one nurse remained in the infirmary, an unpleasant woman who grumbled all the time, as though she were surrounded by patients who meant only to annoy her.

I stopped copying and trying to write. Rumors of bad news raged around us. The deaths of thirty-five soldiers turned the convalescent home into a house of mourning. The few patients walked about with clenched fists, spitting out suppressed words of anger or weeping.

Now my recuperation didn't seem like a determined return to life but, rather, like evading the front lines. I didn't show myself much in the dining hall, preferring to take my meals to my room. I didn't go out onto the balcony until evening.

One of the patients, who noticed my withdrawal, commented, "You've already done your part. You have nothing to be ashamed of."

I didn't know exactly how to reply, so I just said, "It's too bad my recovery is slow."

"Shattered legs don't heal easily. You have to take care of your recovery. That's your task."

"It's hard for me to think of myself at this time."

The patient didn't give up. "It's your duty."

I didn't like this persistent conversation. It clouded my spirit. What did he mean by "You have to take care of your recovery"?

Miri, the physiotherapist, came on time. We did exercises to strengthen the leg muscles. The bedsores were getting better, and she was pleased with my progress; she was a practical and determined woman. Miri was from a moshav, and she brought the fragrance of the fields with her to the convalescent home. Every time she touched me, I keenly felt a hand that gripped and strengthened. After the exercises, I was exhausted. I laid my body on the bed and closed my eyes.

After a sleepless night, I took two painkillers. Cool tranquility fell upon me, and I wrote the following lines at the first light:

Unseen, the changes will come. Growth is slow, almost imperceptible. Only occasionally—at a station, at a temporary resting place, on a balcony—a face will peek out at you. It is encircled with wrinkles and, as on a sawed-off tree stump, you can count the rings of its years.

I read it over and over. From where within me did those words sprout? And how had they joined together into a paragraph? Who was that face that peeked out at you? The wrinkles, the rings of trees? Still, I knew that they had emerged from my pen. Were they mine? I copied the paragraph, and my astonishment only increased.

I was already beyond fatigue. I went into the empty dining hall and made myself a cup of tea. The hot drink erased the night's uncertainties from my mind, and I fell asleep.

Robert surprised me with a visit. Our friends were still on the kibbutz, on alert, and soon they would be going to one of the fronts. He brought me a few sketches. More than anything, they reminded me of lost people from the ghetto.

"Who are they?" I asked.

"Misgav Yitzhak."

"Are you sure?" I couldn't keep from asking.

"I'm trying to be faithful to what my eyes see."

As they used to say back home, a person can't shed his skin. That rule apparently applied to Robert, too. He drew the ghetto and thought he was drawing Misgav Yitzhak.

In any event, the times had left their mark on him. His face was longer, and his eyes had sunk slightly into their sockets, as happens to a person who has been making a prolonged effort.

"I sometimes think about my parents," Robert told me. "At the end of the war, I waited for them and was sure that in a few days they would reach me. Two refugees, passersby, told me they had seen them, with their own eyes, and they were on their way to me. Rumors also reached Italy that someone had seen them. I was going to stay in Naples and wait for them, but because they were so long in coming, I decided to take Ephraim's advice and emigrate. 'All the survivors will immigrate to the Land. You have nothing to worry about,' Ephraim said to me. I'm sorry I listened to him."

They'll certainly find you, I wanted to say, but I didn't.

"I should have stayed and waited for them. During the war, I imagined them returning to me and all of us going home together. My first mistake was that I left Stash's house and went to look for them. Like a sleepwalker, I dragged myself from one refugee camp to another. In the end, I wound up as far away from them as Naples.

"My second mistake was worse, and unforgivable. I should have stayed in Europe, even in Naples, and waited for them and not let them wander. They were afraid to return to Stash, in case they wouldn't find me there. It was wrong for me to leave. I should have insisted on staying at some crossroad to wait for them. Now, go find them! I have no idea where they are. Sometimes I imagine them sitting in one of the abandoned camps and waiting for me. Everyone has already left the camps, but they're sure I'll come to them. Now the sea separates us. How can I cross it?"

Then he addressed me in a different tone. "I want to ask something of you. If by chance my parents come here—by the way, they aren't tall; they're pleasant people; I look a lot like my mother—if they're looking for me, tell them I'm very sorry that I didn't wait for them. I was swayed by rumors and my moods betrayed me. Ask them to wait for me nearby, not to go far away. I hope to return safe and sound from the war. Tell them I'm sketching and painting. Father will certainly be happy. Tell Mother, please, that she is always with me. Do you understand?"

"Very well."

"I have to go back to the kibbutz. They gave me a two-and-a-half-hour leave to see you. Excuse me for throwing myself on you. You're my closest friend. Don't worry about me. We're a solid group now, and we'll watch over one another. 'See you at six p.m. after the war.'"

"Take care of yourself."

"Of myself?" His lips twisted strangely, and he left.

"Robert!" I called after him, but he was already outside.

I went out and sat on a bench. Again I saw his face and that strange grimace as he stood on the threshold. I was angry at myself for casting doubt on what he drew. A person draws what he knows how to draw.

"Watch over him, God," I said and gripped the back of the bench so I could stand up.

59

The days passed. There were battles on every front. No one spoke about casualties, but I could see my friends before my eyes, climbing steep hills and storming fortified positions. They were climbing with all their strength, and while climbing, they reached out to Yechiel and pulled him up so he wouldn't fall or be left behind.

Robert had gotten a lot stronger over the past months, but at our last meeting, he seemed wounded from within. I, like a fool, looked at him with a critical eye and didn't even offer him a single kind word of my own.

I was afraid that when the fighting died down they would send me back to the kibbutz. I would be on display there, and everyone would pity me. That fear depressed me, and not only in the light of day.

At night I dreamed that my friends were dragging me, and I was gripping my bed and screaming, *Leave me alone! This is where I belong now!* But my friends, who had received instructions from the woman responsible for the war-wounded, held me with bony fingers that dug into my shoulders and pulled me. *Don't hurt me!* I shouted with all my might, warning them with my last breath that all of Dr. Winter's work was going down the drain; the connections would be severed and there would be no alternative to amputating my legs. I would remain a cripple all my life. That plea also fell on deaf ears. Fortunately, I then woke up and was rescued from that suffering.

Benno came to visit me and brought me greetings from my friends. All of them were at the front together, and they had already experienced short battles. Some had been wounded, but no one had died.

It seemed that danger had done Benno good. He looked tan and robust. His voice was hearty and a bit hoarse. He spoke about the expanses of the Negev and the beauty of the desert, as if he weren't the Benno I knew but a man who had overcome his sorrow.

"And who was wounded?" I asked.

"Light wounds." He made a dismissive gesture with his right hand.

I didn't believe him, but I refrained from asking for details.

Benno didn't talk about music, and I had the feeling that, to some degree, the progress of the battles, the gains and conquests, compensated for the loss of flexibility in his fingers. But before he left, he told me, "After the war, I'm going to try to get a violin. I haven't given up on playing. Life without playing music isn't a life. If you find someone who's willing to lend me his violin, I'll be very grateful. I'll never be a soloist, but I believe I can play in an orchestra. I promised my parents, before they separated us, that I'd keep playing every day. There were times during the war when music played strongly in my mind. I was sure it would be retained in my fingers, too. I was wrong. If your fingers don't move on the strings, they lose their agility.

"But now I have energy, and I want with all my might to return to the violin. When I was a boy, I didn't like practicing exercises, and I tried to avoid them. But Mother watched over me and sat next to me for two full hours every day, so that I'd do all my tasks. That was that."

Pessimism and sarcasm had fallen away from Benno. For a moment, the child within him resurfaced—the boy whose mother supervised him and worried about his progress.

"And how are things with you?" he asked me like a brother.

"There's been improvement in my walking, but I have a long way to go," I confided in him.

"And the writing?"

I showed him the opening passage I had written. He read it and called out jubilantly, "How beautiful! Even if I copied out seven books, I couldn't manage to write a passage like that. Wonderful! You'll be an author. I have no doubt you'll be an author. Are you pleased with yourself?"

"No. It's a long road, full of obstacles."

"If I were you, I'd be pleased. 'Unseen, the changes will come.' That's a fine sentence. I'm proud of you. A great beginning. After the war, we'll sit and talk. I feel that we have a lot in common."

"Will the war will be long?" I asked.

"In my opinion, it will be short. It has changed us beyond recognition. I, in any event, feel that I have changed. I learned to respect my friends. We're working like a solid team. We help one another and overcome the obstacles the war presents."

"Too bad I can't be with you."

"You have a different task. You're fighting on a different front. You'll be our storyteller. I have no doubt you'll recount everything that life did to us."

"I haven't started yet. I need plenty of grace."

"You'll do it. All your friends support you."

"I don't deserve it yet."

"My time is up. I've got to go. See you soon," Benno said, and dashed out.

An hour after he left, sobs welled up from within me, prolonged sobbing that wouldn't let go of me. Fear crept into my soul that I wouldn't fulfill the hopes they had pinned on me.

I saw the Bible teacher Slobotsky in my sleep. I told him that I had copied many passages from the Bible, even a whole chapter of the book of Job.

He looked at me skeptically and asked, "Copying or studying?"

"Copying," I disclosed.

"And what does the copying teach you?"

"I connect with the words and their melody. I do it with great awareness."

"That's a new invention," he said, chuckling. It was a laugh that pained me.

"Is it forbidden to copy?"

"You're allowed, but what for?"

"I want to become a writer."

"How strange. When did that occur to you?"

"My father was a writer."

"And you want to follow in his footsteps?"

"I don't know what my father wrote. I never read his work. I was a boy. But I want to continue from the exact place where he left off."

"That also seems a little strange to me."

"The Hebrew letters will show me the way. They won't mislead me."

"I can't believe my ears."

"Believe me, Mr. Slobotsky, I took possession of the Hebrew letters through great suffering, and now they are part of me."

"A person mustn't be blamed in his sorrow," he said in a voice that sounded gloomy to me, and close to tears.

I woke up, and I was glad that this had been a night vision and not reality. I kept myself from falling back to sleep, so that Slobotsky wouldn't return and be puzzled by my decision.

60

In the convalescent home the fog of war was very thick. They said that Ben-Gurion was surrounded by excellent army officers. But in the end he would make the decisions, and he would lead us to victory.

"Now the whole world will know that Jews aren't cowards. They know how to fight." One of the patients expressed this opinion, a thin man who could barely walk.

" 'One who puts on his armor should not boast like one who takes it off,' " replied another patient, who was sitting next to him.

The mood around the table fluctuated between high and low, but I, to my shame, became interested in women again. I knew that during those fateful days it was more fitting for me to be concerned about the public good, and especially about my friends at the front. But what could I do? The pretty women of Naples once again agitated my nighttime visions. They were lovely and charming, and one of them invited me to lie with her on the sand.

"I don't have a penny," I told her.

"No matter. Pay next time."

They knew what excited a boy's heart. They didn't talk a lot but wrapped themselves around him, so that every part of his body could feel their warmth.

The taste of that astonishing love in the soft sand came back to me with great clarity, and I was sorry that it was beyond my power to make love as I had. Now every movement hurt me. Once, I asked Dr. Winter if I would ever be able to make love to a woman properly.

"Of course you'll be able to. But only with pretty, attractive women," he joked.

While my life was still stuck at crossroads, the woman responsible for the war-wounded appeared and announced that an appropriate solution had been found for me. Nothing could be more suitable. A man from Tel Aviv with no family had died, and in his will he had bequeathed his small apartment to the defense forces, requesting that a war invalid be housed in it, preferably a young man from Bukovina.

"You come from Bukovina, right?"

"Correct."

"You'll be moving there next week. A woman will come to you every day for three hours. She'll cook your meals, do the laundry, tidy the house, and take you out for walks. What do you say?"

I didn't know whether or not I should be enthusiastic about this, so I just said, "Fine."

"It's better than fine. It's heaven sent!"

"Thank you." That was all I could say.

"Not everybody merits an arrangement like this."

In my heart I felt anxious but not happy. The look of the woman in charge of the war-wounded and her expressions— "from Bukovina"; "It's heaven sent"; "Not everybody merits an arrangement like this"—individually and taken together gave me the feeling that I had left the channel of random events and shifted over to the path of fate.

. . .

Daniel, one of my friends, came to visit me and told me that Yechiel had been wounded in the arm, not a serious wound, and had returned to the kibbutz. He wasn't working for the time being and spent most of the day praying.

"Everybody wishes you well and hopes to see you soon." He spoke as if he'd learned the words by heart.

I confided in him that the woman in charge of the war-wounded had just visited me and offered me a small apartment in Tel Aviv, where I could recuperate and be independent.

"So you won't return to the kibbutz?"

"I guess not."

"Your friends told me to tell you that they're thinking about you and that after the war everything will be as it always was."

It was evident that these words had cost him a considerable effort. He had always been inarticulate, but his awkward way of speaking now stood out even more.

"Was the fighting difficult?" I wanted to hear the details from him.

His face showed that it was beyond his ability to answer my question, but he tried. He put together a few words and said, "We advanced. There wasn't a lot of resistance."

Suddenly, I saw them all, and myself as well, on the burning hot beach of Naples, running with all-out strength and shouting, "*alef* is *ohel, ohel* is 'tent'; *beit* is *bayit, bayit* is 'house,'" trying to bond with our first Hebrew words. The refugees stood alongside their sheds and were amazed, like proud parents. It should be said again: we didn't try to associate with them, but despite this, they were pleased by every achievement of ours. No one could imagine then that the war we were leaving behind would not be our last.

Daniel sat by my side for a long time. I didn't know what to say to him or how to make him happy. His awkwardness of speech clung to me, too. Finally, I asked, "When will you go back to the kibbutz?"

Daniel shrugged his shoulders, as if to say, *Who knows?*

I was annoyed with myself for not finding the right words to draw him out of his muteness, even for a moment. If I didn't have anything to say to a friend who was fighting and who came to visit me, what was all my copying and my lame writing for?

That day I got a letter from Benno:

> *Thanks for the passage you showed me. It's very promising. The first sentence is engraved in my memory: "Unseen, the changes will come."*
>
> *Anyone who has dealt in art knows how slow and small the achievements are. Don't despair. You have anger and determination. They will take you forward. Your father was a writer. Sometimes parents transfer the essence of their aspirations to their children. My poor mother wasn't musical. She was enchanted by music, but the enchantment didn't work on her. She put all her effort into supervising me. My father was an active, practical man. Music seemed to him like work that had no reward. Excuse me for talking about myself. I meant only to cheer you up.*
>
> *As for us, we're living a life of spiritual exaltation. Fear came and went. Now we are constantly happy. The landscapes in the Negev are spiritual. It seems to me that an orchestra is hiding behind every hill, or a fine string quartet. No wonder God spoke to people in the desert and not in the fertile landscapes of Europe. Excuse me for expressing such banal thoughts.*
>
> *I hope the pain leaves you some untainted time for yourself.*

Last night I dreamed about Dr. Winter. He was full of enthusiasm about you. He told me that you're taking giant steps forward, and in a year, at most two years, you'll be walking in the street like everyone else. I believed every word he uttered. Take care of yourself.

Yours,
Benno

61

The very next day preparations began for my move. Dr. Winter had heard about the man with no family who had bequeathed his apartment to the defense forces.

"I can do nothing but agree to an invitation like that," he said. "You, as they say, were fated to live in the city. Nothing to be done. I'll see you every month, and if there are problems, I'll come to visit you. Or else you'll come to see me in the clinic. Adieu."

And so he parted from me. The words I had prepared to say to him dissolved in my mind.

"Thank you." I did manage to throw those words into the air, but I don't know if they reached his ears. It was strange how deeply I'd sunk roots into this un-private place.

Tears welled up in my eyes when I saw the nurses gathering up my clothes and arranging them in the suitcase that had come from Misgav Yitzhak with the rest of my belongings.

Mother often told me that Father had passed his temperament and affability on to me. Whenever she said that, I would see him at his desk with his wrinkled face, and I would wonder if even then he had tried to transmit his inner music to me.

The patients gave me small presents and wished me a life of health and renewal.

"You're young, and your life lies before you," a nurse said, wishing me well. On behalf of the staff of the convalescent home, she gave me two books, one by S. Yizhar and one by Moshe Shamir.

I was moved by the gathering of people around me. One of the patients expressed his opinion about my leave-taking.

"You're lucky," he said. "Not every invalid from the defense forces gets his own apartment." *Woe to my good luck,* I wanted to say, but I didn't.

In the afternoon, a pickup truck arrived. With the help of the sturdy cook, the driver lifted me onto it in my wheelchair, and we set out. If it weren't for the pain that gripped me, I would certainly have been impressed by the sight of the orange groves and green fields, but the pain was intense. I shut my eyes and hoped in my heart that the trip wouldn't take long.

The ground-floor apartment pleased me, but at the same time, I was fearful. Everything in it was on a small scale and coated with a slight dimness: a smallish room with a table, two chairs, and a slender bookcase, and adjoining it, a tiny room with a bed, a cupboard, and a bed lamp. There was also a kitchenette. I looked around and said to myself, *Who heard my cry and provided exactly what my soul needed?*

Rivka arrived and was introduced to me: she was a woman of about thirty, good-looking and simply dressed. The woman in charge of the war-wounded said, "The young man's birth name is Erwin, and he changed it to Aharon. I hope you'll get along. I brought sheets, towels, and some utensils. The late Mr. Arthur Ehrenfeld kept his apartment meticulously, and it was transferred to us in excellent condition. Nothing is lacking here. What else? Rivka will come to you, as I said, every day for three hours. You can rest now and get used to the place."

It was short and sharp and a bit military, but I was happy, as though I had been offered not only shelter but also a hidden run-way from which I would be able to take flight. From now on, I was by myself.

I sat there and didn't move. The tension of the preceding days—saying goodbye to the workers in the convalescent home and to the patients, riding in the pickup truck, and the encounter with my apartment—had shaken me up and made me dizzy.

I shut my eyes and saw the convalescent home and the practical nurse who had always wanted to hug and kiss me and who finally told me about her son—I hadn't seen her before I left and didn't ask about her.

I opened my eyes, but I didn't move the wheelchair. I wanted to imagine the man who had lived there. The books in his library were half in German and half in Hebrew. An educated man, most likely. He read a lot, kept silent a lot, and every time he ran into one of the neighbors, he barely uttered a complete sentence. A tall man. The chairs probably didn't suit his height. Every hour or two he would make a cup of tea for himself.

Now he was in the world of truth, and I was sitting in his apartment. His essence still permeated every corner and told me he was a modest man, monklike but with an aesthetic sensibility. He didn't have close friends and mostly listened to himself and to classical music. There was nothing superfluous in his apartment.

In the evening Rivka returned. She said, "Good evening," and started to make my supper. I saw right away that she didn't intend to ask me questions or tell me about herself. She had cleaned the apartment the day before, and she was now familiar with all the furniture and knew where everything belonged.

For supper she prepared a salad, a soft-boiled egg, cheese, two slices of bread spread with margarine, and a cup of coffee. I thanked her.

"Leave the plates on the table," she said, "and in the morning I'll come and wash them. Good night."

That night I had a long conversation with Mother. I told her I intended to begin my writing with my origins. I would not leave out any part. I'm linked to you and to Father with every fiber of my soul, and when the connection is complete and well fastened, I can go on and search for my grandparents. *Legends of the North*, the book that you would read to me before I fell asleep, that enchanted book, has accompanied me all along the way, and from it, I expect, I will one day take flight.

Putting aside her trepidations, Mother told me in confidence that Father had returned from the camps, and he was now mute. He didn't utter a word. She tried in vain to get him to speak. Most of the day he slept, and when he awakened, muteness clogged his mouth. It was impossible to know where he had been or what he had done or how he had made it home.

"I hope, my son, that you, in your writing, will remove him from the slumber into which he has fallen. I did everything I could and didn't succeed. But you are connected with Father. Only you can bring him back to life and give him voice."

62

I sat at the desk and felt that it was comfortable for writing. The table in the convalescent home was wider but not comfortable. It was too high and it slowed my hand, and the light from outside blinded me. Here the window was narrow and long, the light was moderate, and the curtain was made of thin, airy cloth. Everything reminded me of Father's study.

I made myself a cup of tea. The thought that from now on I would be on my own made me happy, but at the same time it frightened me. My plans for writing suddenly seemed pretentious, beyond my abilities, and precarious. This distress weakened me, and I fell asleep.

I immediately met Uncle Arthur, sitting among the refugees. They recognized me and called out to me.

"Here's the sleepy boy!" they said.

Uncle Arthur didn't know what they were talking about, so one of the refugees explained it to him, with the help of his long arms.

"What's the matter with you?" Uncle Arthur asked with anxious curiosity.

I told him in brief, adding, "I've already left the path of chance, and I'm striving toward a goal."

"And what are you about to do? Do you need help?"

I told him that someone from Bukovina had bequeathed his small apartment to the defense forces, and it had come my way.

Uncle Arthur wanted more information. "What's the man's name?"

"Arthur Ehrenfeld. And that also doesn't seem to have happened by chance."

"In what sense?"

"You and he are namesakes."

"I didn't know a man by that name." Uncle Arthur tried to shake off connections he couldn't understand. "You told me you're striving toward a goal, if I understood you correctly."

"I'm training myself to be a writer," I admitted.

"That's strange," said Uncle Arthur, and a thin smile spread across his face.

"What's strange about it?" I wanted to understand.

"Your father tormented himself for years because he wanted to achieve perfection. That was his one and only desire. For as long as I knew him, he never moved from his desk. He was very meticulous, sensitive to every false note. No wonder his many revisions ate up all his time. Once, he showed me eight versions of a single chapter."

"Eight versions?"

"Even during the last days in the ghetto, he never stopped polishing his writing. At that time, I was sure he was wasting his days, and I asked him to join the communists. He refused. His refusal pained me greatly, and I cut off all connections with him."

"You never spoke with him again?"

"No. I used to meet with your mother. She understood him better than anyone. She admired his writing and used to say he was ahead of his time. I was sure she was only caught up in his charms. I sinned against him. I sinned."

"During the past year, I copied many chapters of the Bible by hand." Like a fool, I revealed this.

"You copied? Did I hear you correctly? What good does that do?"

"I learned to bond with the Hebrew letters. The images of the letters are etched into me now."

"That's beyond my understanding. We always condemned copying. We regarded copying as unworthy. A copy is an imitation, pure and simple. Do you want to imitate the Bible?"

"That's what I need at this time." I didn't know what else to say.

"So it seems to you," he said, raising his voice. "Your father revised endlessly. It seemed to him that he had to strive for perfection, and for that reason he made himself and your mother miserable. Write, yes, but for one purpose—for the good of mankind, for the general good. A grand style is a luxury."

Uncle Arthur had many other complaints about Father, but he now directed them all at me because I was following in Father's path, shutting myself off and depriving myself.

"It would be better for you to bond with the refugees, to serve them a bowl of soup at noon, to sit with them. There's no circle of hell they weren't in. You'd do better to listen to them, to play cards with them, to bind their wounds in the infirmary. Copying the Bible won't cure a single person."

I wanted to raise my crutches and say to him, *I'm handicapped,* but I didn't. I knew he would see that as an excuse. Instead, I said, "Father devoted his soul to writing. True, success didn't come to him, but his devotion to understanding humanity and his diligence in searching for the right mode of expression were boundless." Just as I said those words, I woke up.

.   .   .

Rivka was already in the kitchen, making breakfast for me. She immediately helped me get out of bed. I washed my face and sat down at the table.

"How are you, Rivka?" I wanted to befriend her.

"Fine," she said indifferently. My first impression, that Rivka was reticent and didn't seek human contact, proved to be correct.

She tidied the apartment, prepared lunch and supper, bought groceries and a block of ice, wished me a good day, and left.

The night visions came back to me, but this time while I was awake.

I loved Uncle Arthur—his simplicity, his direct way of relating to people, his belief that action was preferable to words. A complicated or vague statement used to drive him out of his mind. It was no wonder his brother Isidor's ways made his blood boil. Uncle Isidor was a bank clerk. He dressed well, took good care of his bachelor's flat, and read literature and philosophy. He had a subscription to the symphony and the theater and was always surrounded by women. His lofty manners, curiosity, education, and independent thinking created a barrier between him and the Jewish petite bourgeoisie, even though he was part of it. Uncle Arthur used to say that his brother was in love with himself and that it was no coincidence there were ten mirrors in his apartment. Every mirror said, *Me, me, just me!* Barbers, tailors, shoe polishers, and masseurs continually nurtured his egotism. Without them, he would have simply disintegrated.

The two uncles weren't usually invited to our house at the same time, but one time they both came. Father, who was fond of them both, tried to stave off the big fight, but it was inevitable.

"I'm getting out of here," Uncle Arthur shouted. "I don't want to see this toy of a man. Smelly sweat is better than his stinking cologne."

Uncle Isidor wasn't about to be bested. "Anyone who's in love with Stalin can't be a decent human being," he shouted at Uncle Arthur. "Stalin is imprinted on everything he does, and he's corrupt from head to foot."

Unfortunately, this bitter memory stuck in my mind. I prayed in my heart that it would be erased, that I would no longer see them quarreling but, instead, individually: each with his own features, way of walking, tone of voice. It was impossible not to love them. Both Mother and Father loved them with all their might.

63

Once a week—sometimes twice, if the weather was fair—Rivka took me out for a walk in the city. I preferred the afternoon hours. I devoted the mornings to writing—or, rather, to attempts at writing.

My writing still didn't have the right melody. I tried various strains, but one thing was clear to me: I had to start with the first sight of my home, where the music my parents bequeathed to me was hidden away. I had carried that feeling with me for many days, but only now did it take shape. A trip of even two or three miles around the city would bring me closer to that hidden goal.

Rothschild Boulevard was a pleasant avenue that reminded me of my native city. The humidity was oppressive at that hour, but the houses, the plants, and the front doors charmed the eye with their simplicity. I was borne on rubber wheels, without exchanging a word with Rivka. At least she didn't pester me with questions.

On one of these excursions, a man recognized me and called out.

"Unbelievable! Here's the sleepy boy. Where have you been?" His cry tore my heart; it was as though he had rediscovered his brother or nephew who had been lost during the war. To make sure he wasn't mistaken, he came closer to me and said, this time in a whisper, "Is it you? Good God! I wasn't wrong."

Hearing his terrible shout, a few people gathered around and stared at both of us, trying to understand what had happened. But the man just cried out again, "Unbelievable! It's him! I wasn't mistaken!" I was embarrassed and wanted to escape. But Rivka, who was also surrounded by people, couldn't extricate me.

Then the man bent down to my face and spoke in a soft voice. "What happened to you, my friend?"

"I was wounded."

"Where?"

"That's not important."

"You were our secret. We carried you from place to place, and we were sure that when you woke up, you'd tell us marvelous things. We sensed that you were linked to worlds that were sealed off from us. You were dear to us all. True, we didn't always watch over you properly. In any event, you persisted in your sleep. Our repeated efforts to pull you out of it were in vain. Are you normal now?"

I didn't know how to reply. Finally, I said, "Like everybody."

"Too bad."

The man rose to his feet and stood alongside me, as though words had failed him.

Eventually, he left me. The people dispersed, and once again I was borne on the rubber wheels. Rivka didn't ask anything, and I saw no need to tell her. The evening lights were pleasant, and a breeze blew in from the sea.

"You were only a child," Mother sometimes said to me. "You probably don't remember." But to my surprise I remembered not only the paths and the big rusty yellow leaves of early autumn—we called them "blades"—that were strewn along them, but also the peasants we met on the way, whom Father would greet in their own language.

In the evening the upstairs neighbor came in and introduced himself. He told me a few things about the late Arthur Ehrenfeld.

"He was a private person," he said. "We didn't know anything about him. He was polite and pleasant, and he kept away from arguments and quarrels. A solitary, secretive man."

I was still curious. "Was he tall?" I asked.

"Indeed."

But mostly he spoke about what was then going on in the country.

"The war has quieted down, and now we're mourning our dead. Our achievements were mighty, but the pain is hard to bear. How can we console the bereaved parents?" For a moment it seemed as though he was going to burst into tears. I wasn't wrong. Tears welled up in his eyes. He begged my pardon for invading my apartment and left.

From the little news that had reached me, I knew that there had been acts of heroism on all the fronts. My heart was with the thin young men who had immigrated, been sent straight to the battlefields, and did not return. Who would remember them and mourn for them?

During nights of unclouded sleep, I saw Mark again. He didn't die in battle, but his mysterious death lived on in me as a powerful, desperate ascent to the heights. As though he was saying, *This is what I was capable of and I did it.*

I received a short letter from Yechiel, written in charming Hebrew.

"My wound isn't deep," he said, "but it's healing slowly. Too bad

I can't go out and work. Most of the day I'm in my room. May the Lord send us good tidings."

From the few words he had put together, I heard the whisper of his parents' and grandparents' prayers. The ghetto and the forests hadn't torn him from their way of life. He quietly kept the commandments, almost in secret, and if people asked him if he prayed every day, he answered simply, "As much as possible. Sometimes I cut it short." I had the feeling it wasn't easy for him to retain what he had received from his ancestors. When he said the Grace After Meals, he hid his face in his hands, as though trying to hide his whispers. I was sad because my friends didn't see the nobility of his soul beneath his colorless veil.

64

⁓

I made sure to rise early, and when Rivka arrived, I was already
dressed and sitting at the desk. Every movement came with
much effort and pain, but whenever I managed to get out of the
wheelchair without help, it seemed to me that the day was not far
off when I would be able to walk on my own.

Meanwhile, I scribbled, and sometimes I came up with a sentence or two. I didn't for a moment forget my promise to myself:
that if one day I managed to write, I would include Mother's melody in my writing. For the time being, only restlessness throbbed
in my body.

Edward came to visit me. His tall, handsome body was as it always
had been, but his expression was blank, as though he hadn't spoken for many days.

"Edward!" I called to him.

He bowed his head at my cry of joy.

I saw before me the terrace at Misgav Yitzhak and Edward
swinging his sledgehammer. Edward's blows were precise, and
Ephraim praised the way he gripped the sledgehammer. Now
both of them had injured arms. Ephraim had returned to his kib-

butz in the north, and Edward was living in Tel Aviv. The training program at Misgav Yitzhak was a distant vision.

"Sit down. How are you?" I tried to get close to him. I noticed that his injured hand was covered by a simple woolen glove, which called attention to his big hand—the healthy one.

"I've been working," he said, and it was clear that at that moment he had no more words.

I told him about Arthur Ehrenfeld, the man who wanted to have a war invalid live in his apartment, with the first preference being someone from Bukovina.

"Interesting," Edward said, and the surprised expression that I remembered well filled his face.

"Where are you working?" I asked.

"In a bakery."

I saw him standing at the door of an oven, his face glowing from the light and heat. I had no doubt that the owner of the bakery was exploiting him, paying him pennies. But I did doubt that he could afford to rent a decent room and buy nourishing food. People always exploited his height, his strength, and his goodness of heart. Our friends were angry at the refugees who used him for their needs and paid him a pittance. But Edward never got angry. Every time we showed him that the refugees were exploiting him, a soft smile would spread across his lips. This was that same Edward. The wounds had changed the expressiveness of his body but not his soul.

I wanted to offer him a cup of tea and some cookies, but Edward hurried to make the tea himself and serve both of us. I asked him where he spent his nights.

"At a club for people from in and around Cracow," he answered with a smile.

.   .   .

That night I wrote the following lines:

> *Now blood speaks.*
> *The caves spread, and the dams collapse.*
> *Now everything expects to be revealed*
> *In trembling.*

I felt a heavy pressure on my shoulders. My desire to detach myself and be borne aloft had not taken me very far. The four lines I had written were just a momentary opening into what was seeking to come into being.

The days passed. I had already attracted a bit of attention at the entrance to the building. An upstairs neighbor would greet me. Usually, it was a polite greeting, but sometimes I felt that another type of greeting was hidden within it: *Thank God for not placing me among the invalids being pushed in wheelchairs.* Clearly, I served as a living example of his momentary fear.

I wasn't angry. I had learned to accept people's ways. A woman neighbor who came up to me and said, "I dreamed about you last night," made me wonder.

"What was the dream like?" I dared to ask her.

"It was a good dream," she said, flashing her white teeth.

"Did you see me standing on my feet and walking?"

"Even running."

We both laughed.

For quite some time, I had been dreaming about standing on my own and running. In reality, all my movements were measured and cautious, and dreams like those used to sadden and depress me. Now I had learned to value short distances. A walk of fifty yards on crutches made the physiotherapist ecstatic. I was strengthening the muscles of my arms and legs, and I felt that my body wasn't atrophying.

Nevertheless, going out of the house in the afternoon aroused only a slight happiness in me. If a gentle light cloaked my shoulders, or a little bird landed on my palm and pecked sunflower seeds from it, my happiness was greater.

Everyone knew that I didn't have the power to do any harm, but still people avoided me. My frail appearance apparently had a frightening aura. I would tensely watch all the people who fled from me. Some of them did it with abrupt awkwardness; others slipped away as if by chance.

Sitting in the wheelchair, I was under five feet tall; I could clearly see children's faces. But on crowded streets, adults loomed over me. My breath would grow short, and my forehead would become covered with sweat. At first, this distress would depress me, but in time I overcame it with ease.

I could hardly believe that two and a half years had passed since I was wounded. My friends matured, and they finished their army service. Most of them stayed on kibbutz and were preparing to move to another one up north. I was what I was, mindful of my situation and trying with all my strength to climb up smooth surfaces. A night when I succeeded in composing two lines, even rough ones, was a night of brightness.

If it weren't for Rivka, who cushioned me with pillows, bedsores would have done me in. Let me say it loud and clear: thanks to her, I was borne on rubber wheels and got to see the world.

.   .   .

Dr. Winter came to visit me, examined my legs, and concluded that my recuperation was proceeding satisfactorily. I had to keep moving my legs, he said.

"I'm glad you have a place of your own," he added.

I told him about my daily struggles with the Hebrew language and my search for the right melody.

"What will you write about? The kibbutz?"

Again I was perplexed. I didn't have the right words to explain it to him.

"The well I intend to draw from is dark and moist." I finally said. "The water in the bucket is as cold as ice. That is the place that gives me life."

"It's not here, correct? Or am I mistaken?"

"Correct. Since my childhood, the well and the water have enchanted me. But back then I didn't know that I would also be reflected in it when I grew up."

"This is beyond my understanding, my friend," Dr. Winter said, throwing up his hands.

"Didn't I explain myself well?"

"You explained it very well," he said, "but I'm a simple person, and I hear only the voice of what's tangible." Then he chuckled, as though he had succeeded in fooling me.

I wasn't insulted. I had learned to love him and his love of mankind. If there was one person in this world to whom I could turn even in the middle of the night, it was Dr. Winter. With his dedication, he had brought me this far.

The calendar said it was the end of January. Ever since I had been wounded, the seasons passed me by, and I barely noticed them. At Misgav Yitzhak I knew the spring and the summer, the autumn and the winter. The seasons had been imprinted into my skin. Ephraim not only trained us, but he also taught us to love the earth and the stones.

"The trees," he would say repeatedly, "are man's friend. A vegetable garden grows and its produce is eaten, but a fruit tree accompanies us for years—when it blossoms, when its leaves fall, and finally when it tires out. It's a good thing there are trees in the world." Now Ephraim was at his kibbutz, working in the office. He was a man of integrity who tried to plant us into meaningful lives. His life was interrupted, and he was all alone in his little apartment in the north.

65

Rivka was a quiet creature, undemanding and virtually mute. Her devotion was boundless. I was ashamed that I had nothing to give her in return. To the words "thank you," and "thank you very much," she did not respond.

At first I tried to find out who she was, where she came from. My questions were met with lowered eyes. Even the few words that she did utter came at an effort. Most of her speech consisted of "yes" and "no," though she did give those words some variety.

"She's a withdrawn person," said the woman in charge of the war-wounded, when Rivka had been with me for more than nine months. It was hard for me to accept that. A person who served someone else with such dedication and perseverance, day after day, had to have an open heart. I didn't have to tell her what to do or how. She tidied the apartment, bought groceries, cooked, and helped me wash, and in the afternoon, she took me out for long walks. Someone who did all that for another person without once looking at her watch couldn't be called a withdrawn person.

I came to picture Rivka as someone ageless and without a place of her own, as though she had been summoned from out of nowhere to help me. I kept trying to express my gratitude, but my words made no impression on her. She was entirely immersed in what she was doing, as if to say, *I do what I've been assigned. The rest isn't important.*

The woman in charge of the war-wounded asked me on several occasions if I was satisfied with Rivka's service.

"Very much!" I cried out.

"Does she ever ask you anything?"

"There's no need. She does exactly what she has to do."

She didn't react to my replies, as though I was mistaken or being deceptive.

One morning I had the feeling that my shattered leg bones had fused. Not without effort and pain, I stood up and took a step, just as Dr. Winter had instructed me. I wanted to rejoice, but I was cautious. Seven operations had planted the virtue of caution within me. I was experienced with vain hopes, and I knew that even an operation that Dr. Winter considered successful would bring only a slight improvement, sometimes barely noticeable. So perhaps this new feeling was only a wish or an illusion. To his credit, Dr. Winter did not inflate one's hopes.

"Medicine isn't an exact science," he would say repeatedly. "A doctor must be modest and know his place." Indeed, there were times when he did not seem like a surgeon but like a concerned individual.

There was another reason for my caution. When the woman in charge of the war-wounded learned that I was capable of getting out of bed and serving myself, she would discharge Rivka or reduce her hours. In the convalescent home, one of the patients warned me that I mustn't be hasty and show that I could manage by myself, because then they would fire my helper.

The next day Rivka saw me hobbling around on my crutches, and it looked to her like I was walking.

"Good!" she cried out. "Now you won't need me anymore."

"You'll be with me for a long time," I replied, and became frightened by what I had said.

"Won't they fire me?" she asked, staring at me.

"They wouldn't dare," I said loudly.

Later, I revealed to her that I was embarking on a long journey, one that would take years, and to accomplish it I needed to have someone close by, someone who could help me through hard times.

She looked up. "Where are you going?"

I didn't know how to reply. All the answers I could think of seemed absurd. Finally, I said, "I want to return to my parents and to their land."

That's far away and dangerous, said the look in her eyes.

"I have to do it. I can't leave my father and mother, not to mention my grandparents, in a place that is not a place and a time that is not a time. After all, I'm the flesh of their flesh."

I recalled my arrival in the apartment and how troubled I had been, stuck in that wheelchair. I couldn't know what was in store for me. The convalescent home, the nurses, the patients, the books I read and the pages I copied, the few lines I wrote—they all seemed to me like a blessed oasis compared to this jail. But after I spent time with Rivka and observed her ways, her attentive eyes, and, eventually, how she took care of me, I knew that I had been placed in reliable hands. She did everything delicately, even when she bandaged my legs or took me to the toilet. When I began living the in the apartment, my pain was intense, and it distracted me from her, as if she wasn't a speaking creature but a benevolent robot who offered her hand every time it was needed.

We don't know how to love the people who are really good to us. The angels of destruction and the angels of healing were battling over my body. If the angels of healing won out, it was in no small measure because of Rivka. When my body was burning up with fever, she hurried to care for me with damp cloths; she massaged my legs every time it seemed that the power of life was draining out of them. And so, step by step, with silent devotion and perseverance and without boasting, she pulled me out of the pain.

She's pretty. She's still young. Why is she wasting her life on me? I often asked myself. *Your life is no less important than mine,* I considered telling her. But when I saw again how focused she was, how immersed she was in everything she did, my thoughts seemed external and not connected to her. Sometimes she seemed to me like a proud woman whose real life was her inner self. But at other times she seemed like a woman who had decided to forgo her own life and devote herself to others instead. Who knows what she has undergone, where she left her parents? Everyone who wasn't born in the Land had a life full of trials. I often wanted to roar, *You are also a person full of beauty, and you deserve soulful attention.* But every time I was about to say that, I realized it was foolish.

66

Reality soon showed its true face. The woman in charge of the war-wounded announced to Rivka, in my presence, that from now on she was reducing her hours by a third.

"Why?" I didn't hold back.

"I received authorization from Dr. Winter," she said, smiling at my distress.

"And who will help me when I need it?"

"It's not fitting for a soldier to talk that way," she replied, plucking a painful string. "Part of your rehabilitation is to get up and move and be on your own," she added.

The woman in charge of the war-wounded may have reduced her hours, but Rivka herself did not. She came to me every day and did what she always did. I didn't dare ask her how she would make up her lost wages.

I told Dr. Winter about the decision of the woman in charge of the war-wounded, but he ignored my concern.

"You should be happy," he said. "Today I can disclose to you that my colleagues didn't believe you would ever be able to stand on your own."

"Thank you, Dr. Winter."

"We did the best that we could."

"You did more than that."

Dr. Winter responded to that with a forgiving smile.

I confided my concern for Rivka to him.

"Don't worry about her," he said. "She's a young woman, and she'll find other work. You have to take care of yourself." I couldn't believe my ears: Dr. Winter, who had seen her devotion, had shut his heart.

I tried to get out of bed and stand on my own. The effort was painful. Rivka wanted to help, but I tried to do everything by myself. Every time she reached out to me, I felt I was doing her an injustice. In any event, Rivka never asked for special consideration or for me to intervene on her behalf. She just kept coming every day and doing what she had always done.

It took me a while to notice how thin Rivka was and that she was only of average height. With what hidden power did this woman, who did not appear to be very strong, lift my body to lay me on the bed, bring me to the shower or the toilet, and wash me every day?

Thank you from the bottom of my heart, I wanted to say, but I didn't, so she wouldn't think I wanted to part from her.

"I'm glad you can get out of bed by yourself," she said to me one day.

"Thanks to you."

"I didn't do anything special," she replied, shrugging her shoulders.

Once again, Rivka wrapped herself in silence. She tidied the house, bought groceries, cooked, and, because it was Friday, bought flowers. For a moment it seemed she was about to leave me without saying anything.

"Rivka!" I called out in fear.

"What?" she said, and turned toward me.

"I wanted to tell you that you'll be with me for a long time."

"As long as I'm needed."

Then I saw that she was shrinking before my gaze. I wanted to grab hold of her, but my arms were too short to reach her. She appeared to me like a bird in distress, trembling and shaking her head. Wordlessly, she started to leave.

"See you tomorrow!" I called out.

"See you," she replied.

I was relieved, but I didn't allow myself to be happy.

67

That night I didn't sleep. The pain did not abate, but, to my surprise, my body quietly throbbed. I made myself a cup of tea and sat down at the desk.

Rivka's face appeared before me. I felt that she had brought to me not only her silence but also her patience and her ability to live unassumingly. And in fact, she had also prepared me and my legs to follow my life's path.

Pain was still stored up within me, but the urge to move forward surged through my whole body. I was alarmed by the new energy that filled me. It brought to mind the power that coursed through me in Naples while I was running around the camp and the tension I felt in my muscles when I rowed a boat.

As it turned out, the days in the hospital under Dr. Winter's care, the long months in the convalescent home, and, especially, the time I spent with Rivka had equipped me with everything I needed for walking long distances.

The paper lay before me, and the pen. I poured myself a little drink from the bottle of cognac that one of the patients had given me, and I immediately felt the burning liquid seep into me. I wasn't rushing to go out. It seemed to me that I had to gather more strength before girding my loins, and so that's what I did.

I sat tensely, but I saw nothing. At one time, the pain and my visions gave me signs and signals so I wouldn't lose my way, but now I saw neither the road ahead nor even the entrance to the path, not to mention any shortcuts.

The months of preparation had not done their job. Everything was in place, but I was just sitting there like a fool. I was about to stand up and go to open the window, the way my father sometimes did, but even that simple action suddenly seemed beyond my reach. I leaned back in my chair. This was something Father also did in times of distress.

I moved closer to the desk and took another sip of cognac. I took a deep breath, as though I was preparing to start a race. I felt that my own direct efforts were being obstructed, but then another power, far stronger than I, stood behind me and pushed. I smoothed the paper and began to write:

To return home. Who has not heard that whispered inside him? To return home is the sigh of the heart that swells every time a sharp pain attacks you, or when a decision bound up with terrible doubt crushes you, or—usually in the hours of darkness—when you collapse completely beneath the burden of your failures. Just then, a marvelous gate opens before you and invites you into your first house, your eternal house, which waits for you the way you left it.

My first house was built when I was six years old, and there it has stood ever since. The years have passed. I have moved from place to place, from one shelter to another. In all of those dwellings, there was not a trace of the security I felt when Mother sat on my bed and read to me from

Legends of the North, a large book full of splendid pictures. She read slowly and softly, and with my entire body I felt the tall plane trees in the yard, shading the house and filling us with their solid tranquility.

The first house is Father, and it is Mother. They are standing at the entrance. Father will soon leave for work, and I will stay with Mother. Parting from Father momentarily darkens that bright morning. I love the closeness of my parents and everything that emanates from that closeness: the aftershave that Father splashes on his face, the smell of cigarette smoke after meals, the fragrance of the eau de cologne that rises from Mother's neck.

"Why are you leaving us, Father?" I ask, trembling.

"I have to go," Father replies, putting on his white summer jacket. It's clear to me that I can't delay his departure. He climbs up onto the carriage and quickly disappears from sight. But Mother, aware of my feelings, kneels down and hugs me, pressing me to her soft breast and gently moving me away from the realm of sadness.

The plane trees protect the house. I look all the way up to their tops, and I get dizzy. Compared to them, the house looks low and without secure foundations. But there is no need to worry; the plane trees shield us in winter and summer. In the summer they dapple the yard with shade. Sometimes Father climbs a ladder and cuts a flowering branch from one of the giant trees. Mother places the flowers in a blue vase, and this is the giant tree's gift to the house. The whitish-yellow flowers decorate the living room for a few days and then wither. But even withered they have a hidden beauty, and Mother is in no hurry to throw them away.

Later Mother sits in an easy chair and reads, and I sit on

the grass and play with the big blocks that Father brought me from the sawmill. Our dog, Miro, sits and watches me eagerly. Miro is the silent soul of the house. His eyes are big, and his long ears flop to the side. When Mother is busy, he stays near me, and when Mother is worried, he stands close to her legs and worries along with her. If a key or some tool is missing, he joins in the search, and sometimes he finds it with his sense of smell. He seems to see what we can't. In the afternoon, when I am overcome with fatigue, I lay my head on his belly and fall asleep. A person knows this kind of closeness only in his first house.

One day I counted the plane trees, and with a shout of victory, I cried out, "Seven!"

Mother looked at me in surprise.

"We never counted them," she remarked.

There's a tool shed in the yard. Soon the gardener will come and take care of the vegetable plots and flowerbeds. He's a tall man who hardly ever speaks. When Father asks him something about the plants, his eyes widen, but the words refuse to leave his mouth. With great effort, he overcomes this obstacle and manages to join one word to another. I like to watch the way he walks and the way he bends down, turns over the earth, and uproots weeds. His measured movements have a wondrous silence about them.

Once, he asked me if I wanted to be a gardener.

"Yes!" I replied in a loud voice. He chuckled, revealing small, square teeth. I had expected a man of his height to have large, wide teeth, but he didn't.

At sunset he places everything that has ripened in a basket: tomatoes, cucumbers, radishes, and green onions. The smells of the earth and of the vegetables mingle for a moment in the open air. Mother wants to take this gift of nature from his hands, but Chito—that's his name, if you didn't know—won't allow it. He brings the full basket into the house and places it on the counter next to the pantry.

When there's a lot of work, Chito takes a break and sits under one of the plane trees. He spreads a cloth on the grass and makes a simple meal for himself: peasant bread, a small pitcher of buttermilk, and a green onion. Mother brings him a cup of coffee.

When darkness falls, Chito picks up his bundle and goes home. After he leaves, the yard changes. The shadows deepen and the sound of the water flowing in the river can be heard clearly. A white rabbit runs across the yard and disappears under the bushes.

At that hour Father returns from work. The table on the balcony is already set. If he is late, Mother worries. She walks to the gate, turns her head this way and that, and stands and listens. If she detects the gallop of the horses, her face broadens into a smile, and she announces with a slight sigh, "Father's coming."

Father's return from the forests in the evening is a great joy, as though he has been lost and has finally found his way to us. Father steps down from the carriage, hugs Mother, and swings her in the air. Father is taller than Mother and broad shouldered; when he laughs, his body laughs with him.

Before we sit down to our meal, Father waters the horses and feeds them. Immediately thereafter, he washes his hands and face, walks to the balcony, and calls out in a merry voice, "Behold, I am ready!"

Dinner, which is served in the last light of the day, is a quiet ritual with small gestures that will be preserved forever. The first course is vegetable soup, which Father loves and for which he always finds a new word of praise to compliment Mother. The second course is cheese dumplings spread with butter. And for dessert, Mother serves raspberries and cream.

Summer evenings here are long and melt slowly into a starlit night. We sit on the balcony for quite some time. Father tells Mother everything that happened during the day. Sawmills figure in the story, as well as flour mills, and of course the rafts on the River Prut. I don't understand the flow of their conversation, but the few words that I do catch quickly become pictures, and I see before my eyes the noisy sawmill and the strong workers dragging the huge beams over to those enormous saws, which cut them lengthwise into planks. When I hear the word "raft," I see the green and brown water of the Prut, and a secret fear gives me goose flesh.

Then we go down to the yard and sit outside on thick mats. Mother cuts a red watermelon, and Father finally has time for me. Together we build a castle with the large wooden blocks. Miro watches from a distance and doesn't mix in.

It's already late, but red, blue, and gold still flicker in the twilight. Day and night mingle and are drunk with color. Father and I concentrate on building the castle and its outbuildings. Mother leans on two pillows and watches us. She doesn't comment or ask questions. Finally, when the castle stands, tall and broad and surrounded by its offspring, Father rises to his feet and says, "How's our castle, Bunia?"

"A work of art," says Mother.

I'm tired. The wings of sleep already flutter over me, but I try to stay awake and listen to the hawks and owls that pierce the first darkness with their screeches. The calls aren't pleasant, but I'm not afraid. I am encircled by Father's big arms and drift easily into a soft sleep.

It's morning again, and once again Father puts on his white jacket and goes out, and once again I'm saddened by the separation.

"Soon it will be Friday, and Father will be with us all day," says Mother. She knows what I'm thinking. The big castle that Father and I built stands the way we left it. The night rain moistened it but didn't stain its beauty. The castle will stand for two or three days, until a heavy rain comes or the neighbors' big dog invades the yard and knocks everything down.

Friday is a day of cleaning, scrubbing, and commotion. Victoria reports at an early hour, and with her large hands, she changes God's order of creation. Carpets, mats, and bedding are taken out and spread on the grass and the balustrades of the house. The upheaval drives me outside. I can barely find a free space under one of the plane trees. During this crazy time, Miro doesn't leave my side. He sits next to me tensely, ready to do whatever I tell him.

If Mother allowed me to, I would go down to the river with Miro. The boys my age who live in this area regularly wander along the dirt paths, bring potatoes and onions from the fields in wheelbarrows, and even ride horseback.

Those pleasures are forbidden to me. I am imprisoned in the yard and can only follow what's happening outside from there.

"Why can other boys of my age play outside, and I'm not allowed?" I keep asking Mother.

"You have to ready yourself," she says without explanation.

It occurs to me that perhaps my parents are training me to be a prince, like Prince Felix in a story Mother read to me. They imposed grave prohibitions on Prince Felix and even exiled him from the palace so that he would grow strong, overcome hardships, and return home braver.

Finally, I ask, "When can I go to the river with Miro?"

"Next summer, I expect."

"That's a long time from now."

"Not so long."

That night I dream that one of Father's workers has come with his wagon to take me to my place of exile. I am surprised that Mother is standing aside and not intervening. I want to shout out loud, but I feel myself choking, and then I wake up.

In the afternoon, after dusting the house and washing the floors, Victoria brings the scattered contents of the house back inside.

Once, Victoria called out my name and stroked my head. I was frightened and burst into tears. Now I'm no longer afraid, but the remnants of that fear smolder inside me.

Mother pays Victoria with bills and coins. Victoria binds the money in a handkerchief, blesses Mother, and goes away.

Friday ushers in two festive days in a row. Father will come back from work and be only with us, and my world will emerge from its constriction and broaden.

"When will I go school?" I ask Mother.

"You're studying at home, my dear."

"Why do all the other children go to school and only I study at home?"

"Because we're preparing you to study in the secondary school," Mother answers hastily.

Once a week, and sometimes twice, in the early afternoon, Miss Christina comes to teach me reading, writing, and arithmetic. She's young and pretty and wears city clothes. She's a student and attends a school in the center of town. On weekends, holidays, and the long summer vacations, she returns to her parents in the village.

The hours in her presence are a pleasure and a celebration. We read and write and occasionally linger over a single word, such as "heavenly" or "prey." We look for synonyms, but we don't find them easily. I appear to be better in arithmetic. I learn the times table by heart and don't make mistakes.

If the weather is fair, we go for a walk, and sometimes we go as far as the river. Christina teaches me a poem or tells me a folktale.

"Why did they exile Prince Felix?" I ask.

"So that he could become strong and fight evildoers."

"Isn't it possible to become strong at home?"

"Apparently not," Christina says, smiling. I love her smile, which shows her pretty teeth. While we are walking, I notice a small building with a pointed green roof. How miraculous. I've walked on this path many times, and until now I never noticed it. Christina notices my surprise and says, "It's a chapel."

"Did children build it?"

"Children don't build things."

"I built a castle with Father in the yard. Who lives in the chapel?"

"Nobody. People go inside to pray. Do you want to see?"

Christina opens the door, and a splendid sight appears before my eyes: the picture of a mother nursing a baby. On the shelf at her feet, two big wax candles burn. The light of the candles flickers on the picture and brings it to life. Christina bows her head and crosses herself.

"Do I have to cross myself, too?"

"No, Jews don't cross themselves."

Because of my astonishment, I don't look carefully enough at things that happen along the way. A naked young woman swims in the river. She swims quickly and rhythmically. I am about to ask Christina if she knows her.

"It's not proper to swim without a bathing suit," Christina says with suppressed anger. Because of the sharpness of her words, I don't ask her why. The chapel has made such a strong impression on me that all night long I see the mother's large breast and the infant's lips clinging to it.

Twilight has spread over the treetops and tall bushes. The smells of water, soap, and starch rise from every corner. Father is in a linen suit, and Mother is wearing a poplin dress. Miro is happy to see us together. Miro loves each of us differently. He seems to like Mother best. He stays near her most of the day, ready to do what she tells him. He loves Father with respect and awe. With me he carries on; either he runs after me or I run after him, and in the end we roll on the grass. Miro understands my moods. When I'm sad, he curls up next to me and lets his head sink between his paws.

Friday afternoon is devoted to music. We sit on the balcony and listen to classical music. As a girl, Mother played piano. Now she seldom plays. I love to look at her face while she listens. She is wide-eyed with wonder, and her lips are pursed. Father listens differently. His head is bowed, and he makes no comments. Mother loves to describe what she's hearing, and she uses colorful words that create a full picture.

Once, Christina said to me that it was good to listen to music in church.

"Why?" I asked.

"In church it connects you to heaven."

"And at home it doesn't connect you?"

"The church is the gateway to heaven."

At home we don't speak like Christina. Sometimes Mother does say, "Good God," but it's a sign of excitement, not a call to God. Christina likes to take expressions apart and look for synonyms.

"Is 'heavenly' a synonym for 'divine'?" I wonder out loud.

"We'll have to think about that," she says without explanation.

On Friday night, dinner is festive: colorful salads and cheese blintzes topped with strawberry jam, all made by Mother. Our meals are prepared with care and restraint, but their taste lingers with me for hours.

After dinner, we sit outdoors on the wide wicker chairs and provide company for the evening as it departs. Sometimes Father recalls things that happened to him. He relates them slowly, in great detail and in rolling cadences. It's hard for me to follow what he's saying, but I love to listen to his melodic voice, even though his speech is usually sparing, and the silences are considerable.

After an hour of silence, I become restless, and I begin to circle the house with Miro. The walk with Miro puts me at some distance from the house, and I remember the last summer vacation we took in the center of the city. Once again, I see streets paved with dark stones, tall chestnut trees that cast their thick shadows on the sidewalks, the restaurant in the hotel courtyard, and the elegant cinema. Father has a lot of business in the city, and my hand doesn't leave Mother's.

Fear of getting lost in the big city fills my sleep with arrogant and violent people. Because of those nightmares, I'm glad to return home. The carriage that brought us returns us. When we arrive, Miro leaps to greet us with boisterous joy. No anger is evident in him. He welcomes each of us with equal fondness. When the commotion dies down, he turns exclusively to me, and we rekindle the affection that we had missed when I was gone.

On Saturday, Father harnesses the horses to the carriage, and we go off to Count Minitsky's tennis court. Father and Mother play well. Sometimes the count's son appears with his sister, and my parents play with them. They are tanner, and they are better at this sport. This is no surprise, as they spend many hours on the court. Father and Mother quickly lose, and this pains me. But they aren't upset. Their friendship with the count's children, who are younger than they, is a pleasant one for them.

When I grow up, I swear to myself, I'll practice for many hours, and the day will come when I'm taller and stronger than they are, and they won't be able to return my strokes.

In the afternoon, Dr. Wolf, the district physician, arrives to play chess with Father. He's a tall man with a thick mustache, like us in some of his manners, but still different. Unlike us, he drinks beer and smokes cigars. Christina told me that he was born a Jew and converted.

I can't keep myself from asking Mother, "What does it mean to convert?"

"Dr. Wolf goes to church every Sunday," Mother answers, with a haste that's unusual for her. I sense that she has no intention of adding to what she has said, and so I let her alone.

Father taught me how the chess men move, but I don't know how to play. Even so, I like to watch the secret strategies that are woven around the board and played out with the movement of each piece. Dr. Wolf is an excellent player, but Father is no duffer, and he surprises his opponent with a brilliant move. On several occasions I have seen Dr. Wolf raise his hands and announce, "There's nothing to be done. You won!"

Between games, Mother serves a mug of beer to Dr. Wolf and a cup of coffee and some cheesecake to Father. The conversation flows. Dr. Wolf tells us about the peasants' superstitions. They prefer their ancestral witch doctors to modern physicians, and in describing their beliefs, he uses his hands and face and makes us laugh until we cry. "Jews aren't supposed to be stupid," I've often heard him say, "but the Jewish country doctors are frightfully naive. When a patient comes in to be examined by a Jewish doctor, not only does he not pay for the examination, but he also asks for free medicines. When the doctor refuses, the peasant threatens to burn down his house. Everybody says the Jews are smart and sophisticated. I don't know every Jewish doctor, but I do know the ones who work in the villages, and I can attest to the fact that they're frightfully naive."

Sometimes Dr. Wolf changes his tone and tells us about the Jewish merchants, who talk a lot—explaining and interpreting. Because of their passion for talking, they forget that there are things they want to conceal from him.

"I remind them that I was also once a Jew, and I know how to explain and interpret, and how to make a straight line into a bent one. Then they laugh, as if I weren't talking about their weaknesses but about my own. The Jews are a strange people."

I notice that Father and Mother don't argue with him. They like to listen to him and observe his gestures. Once, Mother had a high fever, and Dr. Wolf was called early in the morning. He examined Mother and diagnosed typhus. My parents' bedroom was quarantined, and I was sent to the most distant room, the guest room. Dr. Wolf came to see her every day. His frequent visits imposed an aura of fear on the house.

"Is Bunia getting better?" Father kept asking. Dr. Wolf didn't withhold the truth.

"She's in crisis," he said. "The crisis will pass in two or three days." Indeed, Mother felt better just when Dr. Wolf had predicted she would, and his face glowed. I didn't see Mother for two weeks. When she finally got out of bed, she had to lean on Victoria, the housekeeper. I didn't recognize her.

When I'm sick, Dr. Wolf comes to see me and says, "One day we'll have to get rid of those infected tonsils. We'll give them a bit of a deferment for now, but then we shall see." I know this is a warning, and I'm secretly afraid.

On Saturday night Mother doesn't rush me to get into my pajamas, and I stay up late, listening to the radio or sitting on the floor and playing cards.

Victoria used to play with me. Since she left, the house has felt drained of her vitality. Every time I sit on the floor or on the bench at the entrance to the house, I see her standing in front of me. She wasn't tall, but she was solid, bubbling over with smiles and laughter, and she knew how to imitate animals. She loved Mother with all her soul, and it was too bad she didn't listen to her advice. Mother warned her about her violent suitor, but Victoria loved him. In the end, when she wanted to leave him after they had a fight, he stabbed her with a knife and almost killed her. Dr. Wolf bound her wound, and Father and Mother took her to the hospital in the carriage. The wound was deeper than Dr. Wolf thought, and for a long time Victoria fought for her life. When she recovered, she didn't return to us but to her parents. Mother sometimes goes to visit her. I'm waiting for her to take me, too.

68

At dawn I finished the last sentences, and a fatigue that was more like paralysis gripped me. The first light was still wrapped in darkness. I opened the window and put out my hand to touch the silent coolness.

Suddenly, the melody that had drawn my fingers over the white pages returned to me, and I knew that the gate that had blocked my way had burst open. From now on, I would be quarrying.

I heard Mother's voice.

"Don't be afraid," she said. "You did what Father wanted to. But what a price you paid!"

"How do you know, Mother?"

"I was with you in all your pain, and what I didn't know, I asked Dr. Winter."

"I feel much better. I can even go out by myself."

"May God help you."

I was surprised by those words, but I understood that they weren't hers but those of her father and had come down to her.

Mother, I was about to say.

She looked at me in amazement.

"You're allowed to be happy," she said.

"Mother," I said, "when I think of the path that lies before me, I want to fall to my knees and ask for grace and mercy."

"What path are you talking about?" she wondered.

"I just broke through the gate, and what was revealed to me is beyond my strength."

"Now I'm permitted to disclose to you that Father was certain you would do this."

"I pray with all my heart that I'll be as dedicated as Father was."

"My dear, you've already shown your devotion."

That was Mother, her voice and her concern, but not in her usual clothing. She was wearing white, like a nurse. Suddenly, the operating room—the one I'd been taken to seven times—appeared before my eyes.

"Don't worry," Mother said. "I'll be with you wherever you go."

"And where's Father?"

"Father has not yet returned from the camps. The moment he does so, I'll tell him about your breakthrough. He'll be happy. A father doesn't envy his son. I have no doubt that he'll tell you things that will help you."

I once again saw the opening of the tunnel. I knew I was at the beginning of the path, and from here on, I must dig.

Mother appeared to be alarmed by my fear.

"You'll do the best you can," she said. "A person isn't required to do anything that is beyond his abilities. You began to study Hebrew in Naples, you kept on learning in the orchard and during night training, and after you were wounded, you sat and copied from the Bible. The work in the field and the copying forged your tools, and with such marvelous tools in hand, I have no doubt that God will help you."

"Mother," I said, "where did you acquire that language?"

"I must tell you that in my world everything has changed. The old is no longer old, and what is new sometimes looks out of date to me. I now pronounce with ease words that I heard in my youth, and my usual way of speaking has broken down."

Bless me, Mother? I think of asking her. Mother apparently expected that request.

"I'll ask my ancestors to bless you," she said.

"Don't you want to bless me?"

"In my childhood I knew the prayers and blessings, but over the years I lost them. I can only ask my ancestors to bless you. I'll hug you, and that will be my blessing."

69

I raised my head and saw Rivka. She was standing by the stove, making me breakfast.

"You didn't sleep last night," she said.

"I was writing," I told her.

"What did you write?"

"What I saw."

She smiled a thin smile that filled her face and didn't ask anything else.

Rivka had been aiding me for nearly a year, and she was still a riddle. She apparently understood only the language of action. I was moved by her powers of concentration. All my efforts to get close to her were in vain, and every question I asked embarrassed her. She had been that way since I first saw her. But she was devoted to me in heart and soul. Every time I took a few steps, she stopped what she was doing and watched, as if I were her son who had managed to overcome an obstacle.

"I broke through the gate, and now I have to move forward," I said.

She looked at me in surprise but did not respond.

My fatigue returned, and even more than before. My arms and legs still felt tense. I got out of the wheelchair, sat at the table, and ate Rivka's farina.

Sometimes I felt as if Rivka was trying to tell me something about herself but was prevented by her limited vocabulary. But this time she overcame her inhibitions and said, "I'm glad."

"What are you glad about?"

"That you managed to write," she said. Without looking at me, she burst into tears.

"Why are you crying?" I barely managed to ask before she shrank back into her shell. She didn't raise her eyes, and her entire being contracted.

Dr. Winter came to visit me and told me that he'd made an appointment for my final operation. My legs weren't paralyzed after all. I was able to feel them, although not as in the past. I staggered about, and it was hard for me to lift my legs, but I was no longer a motionless lump.

"Is the operation necessary?" I asked.

In most of our meetings Dr. Winter spoke in High German. But this time his accent sounded exactly like my parents', and for a moment my throat tightened. I was sad that this language, which Mother had cultivated with love and in which Father wrote his stories, was no longer mine. Tears flowed from my eyes.

Dr. Winter was stunned by my weeping. He came over to me and touched my shoulder.

"It's a surface operation, my friend, not like the earlier ones. It's the last one, and from here on, you'll be able to set out on your way. Are you afraid?" He leaned over me.

"A little."

"There's no reason to fear. This will be a lot easier than the earlier operations."

For a moment it seemed as though he wasn't talking about broken bones, torn tissues, and damaged nerves, but about an enigma that was going to be deciphered. But the tears that had been locked inside me for such a long time wouldn't stop.

"Are you afraid?" he asked again.

I was ashamed to say that hearing my mother tongue, which I hadn't heard for a while, had moved me. When I told him, he laughed, hugged me, and kissed my forehead.

"If that's what is making you sad, this is a sign that the eighth operation will do what it has to do, and you will start to run."

70

Robert came to visit one afternoon and showed me some copies he had drawn. He had found a book of paintings by Giotto in the library, and every day after work, he would sit and copy. He had changed over the past months. When he looked at me, I saw that a gentle wonder dwelled in his eyes. But I couldn't be happy because I also noticed that he kept blinking.

"Are you happy when you copy?" I asked.

"I'm doing it willingly."

"It seems that every artist has to learn how to bow his head before the great works in order to feel the secret of creativity," I said.

"Giotto is divine," said Robert, smiling, as though he felt that the word "divine" wasn't one that should be used.

Because of his smile, I asked him what he meant by "divine."

We sat and were silent.

Finally, Robert asked about my writing. I was afraid to tell him about the enthusiasm that gripped me at night.

"I'm trying," I said, and was sorry that I had concealed my exhilaration.

"God sent me Giotto," he said.

"I'm glad."

"I didn't know what painting was until I saw Giotto. He opened the gate for me, and now I know what to look for."

I hadn't heard of Giotto, and I expected Robert to tell me more about him, but he was so fired up by his discovery that he just kept showering praises upon the artist. Then he cut the visit short, as though someone was waiting for him somewhere else. Or perhaps he wanted to return to his copying.

Friends came to visit me, but not as often as before, and I hadn't seen some of them for a year. Edward came. I was alarmed by his appearance. His body had shrunk, and his handsome face had softened. Of all his splendor, only the breadth of his shoulders remained. But that broadness didn't suit the rest of his body.

For years he had known how to give of himself and to be good to his friends. Now he stood helpless.

"Don't you want to return to the group?" I asked, stupidly.

"No," he said with his head lowered.

Eventually, he told me that he was thinking of leaving the bakery. An old-age home called Abraham's Tent had offered him the janitor's job, and he was probably going to move there soon. He would have his own room, meals, and a small salary.

I felt sorry for Edward, bone of my bones, who had given up all his dreams. Now, at age twenty, he was imprisoning himself in an old-age home. He would work, he would serve, the old people would pick on him, and his bosses would exploit his goodwill. His handsomeness would wither even more, and in a few years he would look like a prisoner, with jail stamped on every step.

"Edward." His name popped out.

"What?"

"Why are you going there?"

"It'll be okay. There's nothing to fear."

His words dammed my mouth. The warnings that I wanted him to hear from me slipped away.

"Every place has its disadvantages. No place is perfect." He spoke with a frightening equanimity, as though he had already absorbed the spirit of the place to which he was planning to exile himself.

At night I saw Mother.

"I broke through the barrier, and I intend to return home."

"To what home?"

"To our home."

"Nothing is there," she said and flinched, as if she had been hiding that from me.

"I want to once again be in all the places where we were together. The Carpathian Mountains were with me in all my wanderings, and now the hour has come to return to them, with my own eyes. It's hard to live for so many years alone and exiled."

"My dear, what you say frightens me. Flesh and blood cannot take such a journey upon itself. First you have to get better and stand on your own two feet."

"The journey will make me better. Dr. Winter keeps saying, 'Go, my friend, go.'"

"This is beyond me," said Mother, throwing up her hands.

"Mother, I have to do it. What I don't understand, the trees and the cliffs and the hills will tell me. And if I don't see those marvels, the child who remained behind will show them to me. I saw many sights in my childhood, but I didn't know how wondrous they were. And so I'll go from place to place, until I reach the places where we were, or that I've been told about."

"Wait, dear, until Father comes back from the camps. You mustn't go out on your own. These regions are cold and dangerous. For now, stay where you are living. Let the distant places come to you," she said, and then she disappeared.

About the Author

Aharon Appelfeld is the author of more than forty works of fiction and nonfiction, including *The Iron Tracks, Until the Dawn's Light* (both winners of the National Jewish Book Award), *The Story of a Life* (winner of the Prix Médicis Étranger), and *Badenheim 1939.* Other honors he has received include the Giovanni Boccaccio Literary Prize, the Nelly Sachs Prize, the Israel Prize, the Bialik Prize, and the MLA Commonwealth Award. *Blooms of Darkness* won the *Independent* Foreign Fiction Prize in 2012 and was shortlisted for the Man Booker International Prize in 2013. Appelfeld is a member of the American Academy of Arts and Sciences and has received honorary degrees from the Jewish Theological Seminary, Hebrew Union College–Jewish Institute of Religion, and Yeshiva University. Born in Czernowitz, Bukovina (now part of Ukraine), in 1932, he lives in Israel.

A Note on the Type

The text type in this book was set in Jenson, a font designed for the Adobe Corporation by Robert Slimbach in 1995. Jenson is an interpretation of the famous Venetian type cut in 1469 by the Frenchman Nicolas Jenson (c. 1420–1480).

Typeset by Scribe, Philadelphia, Pennsylvania

Printed and bound by Berryville Graphics, Berryville, Virginia

Designed by Betty Lew